"The street kids the ⸺ grip you, heart breaking ⸺ neart warming, you can't not l ⸺ ⸺ome embroiled into their lives. Expat Naο... adds the compassion to the story as she wants to help these kids so much, and her friend and fellow expat Maggie helps to add a little light humour into a tale that could essentially have been very dark. It's compelling, engaging and at times quite poignant and I thoroughly enjoyed my time in Kyiv with these kids. Highly Recommended." *Alex J Book Reviews*

"An atmospheric read with some beautiful scenes making me feel like I am in the story. I have to admit I have never read a book like this one before. There is something really mesmerising about this story. Along with the crime, the author takes us on an emotional roller-coaster with scenes that pulled on my heartstrings. This is the first book that I have read by this author and it most certainly won't be the last." *Baker's Not So Secret Blog*

"The streets of Kyiv come alive with vivid imagery and the story is raw, sensitive and compelling." *Waggy Tales Blog*

"Don't Get Involved is dark and gritty, providing an insight into the hidden aspects of society that most of us are fortunate enough to not ever have to experience. F.J. Curlew does a fantastic job of painting a picture of the city. From the perspective of outsiders it seems to be a place of wonder, new experiences to be found around each corner. From the side of the street children Kyiv appears stark, inhospitable and corrupt to the core." *Books & Beyond*

"Curlew certainly knows how to draw the reader in and keep them engrossed. I had my heart in my mouth as the story unfolded. Don't get Involved packs so much into its pages, we have crime, its thrilling, full of compassion, and makes for one hell of a read, taking you on a roller-coaster of emotions. My first book by Curlew and with writing like that it wont be my last." *Lost In The Land Of Books*

"The writing style is top-notch, immersive, atmospheric, and full of emotion. Despite the hard topic of the book, I had a great time reading it. This is not a book to leave you with a smile on your face but with hope in your heart that even on the hardest winters there is room to dream and to believe in magic." *Miss Known*

"A novel with surprising action with each page turned, and unfolding on each of those pages is a story that feels like it has been written by an author well established for decades. I feel privileged having been asked to take part in the blog tour and I highly recommend the read." *Page Turner's Nook*

"Don't Get Involved grabbed my attention and I

found it very difficult to put down, reading it in one sitting. It's a dark and often tense novel, written in a manner that I found very involving with short and snappy sentences charged with detail that drew me right in to the culture of Kyiv." *Book Drunk*

"A fantastic thriller with a beautiful insight into Ukraine and in particular Kyiv as a city, its culture and beauty really sing though the pages of this story. I loved the characters in this, they all felt very real...their lives and behaviours felt very raw and very emotional." *Books & Emma*

"Wow, what a read! A really well written tale of hope when you feel like despairing." *The Divine Write*

DON'T GET *INVOLVED*

by
F J CURLEW

For the street children of the world
who deserve so much more

PART I
STANDING

Chapter 1

December 2001

'You?' Igor whispered, wrapping his arm firmly around Leonid's shoulders and pulling him close. 'You, I trust for this. You know these people, how they live. Find them. Finish this.'

'Sure thing, boss,' Leonid replied, his confidence bouncing off the marble floor. He summoned the elevator which hummed open and welcomed him inside. His gold rings sang against the hand rail. He nodded his head approvingly, as he checked his appearance in the mirror, smiling for the benefit of the camera in the ceiling.

When he stepped out onto the pavement, one of Igor's black Mercedes was waiting, ready for use if needed. The driver stepped out, nodded his capped head, gestured invitingly as he opened the door. Leonid shook his head and continued down the hill towards Khreschatyk. He wanted to walk, gather his thoughts; get in the zone. The driver nodded his understanding and slipped back into the front seat.

Soft leather.

The early winter chill brought the promise of snow. Leonid could smell it, almost taste it. He pulled the collar of his black coat up and tightened his scarf. The echo of his handmade shoes shouted above the shuffle and scrape of the residents of Kyiv, mumbling their way to wherever. As he turned the corner from the cavernous indoor market of Bessarabskaya – slabs of meat still dripping blood, the staring eyes of dead fish, pyramids of fruit and vegetables, nuts and dried fruits, too expensive for most – he could feel his cheek beginning to pulse, to twitch, to show his annoyance. *You know these people. Even now!*

Two *militsiya* officers, jack boots, fur hats and weapons, were giving a couple of young tourists – Americans by the look of them – a hard time, checking documents, tutting, anticipating bribes, enjoying themselves with their mocking aggression. One of the *militsiya* caught sight of Leonid and raised his chin in acknowledgement.

'Leonid.'

'Denis,' he replied, with a nod and the hint of a smile, as he walked by.

His pace quickened as he drew closer to Podil, his mindset now where it had to be. He headed down to the metro where he hoped to find his quarry. Sure enough, the pack of street-kids was there, eyeing up their prey. Sad eyes and cupped hands for begging; sharp and quick for stealing. He lit a Marlboro as he stood against the subway wall following their actions, identifying their leader. Unwelcome memories crawled out of the recesses of his mind. He discarded them with his cigarette butt as it bounced off the wall, breaking into a shower of dying embers. He strode across to the leader of the pack. The confident click-clack of leather soles on dirty concrete announced his arrival.

'Dima,' he said softly, the tone ominous, intimidating, wrapping his arm tightly around the kid's bony shoulders, wincing at the stench of dirt and decay. He pulled him to the other side of the underpass, out of the earshot of the others. 'You seen this girl?' he snarled, showing the kid the photo he had been given by Igor.

'Uh,-uh,' Dima replied. 'Don't know her.' He felt a blade prick against the pulsating vein in his neck. The cheeky grin slid off him and slithered into a pool of piss at his feet.

'Wrong answer. I'll ask again, shall I?' he said in menacing monotone, his twitch beating a rhythm, his piercing blue eyes drilling holes. 'Alyona. Where is she? Where does she hang out?'

Dima coughed, trying to control his breathing, his mind working overtime. You don't betray. Never. But you have to survive. 'Haven't seen her. Not since yesterday. I swear.'

'And where did you see her yesterday?'

'At the Saint Sophia, I think, or one of the other churches. She–she...I've seen her begging there.' He knew he was a good liar. He prayed right now that it was good enough. There would be consequences, but he could deal with that later. For now he just wanted this situation gone. The man had a reputation and it wasn't a good one.

'Uh-huh,' Leonid answered, twitching, as he tightened his grip, his voice deepening, almost growling. 'Not good enough. Now? Right now, where will she be?'

'Dunno. I swear.' He shook his head and pulled his best innocent face. It was well practised. 'We don't–I don't know her that well. Just seen her around. Didn't even know her name until you told me. I swear. One of the churches, man.' He shrugged.

'Find her. Bring her here at ten o'clock, or this,' he said smiling, as he drew the blade across Dima's cheek leaving a thin trail of blood. 'This gets serious. Got it?'

'Yeah. Yeah. Got it,' Dima mumbled, feeling his blood seep against the hand he'd raised to his stinging face.

Leonid whistled as he strutted back to the exit. Back to daylight. Back to where he belonged. He wiped the knife and his fingers with a tissue, and tossed it on the ground behind him.

Dima dabbed at the blood on his face with the sleeve of his dirty little bomber jacket that wasn't fit for purpose. The red cotton now more brown, the elasticated cuffs and waistband baggy and frayed. The cut stung like hell, but he couldn't show it. He looked across at the rest of his crew who were watching him expectantly, waiting for a response.

Drawing on the remnants of his strength he laughed and shouted, 'Girls love scars, man. I'm gonna be fighting them off! Cool! See ya!' He waved, turned, and ran towards the exit masking the desperation he felt that none of his gang had noticed the tell-tale stain on his trousers.

To his left was the funicular. The graceful arch over it. The shining glass doors. The gentle climb to a higher place. A place not for the likes of him. He turned instead to the right and ran across the cobbles, over the busy Volodimirsky Spusk intersection, down towards the Dnieper river.

The smell of a McDonald's reminded him that he was hungry. He would love to stroll in, go to the toilets, clean up. But no. He knew from experience that he wouldn't get more than two steps inside the door. Not here. Not in any of the cafes and bars dotted along the waterfront. Not even in the public toilets, where he would be shooed out by a *babushka* who sat, handing out sheets of toilet paper for two *Hryvnia*. No. His was a different world. All he could do was keep running. Running, running, running.

He ran along the wide stretch of concrete beside the river – earth and stunted trees to his left, the low metal fence interspersed with graffitied concrete pillars that bordered the river to his right – until he found a secluded set of steps that led down to the water. He took them three at a time.

Making sure that he couldn't be seen, he flipped his three stripe trainers off – some wealthy person's cast-offs left poking out of a garbage can – removed his grey jogging pants, and hurried into the water. The cold was biting at his skin. He kept going until his legs were covered, and allowed the water to soak away his shame, swishing his pants back and forth, cursing. Cursing at the cold, at his situation. At his life.

He squeezed as much water as he could out of his pants, and pulled them back on. Struggled to get his numbed feet back into his trainers, barely able to feel them as they got caught in the twisted tongue. *Shit!*

His hands were shaking and he wasn't sure why. Cold? Fear? Both? Probably.

He started running again. This time to get warm. To dry himself off. He knew only too well the dangers of being cold. Every winter people died. People who lived on the streets like he did. Their lives were disposable, especially in winter. They would end up covered in a black rubbish bag. A piece of waste. Nothing more. Sometimes he would envy them. The struggle over. He didn't believe in anything else, any afterlife, any God. That was for fools and the rich. He survived, that was all. Survival.

He circled Podil, running like he had seen the joggers do. Trying to keep his head high, his elbows pumping, his step strong. Pretending. Until at last he felt warm enough, and dry enough, to head back to the place he called home. He ran up Andriivs'kyi, past the tourists paying too much for Soviet relics: old army uniforms, hats, *matryoshka* nesting dolls – some of a succession of Soviet leaders: Putin, Medvedev, Stalin, Lenin, Yeltsin, Brezhnev, Khrushchev, Gorbachev. Others the traditional *babushkas* decorated in floral costumes – lace, shawls. Paintings made by ex-cons. Their tattoos telling stories of who had done what, especially the ones on their faces. No hiding that. A life sentence.

Usually he would stroll up this steep little hill ignoring its cobbles and quaintness, the shabby chic buildings, pretty tables decked with their goods. He would be focussed on the people, looking out for easy targets: open bags, fat wallets, mobile phones poking out of jeans and jackets, a back turned, eyes distracted, attention averted. Not today. Today they were a blur of irrelevance. An annoyance.

He cut through an alleyway, narrow, enclosed, smelling of piss. A nasty combination of animal and human. Then across a courtyard of uneven cobbles, crumbling flower pots, dead plants. Finally across the patch of wasteland – rubble, broken bottles, garbage bags ripped open, contents strewn across patches of dirt and broken concrete – to where the derelict building in whose basement he lived stood. It had been left to rot. Appropriate.

He checked up and down. No-one. Skipped over the wall and into his courtyard. Across the remnants of another life, an existence long past, to the makeshift covering that was a sorry excuse for a door. He knew it would be empty. Time was valuable and all those who shared his home would be out begging, stealing, foraging in bins, smiling at women, chatting up strangers. Whatever it took.

*

Sasha checked to make sure no-one was watching. Alyona stood behind him looking up at the sky. A different world. He shifted the corrugated iron aside. Beneath it the decomposing remnants of the wooden door. It clung to its rotting frame by one rusted hinge. He crouched below the splintered wood and pulled Alyona in behind him. The derelict building creaked and groaned; the mumblings of a condemned man. Sasha waited for his eyes to adjust to the darkness. Lifting the hatch in the floor, he made his way down the crumbling steps to the basement, where his breath was caught by the familiar concoction of glue, alcohol, sweat, and garbage. It was foul, but it was what he now called home.

'Sasha! Alyona! What the fuck have you two done?' Dima called – his body draped in a dirty old blanket, his face pale, almost blue – as he made out their faces from the feeble light of the bulb, which hung precariously by its live wire.

'What do you mean?' Sasha replied, taken aback. The usual greeting was a, "Hey man," and a high five.

'That crazy fucker Leonid Lezo paid me a visit at the metro. He was asking after your sister.' He nodded towards Alyona. 'Gave me this,' he added, pointing to the dark, red gash down his face; still wet, still angry, crying out for some stitches. 'Said it'd go a lot deeper next time. What the fuck have you done to get on the wrong side of him?'

'And what did you tell him?' Sasha asked, clinging onto the faith he had in his only true friend.

'What do you think? That I didn't know her of course.'

'Cool. Thanks,' Sasha breathed his reply with obvious relief. He glanced around the basement. 'Can we talk? In private?'

'Sure.' Dima shrugged, open palms. 'There's no-one else here.'

'But there might be. They might come in.'

'Okay, man.' Dima gestured towards the back of the basement. The growing collection of discarded bottles and piles of cardboard was stacked in a corner, waiting to be exchanged for a few *kopeks;* maybe even *Hryvnia* if they'd gathered a decent amount. Along a corridor strewn with rubble. On a blanket lay a straggly bitch and her mangy puppies which snarled and whimpered as the children passed.

'Oh,' Alyona sighed. 'My little babies. Hello little

babies.' She bent down and held her hand out.

The first time she had done this Sasha's instinct had been to pull her away, but he knew better. His sister would need to reach out, to touch them, to connect. It was who she was and there was no changing it. Not that he would want to anyway. She was special. And he loved her all the more for it.

The bitch sniffed and lowered her hackles, her tail flicked, then wagged its acceptance.

Alyona sat beside the puppies and giggled, as they clambered over her frail body. Her spiky boyish blond hair framing a face that could have been sculpted from porcelain. Fine. Delicate. Her eyes, such a peculiar pale blue – a translucence to them – at times appearing as if they held a special wisdom, and at others as if they held nothing. A lost, blank stare. Just now they held a rare sparkle. A sparkle reserved for animals and things of the wild. Things of nature.

'So?' Dima asked. The crooked nose and broken teeth on the fourteen year old's face standing as a reminder of the battles he had fought; the reason he held the respect of his feral family.

'I don't know what happened, but Alyona came back with this.' Sasha handed an expensive looking sports bag over to Dima. The kind you would see slung across the shoulder of the fit and wealthy. It said Hugo Boss but this was Ukraine, so it was probably fake. 'She thinks the car was shot at, but you know what she's like. You never can tell what's real and what's not.'

'What car?' Dima's brow furrowed. 'You're not making any sense, man. What the fuck's going on?'

'Gregor. The blacked out Merc. The man who –'

'Yeah, yeah. Course,' he cut in dismissively with a wave of his hand, as he unzipped the holdall. He pulled the opening apart. Stared. Paused. He dipped his hand in and pulled out a plastic bag of white powder, turning it over, sniffing at it. 'You know what this is?' His voice rose with each word.

'Uh-uh.' Sasha shook his head. 'Drugs, I guess but no idea what.'

'Me neither but whatever it is, this is serious shit. If it wasn't you I'd kick you out on your ass. He'll be back later tonight...Lezo. For your sister.'

'So what do we do?' His voice had risen an octave.

'We? Fuck that, man.' Dima spat proudly on the floor. 'Who said anything about we? That guy's a fucking twisted piece of shit. No way, man. This is a you thing.'

'Come on bro?' Sasha pleaded, calling on a shared history. A brotherhood. 'We need help. Think about it. This could maybe get us out. Must be worth a bit. You want out, don't you? I know you do.'

'Sure. But I wanna live too.'

'So, we go to the States. California!' he grinned. Nudged Dima with his elbow. 'Like we've always said.'

'I dunno,' Dima mumbled, as he kicked at a bottle, watching it spin towards the wall.

'You chicken or something?'

'Fuck off. I ain't afraid of nothing, except maybe the guys that own this!' he said, waving the bag in Sasha's face.

'Chicken. See.' He turned circles flapping his arms and clucking, making Dima giggle.

'Fuck off!' Dima said with a laugh.

'We sell it. We leave. Easy as that.'

Chapter 2

December 2001

Dima, Sasha, and Alyona stood at the entrance to the tower block in Darnytsa. Seventeen floors of decaying apartments; peeling balconies dressed in flaccid laundry and misery. The door clicked open and they headed in. Dima leading, Sasha and Alyona following, hand in hand. It had always been like that. Alyona had sucked the life from their mother with her birth. As Sasha watched her drift away it was as if her life force had slipped from one to the other – mother to daughter. As Alyona grew and their bond strengthened he knew that he would never leave her. He would keep her safe. Always.

His father, the man who had been his idol, the man he had looked up to, listened to, loved, began to slip away that day. It was as if he shrank from the world, his body shrinking too. He stooped under the weight of his grief. "He'll get over it," the neighbours had said. "Give him time." But he didn't. The strip of land that they had been given after the collapse of the Soviet Union couldn't run itself, and their friends and neighbours had enough of their own worries. Their own lives to struggle on with. Kind words, sympathetic faces, and the odd bowl of soup, weren't enough.

Each year, on Alyona's birthday, Sasha prayed to his mother for a miracle. None came. Five years had dragged by. Each one more difficult than the one before. Finally they moved to the big city. To Kyiv. Perhaps here it would be easier to forget. Life would be better.

They moved into an apartment in Podil that belonged to a cousin. It was small and damp and dark. The children were miserable. They knew no-one, no-where, nothing. At least back home they'd had friends. They'd had countryside to disappear into. To play games in. To get lost in for a while. To escape to. But here? Here it was all noise and danger and strangeness. Despite the heat of the summer it felt cold.

Their father's mood sank further. It seemed as though he had vanished, left them, and that they were now living with a complete stranger. A stranger who barely seemed to even notice their existence. He had moments. Moments when he came back and tried to be the father they needed. Moments when they thought perhaps this time? Perhaps now it would get better? The children learned to grab on to those times; to hold the memories, tie them up and store them in a safe place. The darkness always came back and when it did what they held in their memories kept them going. It was like this once. There was a chance it might be again.

After the first year in Kyiv their father brought a new woman into their home. She drank. They drank. They took pills that made them disappear from life, made them something else. The geographical cure hadn't worked. It had made things even worse. Sasha and Alyona were sent out to beg, to steal, to make money for their father and his new partner, Vika. Sasha hated her. Alyona? She didn't have the capacity to hate anyone. It was like she could see nothing bad in this life, despite their situation. Despite hunger and danger and abuse. She smiled through it all. That soft, gentle smile that could break through anything.

Sasha blamed Vika for the decline in their father. For his fall into the darkness of alcohol and pills. He would try to stay out with Alyona until late at night, when the adults were either comatose or too out of it to care. If they mistimed it they would be beaten more often than not.

They had become as good as street-kids. They hung out with street-kids. They never went to school. The closest thing they had to real family were the people of the street. It felt safer out there than in their apartment. The transition, when it came, from house to street was easy, natural, seamless. If anything they were better off. The money they made was theirs. What they went "home" to was more predictable. It was easier and safer to be a street-kid.

*

But perhaps because of this accident, the peculiar fortune of the strange bag that had been dropped into their lives, everything could now really change? No

14

more dreams but a way out. Perhaps this was it? A home, security, warmth, cleanliness, normality of some kind. Sasha didn't like to imagine, not for real; to think of a different life. It was dangerous. Best just to accept. Keep going. Stay alive. But this time...

Of course they had pretended, he and Dima. They had shared stories of what it would be like to live in the States of the movies they had crept in through a back door to watch. There was always a back door. A careless security guard, a friendly woman with a mother's heart.

They had imagined California, New York. Places with names that said, "Life is good here." They had spent so many nights lying head to head in the bleakness of their basement, imagining themselves in a sparkling mansion in Los Angeles. Lounging by the pool. Babes sprawling beside them. They had sports cars and palm trees. Faithful servants and loyal friends. Gucci clothes and Rolex watches. It was all perfect. Purely perfect. Beautiful lives, in beautiful houses, with beautiful people.

It could never be. They knew that. It was just a laugh. A bit of fun. A temporary light in the shadows of their lives. But maybe. Maybe this was big enough? Maybe there was something else? Something for them. He threw the thoughts away and focussed on what was happening now.

'You wait here. They don't like strangers. Okay?' Dima instructed.

'Sure.'

The lift closed behind him and crept defiantly up, despite its baleful creaks and groans. Dima only carried a small bag of the white powder with him. Just to show what they had; just to find out what it was.

'I don't like it here. Can we go? Can we go home?' Alyona pleaded, her eyes in that somewhere else place. The curve of her lips reaching into that almost smile that questioned the world.

'Not now. We need to wait, but it'll all be okay. You'll see,' Sasha replied, putting his arm around her shoulders and giving her a reassuring hug. 'Dima won't be long.'

'I don't like it here,' she whimpered, wrinkling her nose, tugging at the torn sleeve of her sweater, glancing around the bleak stairwell – cobwebs and dust – cuddling into him. 'Mama doesn't like it here.'

Sasha smiled at her. 'You know you shouldn't talk like that. Mama isn't here any more.'

'Mama doesn't like it here,' she whispered to herself, looking at the ground, shuffling her feet.

They heard the lift whining its way back down. The doors opened and two smartly dressed men strode out, clad entirely in black. They stared at Alyona and Sasha. Alyona smiled and looked seductively at them. Her body that of a twelve year old. Her stance something entirely different.

'Not now, Alyona,' Sasha whispered. 'Not now.'

The men muttered something, glanced back and laughed as they left the building.

'Am I bad?' Alyona asked.

'No, no. Just not now, okay?' he replied, trying not to be impatient.

She smiled at him. 'Okay.'

*

When Dima finally came back he exhaled with a whistle and gestured for them to follow, a skip in his

16

step, a smile on his face, a buzz in his eyes. 'It's cocaine, man,' he said excitedly, sniffing, wiping his nose with his frayed sleeve. 'Top quality cocaine from the Colombians. Never had stuff like this, man. It's ace! Phew!' He was buzzing. Words stringing together in a coked-up frenzy. 'Word's out all over what happened. Colombians pissed off about money, or something. A gun fight. Fucking cool. Wish I'd seen it.' He pulled a shooting stance. 'Bang, bang. Blood and guts. No wonder Lezo wants you, or her, rather. Fuck! Was she in the car then? Alyona?' He turned to Alyona. 'Were you there? Did you see it? What happened? Did you?'

'I don't know,' she began, confused, her brow furrowed, a cloud passing over those pale, blue eyes. 'There was a big noise. There was blood. I ran.'

'And the bag? Why did you take the bag?'

'I–I don't know. It was tangled around me. And there was blood. I had to get away, to run. The bag came too.'

'Shit!'

'So what do we do?' Sasha asked, hoping Dima would have a plan, like usual.

'We need to be smart. To think.' He tapped at his head. 'This is serious shit and I don't want no knife in my back! No sir. Not me!'

'So?'

'Right now, we go spend this,' he replied, grinning, holding up five twenty dollar bills. 'Dollars man! Sheesh! We can go up the *rynok* Get some clothes, some food, some vodka!'

'And how did you get that?' Sasha asked, holding his hand out for one of the notes, turning it over, smelling it, smiling.

'For that little bag! Imagine what all of it must be worth. Fuck!'

'And you told them? That we had it?'

'Course not. I ain't stupid! Told them that I saw some guys running and a bag of white powder fell on the ground so I picked it up.' He laughed. Nudged Sasha in the ribs.

Sasha laughed. Nudged him back.

'Who d'ya love?' Dima asked with a big grin.

'You, bro!' Sasha answered.

Alyona was talking to someone, to something that wasn't there. Oblivious.

Sasha was happy at the thought of food and warmth but not vodka. He knew that all of the other kids drank anything they could get hold of, and he knew why. That escape. That lapse into oblivion, but he hated it. He hated what it did to the people he loved. To his father, to his best friend. He vowed that he would never drink or do drugs. No matter what happened, he wouldn't do that.

They headed to the metro laughing and joking, sniffing at a future. Snow had begun to fall. Alyona turned her face up and smiled as the flakes flitted around her and settled on the ground at her feet. Her legs stuck into black ankle boots that exaggerated the skinniness of them. Snowflakes crept in between flesh and leather. She giggled softly.

'Alyona, come on!' Sasha called, gesturing for her to take his outstretched hand. 'The train's coming. Look!'

They ran along the concrete path through what used to be grass, between high tower blocks and low lives, to the station, and clambered on. The doors shuddered closed behind them.

They travelled the rest of the way in silence, each lost in their own thoughts. Perhaps even in dreams. The train rumbled through decrepit stations, across the Dnieper river, its water almost frozen over. Soon there would be people fishing through holes they had cut in the ice. Some for sport; for the peace of it, the brotherhood, but mostly out of necessity; trying to put food on the table.

The train went through Hydropark. A blanket of decaying leaves swirled along the beaches, wrapping themselves around the rusting play park where empty swings swung defiantly. Cruise boats sat forlorn, tied up, awaiting summer, laughter and hope.

*

They got off the train at Kontraktova Ploscha and walked casually but quickly up to the *rynok,* not wanting to draw attention to themselves. Dima was scanning the streets for Lezo, thankful for the man's height and the arrogant strut that he always moved with, making him an easy spot. There could be others after Alyona too. He and Sasha knew that. She didn't. Best kept that way.

A change in appearance had become paramount. One hundred dollars was a fortune to them, but they didn't know how long it would have to last them for. No point in wasting it. They would have loved to walk into one of those smart, shiny shops, smiling back at the disdainful looks, nodding at the armed security guards, flashing their money, sampling the goods. Buying something just because they could. Something that was frivolous, useless, expensive.

In a far corner of the *rynok* was a second-hand stall. It was in a tent-like structure; its walls flapping in the icy wind that crept in beneath the canvas. This was the wise thing to do. Even here, the *babushka* serving – a large woman with an apron tied around her ample midriff, the ubiquitous floral headscarf – was eyeing them suspiciously. Dima smiled at her. He had probably stolen from her before. A hand under the wall. A snatch at something, anything. You chanced your arm. Hoped for the best. Anything could be sold on. Flowers removed from graves and taken to the gates of the cemetery to be bought again. It was just recycling, right?

'We all want clothes. New things for all of us.' He said confidently, showing her that he had money.

She gave them a warm, gold-toothed smile and ushered them in like a *babushka* to her grandchildren.

They chatted and laughed as she pulled out what she thought they would like from her piles of other people's cast-offs. Most of it was from European charities.

This felt so good. A change of clothes. Warmth. It was like having a new identity and they all felt it. They all grew straighter, like they didn't have to hide. But, of course they did. Now more-so than ever.

Alyona chose a pink sweater that had threads of sparkles running through it. It was made of the softest material she had ever felt. She stroked it like it was a much loved pet animal. They all had gloves and boots and socks, and the luxury of warm feet. Jackets with zips that worked. Hats that looked fresh and almost new, and almost stylish. This felt so very good.

'We need to keep away from places where people

know us. We need to be smart. No showing off. Right?' Dima said, confirming his customary role of leader.

'Sure,' Sasha replied.

'I want to show everyone how beautiful I look. Papa will love me now,' Alyona said in a shrill excited voice. An innocent voice. She was twirling around like the dancer she saw in her head. Her jacket undone, despite the cold, so that her jumper could be seen. So that she could stroke it.

'No Alyona. Not now,' Sasha said. 'We're playing a game of hide and seek, okay? We are the hiding ones and no-one we know is allowed to see us or the game will be over. Okay?' He squeezed her hand. 'Okay?'

Alyona sighed disappointedly, then smiled up at her brother with that look of adoration she kept solely for him. 'Okay. I can show Papa later.'

It had been years since they had had any contact with their father, but somehow, in Alyona's mind, he was still a part of their lives. Still someone who cared about them, someone she wanted to impress, someone she loved. Sasha had cut him out of his life completely. He would shrug when asked and reply, "I don't have any parents, they died." And to him they had. Both of them.

'Yes, later,' Sasha confirmed. Sometimes it was easier just to go along with her. To let her believe. He wrestled with it though, not wanting to lie to his sister, to deceive her. But sometimes – sometimes it was for the best.

They were hurrying towards the hill, where they could hide amongst the trees and bushes and wait until darkness, before returning to their basement to pick up the bag. Dima had hidden it in one of the walls, securing it behind a pile of bricks. It would be safe.

The days were almost at their shortest now. The light was weak and dusk was hovering on daylight's shoulders. The discretion of darkness would be with them soon.

'Sasha! Alyona! Hey!' a voice called. It was in the accent of a foreigner – a Westerner.

'Oh. It's Nadia. Hello Nadia,' Alyona called back, standing on tip-toes, waving her gloved hand, forgetting about the game of hide and seek.

'Shit,' Dima muttered.

'It's okay. She is a friend. A good person,' Sasha answered. 'She helps us. We can trust her.'

'Sasha, we don't trust nobody. You understand that? Nobody!'

'Oh, look at you guys,' Nadia said. 'New clothes! Cool!' She stroked Alyona's shoulder and smiled. 'You look beautiful, Alyona.'

'Thank you Nadia.' Alyona smiled back, her face full of pride. 'So do you! But you are always beautiful.'

Nadia laughed, looking disparagingly at her jeans, clumpy boots, and long, thick jacket. 'I don't know about that! But thank you anyway.'

A *militsiya* van drove past, its siren screeching. Angry words spewed out from its loudspeaker. *Get out of the way! Get out of the way!*

Nadia shivered. 'I hate that sound. Bloody intimidating. Even though I haven't done anything wrong it gives me the creeps. Every time!' She laughed a hollow laugh that splintered amongst the ice crystals of her breath.

'I hate them,' Dima spat. 'Bastards. All of them. Just bastards.'

'Can't say as I blame you.' She pulled one of her gloves off, held out her hand to Dima. 'I'm Nadia by the way.'

'Yes, I know. English lady. I know who you are. I know everything.' He didn't accept her hand. His look was one of contempt.

Nadia bit down a laugh. This little kid playing the big, hard man. But then she knew enough about the lives of these children to understand that their ages didn't correlate with their maturity in the slightest. They had seen things, done things, that most people back home couldn't even imagine. She knew how hard their lives were.

Chapter 3

June 2001

Nadia had accepted this job in Ukraine much to the chagrin of her father. She knew what the conversation would be like and was dreading it.

'Ukraine!' her father had said, with a softly raised voice and incredulity. 'You know I support you in most things but...Ukraine! Could you not have chosen a safer place to go to? Why are you going anyway? Could you not just stay here?'

'Oh Dad!'

'Less of the, "Oh Dads", if you please. It's far away. It's as corrupt as–' He shook his head, struggling to find the right words. 'As is. And it's a dangerous place. You know what's happening there? That journalist Gongadze?'

'Of course I do.'

'Got his head chopped off and his remains dumped in the woods and set on fire, all for criticising the government! Come on Nadia! They haven't even found his killer. That could be you. My wee girl. Your ma would...ach!'

'Your wee girl!' She did her best to conceal her laugh, but it crept out anyway. 'Dad, it'll be fine. I'm British. I'm only teaching English, not starting a revolution. Trust me. I'll be fine.'

'You know what you're like. Too nice, too trusting, always getting yourself into trouble.'

Nadia raised her eyebrows and sighed. 'I'll be a good wee girl. I promise.' She planted a kiss on his cheek.

Nadia couldn't wait. She was desperate to get out there. To feel alive again. Okay again. She needed something to take her away from what had become her reality. This felt like it. A second chance at life. Of course it would be hard to leave her dad behind. It was just the two of them now. He had been brilliant. Her rock. But things had to change and she could see no other way. She had to leave.

She had arrived in the early summer, when Kyiv shows its sunny side. When the populace smile and chat in outdoor cafes. When blossom sits heavy on the air. People stroll along broad pavements lined with trees; their leaves casting delicate shadows that dance on the concrete. Buskers and story-tellers hold court for crowds that swell and fall like a tide. Lovers hold hands and talk of happy futures. The sun shines. Life is good. But under all of this she felt something. She couldn't put her finger on it. Couldn't name it. A surreptitiousness perhaps. It was as if the city had another face. A hidden side.

Perhaps all of those years under Soviet rule had

left a stain. A presence. A country, like a person, can't completely erase its history. Remove all of the scars. Something has to cling on. And it was barely a decade ago, in 1991, when Ukraine had voted for independence and secession from the USSR. A free country again, in name at least.

The severity of the border guards hadn't helped with her first impressions of the place, making her feel guilty of some unknown crime. Dirty looks and suspicion. What are you doing in our country? She was probably imagining it. Forget it. For now it was beautiful and she was drinking it in. That's what you should do, isn't it? Take things at face value. Enjoy them for what they are. Live them.

She hadn't started at the school yet, preferring to come across early, to get a feeling for the place and the people before work began. She had been enjoying herself, meandering through the streets, playing tourist, relishing in the Cyrillic street-signs, posters, shop names, and the fact that she could read them, understand them. The sounds of Ukrainian and Russian drifted along the streets, through the starkly different buildings; the feeling almost exotic. She was an expatriate and no-one knew her here. How cool was that?

It was hot and sticky, and she was sitting – like many others – with her feet in the cooling waters of one of the umpteen fountains at Maidan Nezalezhnosti. Freedom Square. It felt relaxed. People sitting, others paddling or just standing in the water, idle chatter, children playing. *See Dad, it's all good!*

It was crowded. She was careful. One hand on her

bag at all times, just as she had been advised. She wasn't about to take chances in this place. Not let her guard down. Not yet. Hopefully it would come, though. That was what she wanted most. Needed. To be able to simply relax without looking over her shoulder. Without fear.

Her attention was casually drawn to a small group of boys who were playing in the water, giggling, splashing, just being boys, but not looking like the rest of the children here. An edge to them. A grubbiness. A young girl, who appeared to be one of their number, sat on the low wall of the fountain, her knees drawn tight against her body, her arms wrapped around them, her head turned up to the sky. It didn't fit with the weather; with the feel of what was going on around her.

But there was also something different about the whole group. A seriousness beneath the laughter. Nadia smiled and kept watching them. Her mind working overtime, as always. Street-kids she guessed. Something else she had been warned about. Watch out for the street-kids!

An urgent whisper drifted through the crowds and the children ran. Them and several other people. The hawkers selling their illicit wares, counterfeit cigarettes and alcohol, disappeared. Huge tartan plastic bags were covered and hastily removed. It was as if she had suddenly been transported to a different place, the change in mood was so tangible.

She stood up and glanced around for whatever might have caused this blatant nervousness and sudden flight. The hem of her skirt, wet from the fountain, clung awkwardly to her legs.

In the distance she saw them. The oversized hats, the army style uniforms. The weapons. *Militsiya.* She had been forewarned. They were to be avoided if at all possible – So many warnings. Look out for this, look out for that – Those with reason to hide did so, others looked away, carried on with what they were doing. The *militsiya* were being purposefully ignored by most. They didn't appear to be doing anything, to be chasing anybody, or on the lookout for anyone. They were simply strolling through the crowd with an air of authoritative nonchalance, a menace attached to it.

Nadia looked back at the hastily disappearing children. They had scampered off into the bustle of Khreschatyk – the main street in the city centre – and disappeared. Her curiosity piqued, she decided to follow. She hastily slipped her sandals back on – ethnic, beads strung through soft leather – and hurried after them. Standing on tiptoes at the edge of the busy thoroughfare, she caught a glimpse of them. Heads bobbing, legs skipping. Trees, buses, people all blocked her view. *Dammit!*

She looked left and right. No sign. They could be anywhere. She decided to head in the direction of where she thought they had gone, out of the centre and right towards Podil. It was on her "to do" list. Why not make it now? She was always happier on the move these days anyway.

She walked past the concrete and glass of the hotel Dnipro. An ugly building where she imagined equally ugly things happened. A place of dirty dealings, of hookers and businessmen.

A circle of the blue and yellow flags of Ukraine

fluttered softly on their roundabout that seemed to draw a line between the built up grandeur and severity of the city centre and something else. Something quieter. Something softer.

She could feel it change as she began the descent. The road became narrower and tree lined. A total contrast to what she had just left. Her spirits lifted with the atmosphere. On one side of her was a steep slope of grass and trees. On the other a peculiar classical arch which seemed to have no purpose. A concrete path twisted off behind it, amongst trees and bushes, begging to be explored. That would be for another day.

As the grass embankments on either side of the road grew taller the sounds bounced back off them, like they were trapped. Cars made a peculiar humming screech on the cobbles. Her footsteps replied to her from either side of the road. It became uncomfortable. Close.

She stopped for a moment to catch her breath; to gather her thoughts, to slow down. This had been going on for too long. The anticipation of something evil. The constant feeling of someone following her. She had to let it go.

Exploring the strangeness, experiencing a life different, that was what she was doing here. A life in which she needed to build a growing sense of purpose, of control, of peace. She exhaled heavily, blowing out the last of unwelcome memories. There was nothing to fear here. Inhale. She was okay. Exhale. Everything was okay. Inhale. Focus on the now. Exhale.

Shoulders back. Head high. Her pace strengthened

with the self-determination she could feel building within her. It was like a long lost friend. This was good. This was all good, she reminded herself.

Finally she could see the Dnieper river at the bottom of the hill, to her right. It was a big, impressive waterway that cut the city in two. Big enough to almost give Kyiv the feel of a city on the coast. Gulls shrieked, boats travelled up and down past sandy beaches – some working, others pleasure boats for merrymakers and tourists.

When the ground became flat and she was on the same level as the water, she glanced along the bank at the peculiar assortment of boats advertising cruises of varying durations and prices. There was an endearing starkness to them. A step back in time to simpler days. But then much of Kyiv was like that. Remnants of Soviet times were everywhere, from the functional severity of the buildings to the elaborate and impressive statues and monuments. There was an odd contrast of seeming wealth and blatant poverty. Of power and weakness.

On the other side of the river were sandy beaches and tree coated islands. *Another day*, she said to herself, *another day*. Today she was looking for...street-kids. She laughed inwardly at the idea and turned back towards the main drag, to Petra Sahaidachnoho Street.

There was an altogether friendlier feeling to this part of Kyiv – like a village within a city. The buildings stood two or three stories high, their facades in faded reds and pinks, blues and yellows. Kiosks were dotted along the roadside, selling alcohol and cigarettes, candies, basic foods, most of what you might need in a hurry. *Obmen Valut* kiosks – money changers – seemed to be everywhere. There were small old-fashioned cafes; places where locals ate and drank. She much preferred that to the recommended expat haunts. This was looking promising and she imagined herself making many return trips. Perhaps even moving down here.

Her employers had put her up in a small apartment on Yaroslaviv, which was fine for now. It was central, quiet enough, and close to everything that she needed, but she could only stay for a week or two. They had lined up some places for her to look at over the next few days. She hoped one might be here, as she pictured herself settling in, becoming a local in one of the cafes, learning the names of the staff in the shops. Chatting. Being known. The reverie pleased her.

The road she was on came to an end at Kontraktova Ploscha, and she had a choice to make. To the right, a vast and seemingly pointless space of tarmac. Some of it filled with parked cars, the rest of it lying useless and empty. She imagined it lined with tanks and military vehicles in Soviet times and shivered. Nestling behind it impressive, elegant buildings with gentle curves, grand pillars and a skirting of trees – pine, birch, chestnut – their leaves softly, mesmerically swishing. Beyond, more roads, apartment buildings, tram tracks.

To the left, a more informal looking road. Intimate, comfortable. She turned towards it, but her legs and their weariness summoned her instead to an open space of trees and grass, and the ubiquitous fountain. They seemed to be everywhere in this place. A seat in the shade of the trees near the cool of the fountain would be good.

She sat on the concrete wall of the fountain and trailed her hand in the water, watching the ripples make their way to the other side, carrying thoughts, dreams. Pigeons, crows, and starlings fluttered and strutted around, marching clumsily towards crumbs, their necks jerking back and forth, back and forth, pecking at something sticky and black.

Young people sat on the grass drinking bottles of beer, smoking, laughing, heads tossing back with the best of laughs. Some old drunks, *bumsh*, as they were referred to, staggered between the groups, trying to join in, to bum a cigarette, share a laugh, or even better, a drink. They were chased off amidst derisory noises. *"Foo!"* Like the stray dogs that hovered around looking for titbits, pulling wrappings out of the garbage cans, fighting over them, the winners hurrying back into the shadows with their prize – the losers continuing their hunt, bellies empty.

Then she saw them, two of the kids from the fountain at Maidan, a boy and the girl, sitting on the grass. There was a strange quality about them. A closeness. An otherworldliness. If not for the apparent age difference they could have been twins. Nadia was fascinated. Drawn. They were eating some dry bread, drinking from a carton of *kefir* – a sort of fermented milk that everyone here seemed to love, but Nadia thought was disgusting.

It had been part of the welcome package in her apartment, along with bread and cheese, cold meats, tomatoes, fruit, chocolates, and Ukrainian brandy. She had felt duty-bound to try it. It disappointed. Even the smell repulsed her and she winced back from the

32

carton before emptying its contents down the sink. She watched, feeling slightly nauseous, as it gurgled its way down the plughole. It was chased away with a torrent of cold water from the tap.

*

She moved closer to the children, sat herself down on the grass a respectable distance away from them, and took some surreptitious pictures with the little Canon IXY that her father had bought for her just before she left.

'There. No excuse now, Nadia lass. It's even one o they digital thingies and it's so small. Look! You can snap away and put pictures on that computer o yours and send them to me. Clever eh!'

'Thanks Dad. It's great, but you'll need a computer at this end too.' She laughed warmly. Her dad the total technophobe.

'Way ahead of you there as well. Got one on order. Stevie's gonna hook me up, or whatever it is that you do.' He grinned with self satisfaction. 'Aye.'

'Wow Dad. The twenty first century has come knocking on your door. Proud of you.' She hugged him.

'Aye, less of that cheek. Just mind and use it now that you've got it.'

'I will. Promise.'

*

A tram rattled past in the distance, crackles of electricity shooting out from its overhead cables. She felt suddenly uncomfortable. That feeling of someone watching her. Someone too attentive, too close for comfort. She was about to turn around when a man sat down beside her on the grass.

'Hi,' he said in English, but he was definitely local. He was tall, dark, and swarthy, like many of the male population over here, but he had a twinkle, a spark and the flashiest of smiles that sat amidst his finely chiselled features. A plain white T shirt clung to a well defined torso. Blue jeans, classic brown leather belt, trainers. An army style bag slung across his shoulders. He didn't fit. The look casual but too clean. It was as if he were trying too hard to look...casual. The hair perfect. The hint of stubble but obviously today's growth. He looked as if he worked out, but he was smoking. That didn't fit either. She couldn't work him out and it annoyed her. He annoyed her.

'I'm sorry. I don't know you,' she replied in Russian, bristling, defensive. Taken aback. She didn't like the fact that this stranger had thought it okay to sit beside her, to invade her space, nor how he had guessed her ethnicity.

*

She had studied Russian at school, and then at college. The country and the language had always held a fascination for her. Socialism had been instilled in her for as long as she could remember. Her father, a shop floor worker, trade unionist, militant. Her mother, when she was alive, equally strong in her beliefs. Marx, Lenin, and socialism were spoken of frequently and with warmth. They had called her Nadia after Nadezhda Krupskaya, Lenin's wife.

'Just you remember your namesake. Get strength from it, lass. You stand up for your rights. Naebody, and I mean naebody is better than you,' her father had said, as he downed his cup of tea and hurried out of the door to his job at the brewery. He made decent money, right enough, but it wasn't what he wanted for his daughter. No. She would do well. She would get an education and he would make damned sure of it. Academics didn't come easily to her, but she worked, burying herself in her studies for her father. She would make him proud. And she did.

She knew that Russian was understood in most of the former USSR countries. That gave her so many places where she could travel to and use her language. Here, in Kyiv, it was still dominant over Ukrainian.

*

'Okay. We shall speak Russian if you prefer.' He smiled, holding her with confident eyes. The type that didn't look away. The type that read you.

It unnerved her. He unnerved her. She stood up, shook her head. 'Excuse me,' she said curtly, and walked off feeling annoyed, intruded upon. Perhaps even threatened.

'Hey! Hold up. I was only trying to be friendly,' he called.

She could hear his footsteps behind her. It was busy enough. There was no danger, not like before, but she was perturbed, perhaps even scared, and she didn't like the visitation to that place she had left behind. It wasn't welcome. Neither was the man following her. She could feel the beginnings of a panic attack. Her chest hurt. Her breathing was short. Her mind slipping. *Oh God, you're better than this! Come on. Get it together. Get it together.* She rummaged in her bag. Her fingers felt the welcome cool and familiarity of stone. It wasn't anything exotic or precious. Just a little white pebble that she had picked up from the beach so long ago. But it meant a lot to her and she used it as a means of grounding herself. Of reminding herself of the simple, good things which were always there if you looked hard enough. There was nothing to worry about.

She had just reached the pavement when a tram came rumbling along the tracks towards her. The stop was a few feet away. She didn't know where it was going, if it would take her anywhere near her place, but it would take her away from here, which was all that mattered right now. This feeling had to be left behind. She jumped on, paid her fare, and held on tightly to one of the handrails. Chipped paint, flaking rust, a nasty metallic smell.

The tram veered away from the square, away from the centre of Podil. After a few minutes nothing looked familiar and it was airless, stifling. Her blouse began to stick to her, a heavy smell of sweat and stale vodka permeated everything. She felt slightly nauseous. All around her was a buzz of strangeness, of foreign sounds and smells. It was as if the world were shouting "alien" at her; that everyone knew she didn't belong. At the next stop she jumped off.

She glanced around looking for a cafe, a bar, a place to sit and gather herself, stitch up the seams. Mostly she was annoyed with herself. *What was that all about Nadia? Stupid. Just stupid!*

Chapter 4

December 2001

Leonid had checked the most obvious churches where children might beg. Holy places. Guilty consciences. Loose wallets. Places where he himself had – no. He tossed that memory away. He had walked around St Andrew's with its green onion domes and ornate gold trimmings, St Michael's famed golden domes, St Sophia's – less audacious and to him, somehow, more holy.

He crossed himself at each, of course, but lingered at St Sophia's, allowing himself a momentary break from his hunt, his dark thoughts. This was such a peaceful place, a clean place. He could feel it in its whitewashed walls and cobble stones, wooden benches in the protection of ancient trees, now bare but gracious. Noble. Shrubs exuded a soft pine smell despite the weight of winter. Voices only in whispers, footsteps light and careful. The swish of a monk's habit, a priest's cloak. All soft. All gentle. All cleansing. Another world.

He offered a prayer on bended knee and left, throwing a few *Hryvnia* into the paper cup of an old, frail looking *babushka* clad in a huge black coat, layers of headscarves, prostrate, mumbling. 'Bless you, my son, bless you. May Christ be with you. Bless you.' No eye contact made.

He turned onto the broad, cobbled grandeur of Volodymyrska Street. Traffic, people, noise, life. Then down the steep hill of Sofiivs'ka Street, dotted with empty plant pots and naked trees, a rumbling trolley bus, a stooped man leaning into a rubbish bin. Then on to the wide, open space of Maidan. The square where people met to debate politics, to protest, to spark the beginnings of revolutions – of love stories. To sell counterfeit cigarettes and alcohol. To oil the machine.

This was getting tedious. He had better things he could be doing with his time than traipsing around the streets, in the freezing cold, on the trail of some good-for-nothing, waste of space, street-kid, like her.

He looked up at the red lights of the digital clock, high in the tower above the square. Nodded his head. Turned around. He had an appointment.

*

He slipped into the back of the *militsiya* car. It was an old beige Lada – insignificant, much like its drivers. They were low standing but hungry for more. More success, more respect, more money than their meagre salary. No-one could live off that. Of course bribes and external work were the norm. These two were loyal, dependable. Leonid had no reason to doubt them.

'Leonid. How are you?'

'Fucking freezing!' He blew on his hands to emphasize the point, even though they were gloved. 'You?'

'Yeah, good. Same old shit, you know? How can we help you then?'

'A street-kid causing trouble. I need her.' He paused and looked from one to the other, eyebrows raised. 'Alive. Tonight.' A slow careful delivery. The words accentuated, their importance stressed.

'And do we know this street-kid?' the driver asked, his arm resting along the back of his partner's seat.

'This girl.' Leonid removed one of his gloves with his teeth, took the picture out of his pocket, and handed it to the passenger. 'Alyona. Hangs out with her brother in Podil mostly, and around Maidan. Begs, steals, you know the score. A bit touched by all accounts. She's done a runner and we need her. I need her.'

'A runner from what?'

Leonid cocked his head, stared, eyes narrowed, brow furrowed. "You know you shouldn't be asking that," written all over his face. 'Just find her.'

They shook hands, the slap of flesh on flesh. Leonid watched as the car sped off down the hill. The chances of them finding her before him were minimal, but it was worth having the extra eyes, just in case. They had different people they could squeeze than he did. It might draw something.

He walked back to where he lived on Kostolna, a quiet little side street off Maidan, inhabited by a mix of expats and the better off locals. He glanced up at the peeling pink brickwork, the odd assortment of balconies, some enclosed in glass, others grey metal, all precarious in their own way. Crumbling. Basements held boutique shops, a gallery, some cafes. It was a desirable area, but not for him. It would do for now, but he wanted more. Much more. He wanted what Igor had. Ultimate respect and more money than he could ever use.

He checked for anything unusual, any tails, before he pressed the code into the entry system and took the stairs two at a time, until he reached the top floor. The apartment was stark, barely furnished. Not out of a minimalist fashion statement. This had purpose. On the outside, his clothing, his car, what people saw of him, that was expensive and flashy. You had to keep up appearances. And Igor made sure of that; made sure Leonid and his comrades showed the trappings of wealth, of success, of power. His power. But here. Behind the scenes. Nothing unnecessary, nothing extravagant. Just enough. It kept Leonid and the others hungry, focussed, driven. That was what Igor wanted from them. The desire for more, and that more was offered by Igor. To betray him would mean death. They knew that.

There was nothing to clutter Leonid's life. He had no family, no girlfriend. Hookers were so available, so abundant, why bother with the hassle of a girlfriend? His whores knew what he liked. He knew the price. A straightforward transaction. Life was best kept simple. No room for distractions, for emotions. He knew that feelings were for the weak, for the emotionally needy. He was neither. He knew where he was going and it was up.

His flatmate – Andrei, another of Igor's men – had left his mug on the coffee table, a used plate beside it. Crumbs, stains, germs. 'For fuck's sake,' Leonid muttered. 'Lazy bastard,' he grumbled, hesitating, before picking it up and taking it into the kitchen. He hated cleaning up after Andrei, but couldn't stand the mess either. This was easier. It was more efficient.

A quick coffee and a bite to eat to boost his adrenaline, keep him sharp, and he was off again. Back down to Podil. He would find them. Of that he had no doubt. It baulked when Igor had said he was one of them. He wasn't. Not any more. But he knew their ways. Some things stayed with you. Some things you cannot shake. He hated it, but it was true. He knew these people. Oh yes, he knew them.

He headed up the hill, checked the church at the top of his street. It was usually gypsies that begged there – persistent and annoying – but you never knew. It was always best to be sure. The inconvenience would be worth it. Another blank. No big surprise.

He cut through the park. A lazy, open space in a busy, closed city; trees, benches, views for those who had the time to ponder. Past the British Embassy – a nod to the security guards, his nod returned – down onto Andriivs'kyi. There were a few places here worth checking. Basements, derelict buildings, hovels that he had once known intimately.

Digging around in the dirt and desperation of those places wasn't something he wanted to do, but it was what had got him this far. What Igor said, he did, no questions. And he did it well. He was tidy and efficient and as mean as they came. Feelings weren't an issue. Everyone knew he didn't have any. The sun

41

was sinking low in the sky. He was in a hurry.

Chapter 5

June 2001

They had found Nadia a place in Podil. It was small with a friendly atmosphere, and she loved it. There was nothing modern or pretentious about it. Old Soviet style furnishings. The monumental, heavy-duty wall units with glass fronts, housing all kinds of peculiarities. Ornate, over the top tea-sets, which seemed to be everywhere. Books, classics mostly. Pushkin, Tolstoy, Shevchenko. An inordinately large collection of encyclopedias. Plastic toys and dolls, even clothes.

It was odd and she felt like she had stepped into someone else's life for a while. It seemed too intrusive to go through the landlord's possessions that remained in drawers and cupboards. She had gone as far as to open them, briefly touch their contents. Tempted. Her fingers lingering. No. Doors and drawers were hastily closed as if she might be caught doing something illicit.

There was a smell. Old books. Old lives. Old dust. A time passed. Everything was old, functional and she liked it. It made her feel more like a local. More like she belonged.

The plumbing was ancient. The pipes gurgled and mumbled as if in complaint at being used. There was a gas water-heater above the bath which gave off an ominous smell. The first time she had used it she held a match at arm's length, turned the dial to "on" and winced as it boomed into life. The whole contraption shook as the water passed through it. But, like most things here, despite its appearance and apparent overused state, it worked, and the water spurted out of the shower-head with a satisfying strength. An effective means of unravelling tension, almost as good as a massage.

She had enjoyed finding her way around the area, chosen a favourite shop, kiosk, and cafe; made herself known through persistent smiles, good-mornings and pleasantries. It took time but, eventually, after initial confusion, they were well accepted, the smiles warmly reciprocated, the greetings returned from most. Yes. She could relax here now. Anxiety turning into a memory.

*

It had been an uncomfortably hot day, and she was sitting at the fountain on Kontraktova, listening to the cawing of the crows, watching them flit from tree to tree, fighting over a scrap of food, tumbling through the sky, righting themselves, swirling, swooping. Their relentlessness impressive. She was people-watching as usual. It had always been one of her favourite ways to while away a few lazy hours. Inventing lives, making up stories, wondering.

She had taken countless pictures of the park, of people, of everyday life, partly because it was just something that she liked to do, but also to send to her dad, confirming that everything was just fine and he needn't worry. Of course he did. That was a father's job. But he was, at least, reassured. As long as the pictures kept coming it was okay. His daughter was coping.

*

'Hey disappearing lady. You are really hard to keep track of. You know that?'

It was that man again. She really didn't want this. Didn't need this. And what did he mean, "Keep track of?" Warning bells were flying off in all directions.

She smiled, but not warmly. 'Um. Perhaps that's on purpose. You know? I don't want to be pestered. If that's okay with you I'd sooner just sit here on my own.' She turned away.

'Oh. No harm meant.' He put his arms up in submission. 'I was just trying to be friendly. Even bought you a beer. Look. *Baltika* number 3. That's the one you like, yes? And it's cold. Look!' He pointed out the trickle of condensation.

'How did you–?' She was getting really uncomfortable. What kind of game was this man playing?

He laughed, his eyebrows raised, a bright sparkle in his blue eyes. 'It's what you're drinking. I saw the label and bought you one, that's all. Why so suspicious? Are Western women all like this? Ah, of course! I remember from my English lessons. You are

British. I need to introduce myself, yes? Hello. My name is Artem. I am pleased to meet you,' he said mimicking a posh English accent. Badly. He held his hand out and looked comically expectant.

Despite herself, she found that she was smiling. What harm could it do? 'Nadia. Not sure if I'm pleased to meet you but–'

They shook hands. His shake strong, firm, confident. She noticed how perfectly manicured his hands were. Fingers long and slender. Musician's fingers, she wondered.

'We kiss. In Ukraine, when you meet a beautiful lady you kiss her on both cheeks.'

'Well we shake hands, okay?'

He pulled a crestfallen face.

She laughed.

'May I?' he asked, pointing to the space on the fountain wall beside where she was sitting.

'I guess.'

Apparently they had quite a lot in common. People-watching, making up lives, stories to go with their subjects, photographing them. His was a more serious hobby than hers. He had a darkroom where he developed his own photographs, even sold a few of his pictures to the press. The anti president Kuchma demonstrations, the tents of protestors pitched on Khreschatyk demanding change; an end to the corruption and dishonesty that had been a trademark of Kuchma's government.

The haunting devastation left by the nuclear accident at Chernobyl power station in 1986 – Pripyat, the city built to house its workers, deserted after the accident, now left like a post-apocalyptic scene from a dystopian movie. The buildings crumbling and overgrown with the wildness of nature left to its own devices. Everything empty, skeletal, desolate. The *babushkas* who had moved back to the exclusion zone – two and a half thousand square kilometres surrounding the power plant from where everyone had been removed and forbidden from returning to – walking for weeks to get there. Hiding, skulking. Where else were they to go? What else could they do? A room in a high rise block in a strange city far from all they knew? No. They were old. Their lives would be over soon enough. A little bit of radiation wasn't going to make much difference now, was it? They returned with the street-dogs and wild things and life carried on.

'You must come to my place and see my pictures. I think they'll be interesting for you.'

She burst into laughter. Beer trickled from her mouth as she did so. She wiped it off with the back of her hand. 'I can't believe you just said that. The oldest pick-up line in the world and you've used it!'

'No, no, no, it's true!' he protested, a blush bursting onto his cheeks. 'And you have beer all over your top.'

'Don't you dare try and dab it off. That would be just too much!'

They both laughed.

He was full of questions about Scotland; about the West in general. His dream was to travel. To be an international photojournalist. To work for some big newspaper, or better yet, Reuters. To uncover some great wrongdoing. To do good.

'But then I would have to leave Ukraine and I love

my country.' He shrugged in acceptance of his fate. They talked of Gongadze, of the dangers of honest journalism in this part of the world. He was frustrated by it all, but what could he do? What could any of them do? He worked for the city, for the council. He could live off it. Just.

'These people here, look.' He nodded towards a middle aged couple who were sitting on a bench quietly, not talking, not looking at each other. 'You see how they are so close. Their hands are touching but they are not holding each other's. Something illicit. An affair.'

'No. They haven't done anything. There's an innocence. They're just friends but they would like to be more,' she said.

'He was KGB. Arrested her. Had her locked up. And now he can't bear it. The guilt. She can't forgive him. Even though she loves him. She can't forgive him,' he added, his voice overly dramatic. Emotional.

'And so they just meet every day and sit in silence. Almost touching but not quite,' she concluded.

'I could cry!'

They laughed.

'And what about those two?' Nadia asked, pointing out the children who were becoming a preoccupation for her.

'The boy and girl?'

'Yes.'

'Street-kids. There are many of them here. No funny stories for them.' He grimaced. A look of sad resignation.

'Hmm.' She was warming to him. That was dangerous. Not part of her plan. 'I need to go,' she said suddenly, with no warning, no build up.

He looked surprised, stood up and stretched. 'Let me walk you home. It's getting dark.'

'I'm a big girl.' She smiled. 'I'm sure I'll be fine.'

'No really. I won't sleep if I don't know that you are safe and at home. This is Ukraine. You don't know the way of things here.'

She laughed. 'Oh, I think I do. I'll be fine.'

'At least give me your number so that I can call you?'

She hesitated, weighed up the situation. 'I guess that's harmless enough.'

'And let me follow you until you're almost home?'

'You are incorrigible! I am almost home and I'll be fine! Good night.' Her voice strong, determined but slightly amused.

She walked quickly away, without looking back, waving, confident that he was watching her leave and not sure how she felt about it. A couple stood in the shadow of a doorway wrapped up in each other, bodies intertwined, tongues twisting, hands exploring.

An old woman shuffled past mumbling to herself, but in conversation with something unseen. She stopped. Shouted. Raised her fist. Spittle flew from her mouth. Nadia crossed the road, skipping between cars to avoid any possible uncomfortable confrontation. Her phone rang. It was him, Artem.

'You are okay, yes?' he asked.

'Good grief! You can see me!' she answered, with an annoyingly girlish giggle. 'Really! Goodnight!'

She turned the corner, ducked into a doorway that wasn't hers, held her breath and waited. This was normal wasn't it? To be careful. To be cautious, especially in a strange place. *Please let this be normal.* She listened to the hum of distant traffic, the crackle of tram and trolley bus cables, snippets of conversations drifting out of open windows. Footsteps, laughter, a couple arm in arm with eyes only for each other. A world away. *Okay. Enough Nadia!* She stepped back out, head held high, and walked briskly to her own apartment, checking left and right before she went in and closed the door behind her.

It would have been good to have someone to talk to. A late night chat. She thought about her dad. No. That would spark unnecessary concern. She would be fine. She sent a text to Artem.

At home. No bad guys. Good night.

He replied instantly. *Good night my beautiful Nadia. I will see you tomorrow.*

Oh...

Despite being close to midnight it was still hot and sticky. There was an electric fan, but its noise would keep her awake. She opted for opening the windows wide. Barely a flutter of the curtains. A quiet hum of distant noise outside. Lying in bed, her nightshirt stuck to her sweaty body. Clinging, twisting, uncomfortable. It was a night when to be naked would be best, but she felt strangely vulnerable. Too vulnerable not to be covered up. Clothed. Protected.

She rationalised it. Nothing untoward had happened. There was no reason to feel perturbed, nervous. No-one was after her. No-one was trying to get into her apartment. He was just some guy – some cute guy – and it was all normal. It could even be fun if she would allow it. Drop her guard. Trust someone.

That was a big word – trust.

Chapter 6

December 2001

'Can I buy you a burger?' Nadia asked. 'Come on. It's cold and I'm hungry.' She shivered and made a "brrr" sound to stress the point.

'Ooh, yes,' Alyona enthused and grinned, clapped her hands.

Nadia held out her arm and Alyona slipped hers through it. They smiled at each other. The buildings were tinged a pale, pink-orange by the tired rays of the winter sun. Its light feeble. Its strength all but gone. Its ability to create beauty still there.

'We need to be somewhere else,' Dima said testily. 'Remember?'

'A takeaway then,' Nadia put in hopefully, expectantly. 'Come on.' She didn't like happening upon these kids and not doing something, anything, however small.

Dima and Sasha exchanged glances. Sasha's

intimating that this was normal. That this was what they would do. Perhaps they should. Dima's more of concern. He didn't know this woman by anything other than here-say. She was a foreigner, a stranger to him, and he was nervous of her, of their situation, of the need to hide. Now.

Force of habit and the mouthwatering smell of cooking burgers made Dima go against his better judgement. When people offered you food you accepted. Always. Who knew what the next day might hold? It was winter and pickings were light, pockets deeper. Hunger was a regular, unwelcome companion. Yes, they had some cash now, but they couldn't flash it. Not out here. It had to look like nothing had changed.

They were standing at the kiosk; one of a row of single storey pre-fabs. Most of them white, some with red and white striped awnings. Small ledges on which people leaned with bottles of beer, plastic cups of vodka, French-fries, kebabs, chicken, burgers, ashtrays full to overflowing. The mumblings of men. Laughter.

Nadia was handing the burgers, wrapped in napkins, across to the children. The woman behind the counter was all smiles and soft words. She knew what was going on here and she approved. She had given Sasha and Alyona scraps at the end of the day on more than one occasion. It was to be kept secret though. She cared, but she didn't want a whole bunch of street-kids hanging around. It was bad for business. And these two? They were quiet, well-behaved, not like the rest of them.

Dima suddenly nudged Sasha in the back. 'We

need to go. Quickly. See?' he whispered and jerked his head backwards.

Two of the wardens, whose job it was to find street-kids and runaways, were walking across the square. There was nothing to identify them as such other than their eyes scanning for known faces, for escapees, for children running. And experience. Sasha, Alyona, and Dima had all fallen prey to them before and been hauled off to their office. Stuck in a bare room with barred windows and emptiness. Questions, the talk, phone calls. It was always the same. Always pointless.

'What is it?' Nadia asked, turning to look at the cause of their nervousness. 'Ah.' She knew who they were. She knew the score. If they were caught, an orphanage would become their destination. Not good places apparently.

Sasha, Alyona, and Dima would spend as little time as possible in care, plotting their escape immediately upon arrival. They preferred life on the streets to being locked up in one of the orphanages, where they faced abuse from the older kids, from some of the staff. It might be hard on the streets but it was their choice, their life. They were in control. At least in some way.

Nadia wrapped her arms around the children, as a mother to her own, and led them away from the wardens. It was winter, it was getting dark, it was commonplace to be in a hurry. They didn't look back. Act normal. Chat, laugh, be a family.

They got to the bottom of Andriivs'kyi.

'You go now, lady. We're on our own from here,' Dima growled.

'But–' Nadia began to protest, but there was no point. She could feel that. Instead she stood and watched as they scurried up the beginning of the hill – Alyona's confused face looking back at her – and disappeared. The wardens were nowhere to be seen. That was good. But she felt a sense of uselessness. She wanted to help but didn't know how. Something was obviously going on and it bothered her. They were often skittish, often wary or nervous, but today they were scared. Very obviously scared.

'No more of that shit!' Dima hissed angrily. 'You understand me? We don't trust no-one. We don't talk to no-one. You got that? And you!' He pointed his finger at Alyona, raised his voice. 'You don't say anything at all.'

'Come on. There's no need for that.' Sasha cast a disapproving scowl at Dima. 'It's okay Alyona. You come here.' He held his arm open for her and she snuggled in.

'I don't like this,' she whispered to Sasha.

'It's okay. We'll be okay.' He stroked her hair.

'Fuck's sake,' Dima mumbled to himself. 'What the hell have I got myself into?'

He thought about leaving them. He could get the bag and disappear. Just him. Nothing to slow him down. Get him caught. But that would be a really shit thing to do, wouldn't it?

'Come on then. Let's move it,' Dima said, resignation in his voice.

They dipped in and out of alleyways, and across wasteland, until they found a place where they could hide, but also see their basement from. They were at the top of a heavily wooded hill. Ancient chestnut trees, naked, stretched around them, tangled, twisted. No-one could sneak up on them. Peering through the trunks – sap silent, sleeping, but holding on to a heartbeat – they could just make out what was happening below. Catch any movement large enough to be human. Shadows disappeared into darkness.

'You two wait here. Safer if I go down on my own. Right!' Dima stated.

'Uh-uh. We need to stay together. And it's freezing out here. Come on bro. Together.' Sasha smiled at Alyona and squeezed her shoulders.

'Jesus!' Dima looked skywards.

'I'll be very quiet, I promise. And I'll run like the animals. You won't know I'm here. You won't. You won't know I'm here,' Alyona pleaded.

They climbed down as quietly as they could, but twigs snapped, quiet curses were mumbled. The shouts of a drunk echoed through the woods. Some music fought its way out of a cellar bar. When they reached their house there was silence. At the door, whispered words, barely audible, crept through the floorboards. That was normal. They all knew to keep their voices low, their lives a secret.

The trio didn't risk using the main entrance. Better to be cautious, safe. Dima led the way towards the back of the house. Sasha and Alyona followed. He slowly, and carefully, pulled aside some shrubs, shifted a couple of large stones, and pulled at the handle of a metal trapdoor. Under it was a cellar that had been used for storing coal when the house had been in proper use. Dima jumped down landing with a soft thud, coughing lightly at the plume of coal dust that flew into his mouth, up his nostrils. He wanted to spit it out, but wiped his tongue on his hand instead. Quieter, if less effective. Sasha lowered Alyona into Dima's arms and then jumped down beside them. The walls were black. The floor was black. The air was black. But tonight it cushioned their landing, muffled their sounds. It was welcome.

'Hide and seek game, Alyona,' Sasha whispered, putting his finger to his lips.

Alyona smiled and copied his gesture. 'Who is seeking?' she asked.

'The other children. They are seeking.'

'Okay,' she giggled and pulled her shoulders up. 'Shh...'

*

Leonid was at the bottom of Andriivs'kyi. He was crouched down, talking to an old man who was dressed in layers and layers of coats. His feet in thick sheepskin boots, his head covered with an old Soviet army fur hat, moth eaten and rotting. The real thing he claimed. Stories of Afghanistan. Lost comrades. All around him were dogs. Ten, maybe twelve of them lying on dirty old blankets, their coats matted, all on leads of string and rope. There were small terrier type dogs, large Afghans, motley street-dogs of all shapes and sizes. The stench coming off them made him wince, but he choked it back. Smiled.

There was a handwritten sign on a piece of cardboard asking for money to help feed the dogs, a plastic tub with a few steel and brass *kopeks* sitting in it, a couple of paper *Hryvnia*. Like everyone who made their living on the streets, life was so much harder when the tourists left and the cold and dark settled in their place. He was always here and, when he was lucid, he saw everything, everyone.

Leonid had taken up the habit of being generous when he passed by. He took the time to pat a dog or two, hiding his distaste. Slipped a few notes into his grimy hands, the nails yellow, encrusted with black. It was disgusting. He listened to the nonsense he spurted. It was necessary. It was worth it. Sometimes amongst the nonsense, a pearl. Yes, he had seen them with the foreign woman. The English one. No, he didn't know where they were going.

'What is so special about these children? So many people asking.'

'Who?' he asked, perturbed but masking it.

'I told them nothing.' He spat on the ground.

'You told who nothing?' Casual. Like it didn't matter.

He looked up at Leonid and grinned. Narrowed his eyes. 'They came. So many of them.'

'Who came?'

'So many of them. Dirty. Buzzing like bees. A swarm of bees. Everywhere!' He swatted his hand above his head, in front of his face. Grimacing.

'You were telling me about Alyona. Who else has been asking about her?' Patience slipping.

'Can't you see them?' His voice had changed, slipping into angry accusation. 'Did you send them?'

Damn it! He had lost him. His train of thought somewhere else. His words becoming unstuck, losing cohesion, comprehension. It was time to leave before he started screaming and shouting about things known only to him. At things unseen. Battles in his head. Leonid stuffed a ten dollar bill in the old man's cup and headed up the hill. At least he knew that they had been here. He wondered about the others who had been asking. Were they real or just in the man's head? There was no way of knowing, but he would have to be careful. Extra careful.

He was scanning basements, deserted courtyards, waste-ground, looking for an out of place light from a dark space. The careless use of a match or a candle. The flicker of a fire. Mostly they were *bumsh* – old vagrants, useless people. The street-kids were smarter but sometimes; sometimes you struck lucky.

Chapter 7

June 2001

Nadia had no intention of meeting up with Artem that day. One of her fellow teachers, Magnolia – an Australian who had been here for a year – had offered to take her around some of Kyiv's famous places, tourist spots. The must sees. It was a good enough excuse and although she wasn't so keen on doing touristy things, some English speaking friends might not be such a bad idea. Yes. She had come here to mix with the locals, to culturally submerge herself but sometimes...

Artem phoned again and again. She rejected his calls, and was both amused and annoyed by his persistence. Eventually she turned her phone off. The constant unanswered calls were being noticed. She'd rather they weren't.

The day was spent looking at a plethora of important buildings, places and monuments. They went up to the Motherland statue. The woman made of stainless steel, a sword held aloft in one hand, a shield in the other. It stood sixty two metres high, immense and impressive, from where the multitude of churches and domes, monasteries, and the Lavra, could be seen. All gold and green, audacious in their opulence.

'It's always a good idea to do one of these touristy things just to get your bearings, I reckon. I prefer going walkabout though,' Magnolia said with a laugh. 'It's the best way to find out about a place. Get lost in it.'

'Yeah. It's appreciated. Thanks Magnolia,' Nadia said, thinking that she might well like this woman. She was the archetypal Australian. Tall, blonde, and effervescent, as if she'd just walked out of an Australian tourist board poster.

Magnolia laughed. 'Maggie, please. I never use Magnolia unless I'm at home and have no choice in the matter. Even then I argue.'

'But it's such a beautiful name.'

'Ha! Yeah, yeah. And who made my mum suddenly pop into your brain? She takes great pleasure in telling everybody how she and dad had conceived me one drunken night under a magnolia tree – hence the name.' She looked over with a pained expression on her face. 'The story is accompanied by way too many unspeakable, too-gross-to-be-talked-about, details. And seriously, I really don't want those images popping into my head every time someone says my name. I mean! Really! It's not a nice thing to do to your child, now is it?'

Nadia laughed. 'I don't know. It's romantic.'

'Disgusting is what it is. So, changing the subject completely and irrevocably,' her eyes reinforced the statement. 'Where have they put you?'

'I'm in Podil, just off Kontraktova Plosha. It's a really nice wee place. Quirky, I guess. Do you know it?'

'Oh, ripper! Too right,' she answered in an overly exaggerated Aussie accent. 'We're as good as neighbours then.'

'Oh, cool!' she laughed. 'Which street are you on?'

'Bratska. The one the tram goes along. You get used to the noise after a while.' She grinned, raised her eyebrows.

'Okay. We are close then.'

'That's a cute accent you've got there. What is it? I'm guessing Irish or Scottish.'

'Scottish. I'm from Perth.'

'Ha! Ripper!' She slapped her thigh. 'Me too. Only on the other side of the planet. You see? We were meant to be mates! Destiny!'

That evening they went to O'Brian's, the Irish pub. Guinness and vodka, expats talking loudly, eating familiar food, drinking familiar drinks. Locals joining in, being something else. Somewhere else. Irish music mixed with classic rock, shamrocks and the tricolour. A smell of cigarettes, expensive aftershave, cheap perfume, stale alcohol, and furniture polish. Smiling bar staff. Provocative women. Lecherous men.

Nadia failed in her attempt to hide her dislike of the place.

Maggie picked up on it. 'You just never know. Trust me. When you're far away from home, in a country like this, sometimes you need that familiarity.

The expat bar. A familiar language. An easiness. Get yourself known. It can be a lifesaver. You'll see,' she added with a knowing smile. 'They may have their distasteful side but a good one too.'

Nadia would keep an open mind, listen to advice, for now. She was new to all of this and Maggie? Maggie had been about. Ten years of travelling. Australia to Asia, the Middle East, Turkey and now Ukraine. It would be smart to listen to her, she decided. This wasn't something she could see herself doing on a regular basis though. This wasn't why she had come so far from home. It was precisely the strangeness, the difference, that attracted her. The chance to be someone new, somewhere new. To change. And then there was the language. She was determined to become fluent and that wasn't going to happen hanging out in expat bars.

She and Maggie had shared a taxi back. The driver, who was recommended by the school, was full of questions and chat. He was obviously proud of his English, enjoying showing off. That was fine. There was a set fee. It was expensive but it was safe.

'Next time I reckon we should do the old Gypsy-cab thing,' Maggie said. 'You and me, standing by the side of the road, flagging down random cars. It would be a laugh. Right?'

'I'm willing if you are.'

It was one of the many things that had struck Nadia about Kyiv. How people stood at the side of the road waving their hand, waiting for a random car to stop. It seemed so trusting, so...different. Of course, everything was different. She had learned that it was the way some of the locals made their living, driving little Ladas around, picking up fares. If you were lucky you might get picked up by something flash, something expensive, a Mercedes, a BMW. Someone being kind or looking for a cheap thrill? All part of the fun.

When she got home she turned her phone back on. Twelve missed calls, all from Artem. Softened by the drink she was about to return his call. 'Nah,' she mumbled, switching it back off and climbing into bed. He could wait. Maybe she wouldn't call back at all.

Chapter 8

December 2001

Alyona tugged at her brother's sleeve. First gently, then urgently. 'No! This is bad. A bad thing. We mustn't go in there,' she whispered.

'It's okay, Alyona. Shh.'

'No!' She dug her heels in and pulled backwards.

'You need to keep her quiet,' Dima grumbled, barely audibly. But the feeling was easy to pick up on. The urgency blatant.

'Do you want to wait here, Alyona?'

'Yes, but with you. You must wait too.'

'Dima?'

'Okay, okay. I said that, didn't I? Just keep quiet and wait. No sound. No movement. Nothing. Got it?'

'Sure. Take care bro.' A softer than usual punch of fists between him and Dima. 'Sometimes she knows things.'

Dima tutted, shook his head, and edged out of the

cellar, his back against the wall, his eyes and ears straining. He could see nothing but black. The silence was equally heavy and dark. He felt the corner of the wall, the absent door, the bricks, and the rubble.

He was in the part of the basement where the bag was hidden. No light was needed. He knew exactly where everything was. More importantly, no-one could see him, and if he was careful they wouldn't hear him either. He hoped it didn't matter. He hoped that no-one was in the basement apart from his crew, but Sasha was right. Sometimes Alyona knew things. In her own messed up way, she knew things.

Sasha and Alyona had edged further forward. A movement. Something brushed against their legs. Sasha jumped, swallowed a squeal. Alyona dropped his hand, leaned forward, let her hand run along the dog's bony spine.

'Hello dog,' she whispered.

It stopped for a second, sniffed, a light wag of its tail in recognition, then moved off again, back to its puppies.

Dima had returned, the bag clutched in his arms. Another sound. Footsteps. Heavy. A torchlight. 'Shit! Move!' he whispered. 'Go!' He pushed past them and led the way back to the trapdoor. He climbed up the rope, the bag now slung over his shoulder.

Sasha hoisted Alyona up, then followed. They pulled the rope out, lowered the hatch, secured it, and ran. Back up the hill. Back to their vantage point amongst the trees.

'What was that all about?' Sasha asked.

'Maybe just one of the others managed to steal a torch. Maybe not. Wasn't about to wait to find out.'

He was panting and it wasn't just through exertion.

'It was something bad. I told you it was something bad,' Alyona whispered, looking at the ground.

'Yeah, right,' Dima muttered.

*

Leonid had drawn a whole bunch of blanks. An old *bumsh,* well, you couldn't tell, they all looked old. A mess of rags and matted hair and dirty, scaly skin. An air of resigned desperation. Desperate for what? A reprieve? A cigarette? The dregs left in a discarded bottle? Shit! What a state to get yourself into.

Another empty basement. A family huddled in a corner. Miserable and frightened. The man and woman drinking from a bottle, whispering. The children wide-eyed. They hadn't been living out here for long. There wasn't that resignation. That acceptance of their fate. That stare of no hope.

Teenagers full of mock bravado, indifference, and chemicals. But not his teenagers. He knew they were here somewhere. It was just a question of time.

Leonid had just been to St Andrew's church, the open ground behind it. Grass and bushes. Places to hide. More blanks. There was one last, likely place to check up here. The decrepit old building on the edge of the park. He shook a Marlboro out of his packet, stuck it between his teeth, flicked open his Zippo – that sound did something for him. It was the strength of it, the masculinity of it – spun the little brass wheel, sucked at the flame, inhaled and held it. The cigarette turned a bright fiery red. *You little fuckers.* He blew out the plume of smoke and it trailed behind him, like an apparition, as he strode down the hill.

When he reached the courtyard a shiver ran down

his spine. It surprised him. Disconcerted him. He pulled his gun out of his holster. He preferred a knife to a gun. Quick and quiet and less evidence left behind. No shells, no bullet to tell stories. Only his blades, that he cleaned meticulously and never left anywhere, other than on him or hidden under the floorboards in his apartment. The gun was for emergencies only, and for instilling fear. This was a time for intimidation. The gun it was.

He shifted the excuse for a door aside, climbed down the stairs that he hadn't set foot on since he was a teenager. That stench! Christ! He tried to breathe lightly. Quick breaths. Keep the stink and disease out. He pulled one arm across his nose and mouth, the other moving the torch back and forth, and headed down, wishing he wasn't.

Result! This was the right place. He recognised some of the kids from the Metro. Eight bodies huddled in sleeping bags and dirty blankets. Their state of intoxication dripping out of every pore; their heads hanging limply as if too heavy for their necks.

'Don't piss me about,' Leonid snarled acrimoniously, picking out each figure in turn with the beam of his torch. Malice blatant. Intimidation palpable. 'Dima? I know he stays here. Where is he?'

He was met with shakes of the head. 'Uh-uh. Haven't seen him. Not since the Metro. Swear. Uh-uh.'

He kicked at an empty sleeping bag. 'This his?'
'Yeah.'

Kicked at the rubbish that lay around it. Shone his torch again in the faces of all of the residents. In all the corners. At the dog and the puppies, the cardboard, the bottles. Into the empty rooms. The old coal cellar. Footprints. He followed them into the centre of the cellar. There was a mess of them. Like there had been a disturbance. Jumping. He shone the torch up. Its beam picked up the outline of a trapdoor. There was no ladder. Nothing to climb on. *How the hell?*

He hurried back out through the silenced children, their faces expressing nothing but fear; up the stairs, round the outside of the building to where he knew the hatch for the coal cellar was. He found the trapdoor, the rope, the rocks. 'Clever,' he mumbled. He stood still. Scanned the area with his torch. Trees, shadows, a line of flattened shrubs, a sooty trail. He followed. Slowly, meticulously. Twitch.

Chapter 9

July 2001

Nadia and Artem met up a couple of times a week. He showed her the places that were popular with locals. Hydro Park, the island in the middle of the Dnieper river, with its beaches, and play-parks, and perpetual smell of *shashlik*. Its tracks and paths that disappeared into dense trees; into complete wilderness. The packs of dogs that hung around nervously waiting for food. Slinking down close to the ground as if their emaciated bodies were too heavy for their spindly legs.

He took her up Zamkova Hora. They sat on one of the high, grassy slopes eating the picnic he had prepared, drinking beer.

'Kyiv is a city built on hills. You see?' He pointed out the undulating landscape around them. 'And this one is Castle Hill, the most important of the hills. It was once a fortress for the Lithuanian invaders,

Vytautas the Great had his castle here. The founders of our city had their vision here back in the fifth century. And now, beautiful churches, green trees, the river, the bridges, the monuments. All there before you.' He looked across at her and smiled.

She could feel his pride. 'It's all very beautiful,' she confirmed.

'And if I were to tell you of witches that meet here and black magic and devil worship?'

She pulled a face of disbelief, as if he were playing a trick on her and she had found him out.

'You don't believe me? They say that, historically, the souls of witches gathered here. And now? It wouldn't be wise to come up here after dark...' He pulled a comical, scared face. 'For they walk–here–at night.'

She slapped his thigh. 'Oh stop it.'

He laughed. 'Seriously, I wouldn't come up here, on my own, at night. There are hidden places, stories of underground caverns, passageways where dark things happen. Where people have ventured never to be seen again.' He shook his head. 'Dangerous places.'

'You're still winding me up, right? I mean, it's not true, is it?'

'Maybe. Maybe not. It's just what I've heard.'

*

Nadia had agreed to meet up with Maggie that night. They had thought about going for a Mexican at Tequila House, but decided on going local instead. Just off Kontraktova there was an interesting looking little bistro that had tables and chairs out on the pavement. Canvas umbrellas stood above the tables, gently flapping in the welcome breeze. A couple of men sat drinking shots from a bottle of vodka that was on their table. Their mood was serious, as if they were talking business. At another table two young couples, flirtatious, jovial, intimate.

'Shall we?' Nadia asked.

'Oh, why not?'

Inside was dark and old fashioned. There was a smell to it of permanence, of something from times gone by but hanging on, refusing to change, to move on. It felt like there were stories, history, clinging to the place. It was peculiar, almost unpleasant. Almost. The walls were clad in dark wood panelling, the table and chairs matched it, but were scratched and stained by an assortment of circles and scars. More stories.

Behind the counter two formidable middle-aged women dressed in overalls stood, arms folded, deep in conversation. They glanced across at Maggie and Nadia, ignored them, and returned to their conversation.

'Hmm. Ever get the feeling you're not welcome?' Maggie muttered.

'Maybe they're just wary of strangers. Let's persevere.'

Nadia walked up to the counter and spoke in Russian. The women began to drop their scowls and slowly broke into smiles and almost friendly chatter. Reticence and suspicion still lurked beneath the surface. Westerners were not to be trusted.

Nadia returned with a smile and a menu. 'Mission accomplished.'

The evening was warm and sultry, so they sat outside.

'I am just so impressed with you, girlfriend! Jeez!'

Nadia translated the menu and they ordered green borscht, stuffed cabbage leaves, and a couple of beers. It wasn't what either of them had planned on having, but the waitress had been quite insistent in her recommendations.

'Best in all Kyiv,' she had said proudly, in English, wiping her thick hands on her overall. 'Very best.'

They decided to go along with it. Why not?

They sat in the shade of some chestnut trees which kept them pleasantly secluded, the sounds of the street slightly muffled, apart from the rude interruption of intermittent trams.

'So who's this mystery man that's keeping you so occupied?' Maggie asked with a grin and a wink. 'Tell all!'

'There's not much to tell really,' she shrugged her shoulders in a nonchalant kind of a way.

'Oh right. You're hanging out with this tall, dark, and handsome local dude and there's nothing to tell?'

'How did you know he was tall dark and handsome?'

'Well, it wouldn't be too big a leap of faith now would it? I mean, so many of them are, aren't they?' She laughed. 'But, I saw you two all cosied up on Castle Hill when I was checking more of the "must do's" off my list.'

'You should have come and said hi.'

'Uh-uh. You guys were giving off such a vibe. It was intense and it was a no-go. He's a bit cute, isn't he? Very easy on the eye. The bod looked pretty impressive too!'

Nadia laughed. 'You're awful, you know that?'

'Nah. Just honest. So...' Her eyes were expectant, her smile wicked.

Nadia sighed. 'He's called Artem. I met him in the park at Kontraktova, not long after I'd arrived. We just hit it off. He's charming, and fun, and yeah, I like him.' She shrugged and pulled a face. 'We get on. That's all.'

'And have you done the deed? Marks out of ten.'

Nadia had a mouth full of cabbage which she almost choked on with her laugh. 'Oh my God! You don't mess about do you?'

'What's the point in that? Get right in there. Speak your mind. Live your life. That's my rule of thumb.'

'Fair enough. Well, A, I haven't and B, I wouldn't tell you if I had.' She cocked her head. 'We're friends, that's all.'

'Oh, girlfriend. Come on.'

Walking along the pavement towards them Nadia spotted the street-kids. The boy and the girl. 'Come on. Let's pay and go.'

They took their bill to the counter and paid there. You could wait forever to get the attention of the staff over here and Nadia had decided that she was in a hurry. Maggie wasn't too sure what was happening but was up for a bit of excitement.

'I want to see where they go. What they do. I don't know what it is about them, but they fascinate me.'

'Fair dinkum!' she said, in her exaggerated Aussie mode.

They followed at a discreet distance, not sure why they were being surreptitious but doing it anyway. It made it all the more fun. Nadia was taking pictures as they went, her camera a constant companion, as promised. Pictures of Maggie, of the architecture, of odd street lights. Random things that caught her eye. And of the street-kids.

They had almost turned into Kontraktova. A black Mercedes pulled up. The girl got in. The boy stood and watched it drive off. Sat on a wall. Waited. Head hanging.

Music was coming from the square.

'Buskers! They sound good. Shall we?' Maggie enthused.

Nadia was still watching the boy, distracted. She suddenly realised that something had been said to her. 'What?'

'You're miles away. Jeez! What is it with you and street-kids? Music! Come on. Let's go!' She linked arms with Nadia and pulled her off towards the group of buskers. Nadia still looking back, wondering. That whole scene just didn't look right. Didn't feel right. Street-kids. A black Mercedes. There was something dirty about it.

Chapter 10

December 2001

Dima picked up a Marlboro butt from the ground, examined it, straightened it out and lit it up. He struggled to light it through the damp that had seeped in with the falling snow, but he persevered and eventually succeeded. Puffing and puffing, his lips smacking.

'You know you can buy your own now,' Sasha whispered, allowing himself a light laugh.

'Old habits, man. Old habits.'

'Here is not a good place now. It is not safe,' Alyona said with an unfamiliar strength, a purpose to her voice.

Dima took a final drag on his cigarette end and ground it into the snowy earth with his heel. 'Yeah. We need to keep moving. And we need to deal with this.' He patted the bag slung across his back. His mind was ticking away, trying to come up with answers, solutions, a way to convert the contents of the bag into money without getting grassed, or killed, or most likely, both.

They started to make their way back down the hill, but in the opposite direction from the house, away from Podil and the people and area they knew so well. Into the relative safety of less obvious places. The trees were thick enough, although bare, the only leaves in a mulch of decay at their feet. Slimy and slick. Each footstep squelching out a waft of leaf mould sticky with snow. Their progress was slow but they felt safe, hidden.

No-one said anything. Silence was natural. They listened to the sounds around them. The scurry of an animal that made them freeze, focus, until they were sure it wasn't made by something human. Further away, the sounds of people in another world laughing, eating, drinking. The muffling of the darkness, the blurring of the falling snow, made it all the more eerie. Their lives more separate. Ghostly.

All three of them heard it. A different noise. An intrusion. They stopped, stared at each other, tuned their ears in. There were footsteps. The breaking of branches. A curse. It was close. Dima placed a finger on each of their mouths. No words. Just a feeling. A feeling that left no doubt. *Be quiet.*

Dima was leading them to Vozdvyzhens'ka Street. If they could get there, across the road and onto Zamkova Hora – Castle Hill – perhaps they could hide, seek refuge like their ancestors had.

Amongst its solitude they could easily hide, at least until daybreak. Then what? Perhaps to travel at night? To sleep during the day? Dima didn't know and it bothered him. The volatility of his life had made it important that he knew what to do, where to go, how to survive. But this was a bigger survival. This was a different kind of life or death, and he found it more difficult to make sense of it, to see a way forward. To get through it.

The snow had begun falling in earnest now. It would soon be thick enough to leave tracks of their footprints. The need to hide, to break their trail, had become all the more urgent.

The narrow cobbled elegance of Vozdvyzhens'ka Street was quiet. They stood in the shadow of the buildings, out of the flickering glow of the erratic street-lights, and waited, just to make sure. Nothing. The snow brought with it a silence, a deceitful covering of softness and beauty.

'Are you all right?' Sasha whispered, looking closely at his sister's face. Her chin in his hand. Reading her eyes. They held more honesty than her words. He had always been able to find the truth in her eyes.

'Yes.' She cocked her head.

He believed her. The smile was there. The smile in her eyes. She was caught in a reverie, remembering their first winter in Kyiv, when Papa had brought them up to Zamkova Hora. He had bought a wooden toboggan from a *babushka* outside the *rynok*. The old woman's coat so thick and heavy that she could barely move. Everything but her face covered. The face full, with more than a lifetime's wrinkles. The eyes sharp and wise. "The best quality," the *babushka* had said through gold teeth, smiling, her odd assortment of items for sale laid out along the wall behind her. Some boots, a saucepan, a pair of slippers, some pickles, cutlery. Some of them found, scavenged, others things that she could live without. A trade for food, for warmth, for life. She, like many of the older generation, hankered for the times of the Soviet Union. For communism. Life was better for her in those days. She had enough then. Not much. Nothing in excess. Nothing luxurious. Enough. Now she struggled. Life's essentials were a constant struggle.

The toboggan was old and well used, but Papa could fix it. He took it home and smoothed down the wood, sanded off the rust from the runners, tied a new rope to the front. It was like it had given him a purpose. He smiled, and whistled, and chatted like the Papa of long ago. The Papa Alyona had never known.

The next day he had packed some bread and meat and a flask of soup into his old army knapsack. A blanket was placed on the toboggan. Alyona and Sasha sat on it, muffled in snow-suits, as their father pulled them along the snowy pavements towards Zamkova Hora. This was the best! The pride. The joy. The love. It was the best.

Papa took his time, searching out a perfect slope for them to go down. It had to be safe, but fast enough for excitement, for fun.

'This one Papa?' Alyona had asked.

'No. You see the roughness there? There could be rocks hiding. It is too dangerous.'

When he was finally content with the area around, with the steepness of the hill, the smoothness of the descent, the safety of the landing, he climbed on behind them, held the rope, and off they went. Again and again. Laughing. Screeching. Shouting. Falling off. Hearts pounding. Clambering back on. It was pure fun. The best kind of fun. They were all so very happy.

At first Alyona and Sasha had held on tight. Then, as their confidence grew, they loosened their grip.

'Look, Papa. No hands!' Alyona screeched, a huge, rare grin breaking up her face, her hands high in the air. Sasha copied. Papa joined in. The toboggan tumbled. So did they. They lay in the snow laughing. That was what she remembered most. Laughing and laughing. It wasn't something they did any more. Laugh. Not proper big laughing like that. She suddenly felt cold and sad. It felt like it had been a different person, a different family. Her memory left.

*

Sasha and Alyona held hands and ran after Dima, across the cobbles, feeling like the street-lights were shining just on them, picking them out for whoever might be after them. They slunk past people's houses, not glancing in the windows, not thinking of anything other than somewhere to hole up, to camouflage themselves with their surroundings. A place of sanctuary.

They reached the gap in the buildings that Dima had been heading for, hurried round the corner and into the welcome darkness of the hill. It was criss-crossed with dozens of paths and trails worn down by sightseers, picnickers, families playing, exploring, and the unseen people of the streets. Obscured, now barely visible through the snow. A slight indentation. A scar.

They ran through the shrubs. The trees. The slope was steep and they scrambled on all fours, like dogs or wild things. Alyona didn't complain, despite the thorns that snatched at her face, despite the fear she felt from her brother. Despite the breath she could barely catch that made her lungs feel like they were on fire.

At the top of the hill they could see Kyiv stretching out in all directions. Lights everywhere. Rows of street-lights. Tower blocks reaching up to the sky with a chequerboard of lit and unlit windows. It all looked so unreal, so distant. Separate. Everything softened by the falling snow. The lights blurred. Buildings less defined, no edges. There were no lights up here on the hill. And they were thankful for that.

They had criss-crossed, doubled back on themselves, waited and moved, waited and moved, until they were as sure as they could be that no-one was following them. That their trail was suitably confusing.

'What are we going to do?' Sasha asked, a tinge of helplessness, hopelessness, seeping into his voice.

Dima picked up on it. Felt it too. Fought against it. Smothered it. 'Dunno.'

Dima knew this place well. It was where he often came in the summer. Pickings were good up here. People relaxed, sitting on the grass drinking. Tourists paying attention to the view – the domes sparkling in the sunshine, the river twisting dark and blue – not to their belongings. If the day had been good, enough found, or stolen, or scavenged, he could just lie in the sun like normal people did. His arms folded behind his head, a piece of grass in his mouth, his eyes closed, the sun stroking his body.

*

There were tracks and trails and different exits

giving them a choice of escape routes, if it came to that. It also meant that there were more places to keep an eye on. To stare through the blackness at. To imagine images, shapes, shadows, assailants.

Dima had heard and told so many stories about this place. About black magic and witches' covens and evil doings. They had shared these stories as entertainment, amusement, during long, cold nights. It didn't seem so funny now. He didn't like to admit it, but he felt scared. Scared of things he didn't know.

He stood still, looked around. 'We need to keep moving. There's no place to shelter up here. It's too damned cold. If we don't get caught by Lezo and his bastards we'll probably freeze to death,' he mumbled.

'Maybe we should go back to Podil?' Sasha suggested. 'Down to the metro, some shelter, get a bit warm?'

'No way man. The *militsiya* would pick us up in a second.'

'You think they're looking for us too?'

'Course man. Everyone knows they're the same thing. Mafia and *militsiya*. They'll all be after us, for sure.'

They talked through as many options as they could think of. Places where they could steal a bit of warmth, a bit of shelter, without putting themselves in danger. Nothing feasible was opening itself up to them.

Sasha suddenly felt an absence, a panic. He looked around, his heart racing. Trees, shadows. 'Alyona? Where the hell is Alyona?' An urgent whisper.

'She was there. A second ago. She was right behind you.'

'Aly –' he began to call her name but Dima clasped his hand over his mouth.

'Shh, man. You stupid? You can't do that.'

Sasha pushed him off. 'Fuck you. She's my little sister.'

'Right. Right. But you need to be smart, man. Quiet and smart.'

They walked around in a widening circle but couldn't find any trace of her. They had no torchlight and what had been their saviour – the thick, heavy darkness – it was an enemy now.

Chapter 11

July 2001

'So what's your story?' Maggie asked. 'What are you running, or hiding from?'

Nadia bristled slightly. Maggie was brash and that was part of the draw. It was refreshing, but this was a bit too close. Uncomfortable. She laughed nervously. 'What makes you say that?'

'Well, you're not on a gap year. I'm guessing this isn't a between uni and work thing. You're not a missionary, nor married to a big businessman. Which means you must have a story. Everyone who comes to live in places like this does. Hiding from someone they don't like, running from a past they're trying to escape. Logical really.'

'What about you?'

'Oh, now, that doesn't include us Aussies. Australia's so damned far away from everywhere else that we do one big travel. A few years. Then we go home and stay there.'

'So I have to have some big, dark secret, do I?'

'Something like that. It would be so much more fun if you had, right?' She nudged her in the rubs, raised her eyebrows.

Nadia had looked away. Thoughts slipping back through dark windows. Her child. Unwanted. Unloved. His face. She didn't want to see his face any more. There was no fun in this.

'Hey,' Maggie put her hand on Nadia's shoulder, realising she had overstepped her mark, yet again. 'Sorry. It's just me being insensitive as per. Beer makes me even worse. Mouth before brain and all that. Just forget I said any of that. All right?'

'No problem. I've got nothing to hide.' She shrugged trying to appear nonchalant.

Maggie doubted that, and she was desperate to know, but it could wait. Meantime she would just make up her own history for her new friend. Messy divorce she wondered. So messy that she had to run. Or she was the other woman and they got found out. She got dumped. Couldn't stand it. But then there was the whole fascination with children thing...

Nadia had come over here to forget. To get on with a new life. Be a new person, and she wasn't about to go back over it all. She had been trying so hard to resign it to history. When it did creep in to the present she pushed it back. Away. Someone else. Somewhere else. Not her. Not here. Not now.

A passable explanation had been practised, and it was true. Not the whole story, but most of it. Enough of it. 'You want to know? It's nothing exciting. I've always had a thing for this part of the world, that's all.

I decided to come over for a couple of years so that I could improve my Russian, experience a bit of the culture. And that's it. Sorry to disappoint!' She smiled.

Maggie remained unconvinced but she let it slide. For now.

They stood and watched the buskers. A full band of talented young Ukrainians. Drums, bass, guitars, the lot. Crowds formed, swelled, and drifted away with each new song. Some stayed longer, like them. They drank more beer, enjoyed the air of this place. When it was time to leave they put some notes in the buskers' open guitar cases.

The singer smiled, nodded his head at them, 'Thank you.' His English heavily accented. Cute.

'No. Thank you. You guys are good,' Nadia replied. 'Do you play here often?'

'Here or sometimes on Khreschatyk.'

'Great. We'll maybe see you again then. Cheers!'

Maggie was busy flirting with the guitarist. Nadia glanced around. Behind them was a long row of kiosks, maybe twenty of them. There were people, young and old, sitting on benches, standing in groups, drinking from bottles of beer. Others stood at tall tables close to the kiosks, drinking vodka. Her nose caught the now familiar scent of roast chicken, burgers, French-fries, kebabs. It was a peculiar mix along with the blossom, the trees, alcohol, and body odour. It was heavy and sat on the air. She wasn't sure if it was pleasant or not, but it was definitely different. Very different from what she knew and she was reminded of how far from home she was. How far *she* had come. And she smiled. She felt good.

'What a cutie!' Maggie breathed as she took Nadia's arm and they left the square. 'Who wouldn't, eh?'

'You've got such a one track mind.'

'I know!' she said with a wink. 'Don't know about you but I'm done in. I'm going to head home, okay?'

'Yeah. On you go. Goodnight.' She gave her a hug. 'And thanks. It was fun.'

'It was, wasn't it? Later!' She waved and headed in the opposite direction.

Nadia turned towards home. It wasn't until she started focussing on her walking that she realised she had had too much to drink. She was swaying. That wasn't good. She fought it, but that only made it worse. The sway became a stagger. She laughed at herself, then felt slightly embarrassed. Checked around for any unwanted witnesses.

The boy was still there, sitting on the wall. She smiled at him. He looked around, stared, then smiled back. A half smile. An unsure smile. A "were you smiling at me?" smile. The connection didn't linger as he turned his attention back to the road. She stepped into the shadows of some trees and watched, taking pictures. Watching.

He jumped off the wall. The Mercedes pulled up and the girl stepped out. He hugged her. They walked off together, arms wrapped around each other. The girl's head on his shoulder. She was sure she felt a sadness. A pain.

She didn't know why but she had to follow them. It was probably very unwise. It was late. She was tipsy. Light-headed. She didn't get to follow them far. It was as if they had just disappeared.

Oh well, so much for that.

She turned back towards home. Again she had that unwelcome feeling that someone was watching her, following her. This time she wouldn't let it get to her. She wouldn't hide. Regress. *I am not a victim.* She stopped. Sat on the wall where the boy had been sitting. Took deep breaths. Lit a cigarette. Blew the smoke out and watched it dissipate with her irrational fear. The trees rustled as a welcome breeze struck up, clearing the air, lifting the fugue. *I am not a victim.*

Chapter 12

December 2001

Leo couldn't see a damned thing up there on the hill. No tracks, no tell-tale signs. This place was too big, too desolate, and it felt futile without a trail to follow. *Fucking snow!* He flicked his phone open. Called his *militsiya* contacts.

'Anything?'

'No. No-one has seen them. No-one knows anything. No sign.'

'Shit! Check the metro at Poshtova at ten. You might see Dima. If he is there grab a hold of him and do not let him go. And be careful. He's a slippery little bastard. Whatever happens meet me at the cafe on Spaska. Ten thirty.' He hung up. 'Shit, shit, shit!' He knew Dima wouldn't show. Not now. He was obviously in on this too. But he had to cover all bases. You never knew. Kids like them were unpredictable. Nothing normal about them.

He heard something behind him. A squeal. A rustle. He held his breath. Stood still. Listened. Silence. Another rustle. A dog darted across the path in front of him. He swung a kick after it. It yelped in anticipation of pain, but no connection was made.

The snow had turned serious now, covering everything, falling almost horizontally in the vicious wind. There was nothing pretty about this. This snow was painful, cutting its way into the flesh of his face. He pulled his scarf up over his mouth and nose. Uncomfortable. The stickiness of his breath now harder to catch. But it offered some protection. He carried on, head down, shoulders hunched, body tight, as if making himself more compact could reduce the impact of the cold. The weight of the snow.

He checked the time on his wristwatch – imitation Rolex, but a good one – glanced up at the slope ahead of him. He would carry on across the hill, hope that a trail would show itself. A carelessness – they were only kids after all – that would give them away. Something. He would come back off the hill at the other side, on Khorvya Street, where he had planned to be anyway. He slipped the scarf down, lit up again and trudged on through the snow, treading carefully but purposefully. He would not be beaten.

Snow had that ability to bring a hush with it, and it was like that now. Unnaturally quiet. He could hear everything. Every snap of a twig, scurry of a nocturnal animal, yelp of a street-dog. There were no decent tracks in the snow, no footprints, slight indentations which may, or may not, have been made by human feet. Nothing of any definite consequence. No human voices. He would be alone up here. Him and the children, if they were here at all. But he had a feeling. A feeling that they had passed by here, gone up the hill. It's what he would have done in their shoes. Gone somewhere so inhospitable, so isolated that only a fool would follow. A fool or the best of predators.

He swept his torch in an arc in front of him. The skeletons of naked trees, sleeping shrubbery, a barely visible path. He knew this place well enough to know that he was heading in the right direction. His torch now off. The brightness of the snow giving off enough light to see outlines by. To know. He stopped at regular intervals to listen, to feel. It was bitterly cold now. Surely the kids would think about making a bolt for somewhere sheltered, somewhere they felt safe? You could die out here.

Chapter 13

August 2001

Nadia had been spending most of her spare time between Maggie and Artem. But she also valued her solitude, her growing independence, and much though she enjoyed both of their company she felt it important to be herself. To nurture herself. She saw more, learned more, felt more, when she was by herself. It gave her a sense of achievement, of putting her past behind her and getting on with living, of being a real person. No crutches, just her.

Today, however, she had agreed to go on a trip with Artem. His enthusiasm had been such that she hadn't been able to turn him down. Something special was in store, but he was keeping schtum about it, despite her probing, pestering. She had no idea of what the day ahead might hold.

He picked her up at eight in the morning in an old orange Lada Niva.

'My brother's,' he said, grinning, opening the passenger door for her with a flourish, gesturing her in.

'And he trusts you with it?' she asked, cheekily.

'Huh! My driving skills are legendary.'

'Uh-huh. We'll see, shall we?'

They both laughed. She was enjoying the ease of their relationship. The friendship that was developing into a good one. A comfortable one. She felt that she could almost trust him. Relax with him. Let go. Almost. That was a big deal.

It didn't take too long to get out of Kyiv. The change in the feel of the air was dramatic. She opened her window all the way down and stuck her head out, her arms. This was good. The land was flat, the air clean, the road quiet, and straight, and lined by row upon row of hops, then sunflowers. Everywhere masses and masses of sunflowers. The sky was a rich, pure blue, the flowers vibrant yellow, gold, stunning.

'Your flag,' she said excitedly. 'It's your flag.'

'Yes. Now you see where the colours come from. Officially the yellow is for the fields of wheat. Ukraine is the breadbasket of Europe. Well, it used to be, and it shall be again, once we get our country working properly. Back to its glorious past.' He grinned at her. 'The land is very fertile, you see. Very rich soil. The best! But the sunflower can be the yellow as well. It too is very Ukrainian. It's our national flower, you know. We love our sunflowers.'

She could feel more than pride from him, a strength that she hadn't felt in Kyiv. She smiled.

'What?' he asked.

'Just this.' She spread her arm around at the

surroundings. 'Thank you.'

'You are very welcome. I am happy for you to see the real Ukraine. My Ukraine. Capital cities are capital cities, yes? Not like the real country. I mean, I love Kyiv, but here, here is home. Here is real.'

'I understand that.'

He pointed to a small house on the side of the road. On its roof the chaotic mess of sticks that made up a stork's nest. 'You see that? The nest? It means good luck. The nesting storks bring good fortune to the residents.'

'You believe that?'

'Why not? Perhaps they sense things. Know things that we don't.'

'But they are only birds.'

'Nothing is only.'

'Nothing is only. I like that. Deep!'

He smiled. Shrugged his shoulders.

They pulled onto a side road. It was little more than a dirt track. Pot-holes outnumbered even ground. He gestured that she should close her window. She soon found out why. Dust began to cover everything so that she could hardly see the road any more. She could hardly see anything at all.

'Don't worry. This road is like an old friend to me. I have walked it and driven along it so many times. I could do it with my eyes closed. See?' He closed his eyes without adjusting his speed.

'Eek!' she shrieked. 'Don't do that! There might be someone coming. Something coming. Jesus! Open your eyes. Really!' She grabbed for the wheel.

He laughed. 'Oh, and I thought you were more fun than that.'

'Fun, yes. Suicidal – not so much.'

He slowed down. The dust settled. They turned onto a track that was only just identifiable as such. On both sides sunflowers higher than the car. There was nothing else to see but thousands of sunflowers, their massive heads turned, smiling at the sun. Eventually a clearing. A small gathering of buildings. This was more like it. This was idyllic. A little piece of magic.

The cottage was whitewashed, the roof thatched, the windows had green wooden shutters. Paintings of flowers and leaves trickled around the building. Artem pulled up and parked beside one of the barn-like structures. Dishevelled but standing. A bit like the old man who had come to greet them.

Artem smiled as he opened the door for her. 'My grandpa.'

'Oh, how gorgeous!'

So, this was it. The big surprise. A step into another world. It hadn't disappointed. She felt honoured, touched, if slightly uncomfortable at the connections, the intimacy it brought with it. His family. Suggestions of something more than friendship. She was probably just being paranoid. Over-sensitive. This was lovely. Nothing to fear.

The old man walked with the aid of a gorgeous hand carved stick. Flowers and leaves and symbols she didn't know. His back was stooped, his legs bandy. On his top he wore a traditional white Ukrainian shirt with embroidered collar, yoke and cuffs, the sleeves full. It looked like an antique. His trousers were held up with a red cummerbund. His face was adorned with the most splendid moustache. White, thick, curling over his lips, up his cheeks. His white hair collar length, thinning but showing it had once been lusciously thick. Eyebrows, luxuriant, curling above his eyes to complete the look. His skin was leathery and liver spotted, his eyes a tired blue but with the brightest sparkle. Everything was a bit squint, a bit skew-whiff which made it all the more endearing. It was like he had tried so very hard to look perfect but hadn't quite managed it.

'Wow,' she whispered, not meaning to externalise it, but the sight was so extraordinary she couldn't help herself. He was quite simply beautiful. 'Was he expecting us?'

'No. This is a surprise.'

'But his clothes?'

'He always dresses like this.'

Artem embraced his grandpa and they kissed each others' cheeks three times, warmly, strongly.

'Come,' Artem gestured to Nadia. 'Grandpa, this is Nadia.'

'Ah. I can see why she has stolen your heart.'

Artem blushed and smiled. 'Grandpa, we are friends, nothing more,' he said gently but firmly.

The old man grinned. Gold teeth outnumbering real.

Nadia held out her hand but was pulled close and kissed also. 'Welcome to our home,' he said. 'Come, come. I have food ready for you. You must be hungry, no?'

'Wasn't expecting us, huh?' Nadia whispered to Artem, as they climbed the wooden steps of the terrace that surrounded the cottage.

'I lied!' he whispered back, a mischievous smile on his face, a twinkle in his eyes.

They sat down at a table on the terrace. It was made of wood, hand carved with flowers and leaves, as were the chairs. She found herself stroking them and smiling. Artem and his grandfather, Bogdan, broke into Ukrainian every now and again. At times it sounded like Russian. She found herself understanding snippets, thinking she had it, then losing the flow with a string of unfamiliar words.

'Grandpa, we should stay with Russian. Nadia can join in then. Can understand.' He squeezed her hand under the table.

'Of course, of course. Forgive me. It is our habit to speak Ukrainian when we are together,' Bogdan replied, slightly abashed.

'It's no problem at all. It's your country after all. I'm just sorry that I can't speak your language. It's Russian that I hear in Kyiv, isn't it?'

'Yes,' Artem said. 'It's easier, that's all. In Soviet times everyone had to speak Russian and it stayed in the city and in the East. But in the countryside, like here, Ukrainian is more common.'

'So am I offending people by assuming they speak Russian?'

'No. Not at all. Not in Kyiv. I speak Russian there. All Ukrainians can speak Russian but not all Russians can speak Ukrainian.' He shrugged. 'Anyway, Grandpa wants us to stay for the night. He says we can't come to visit and not drink some of his *samohon*. It is legendary and very good, and very strong.'

'I've heard about this stuff. It can kill, can't it?' she said, half jokingly, in English.

'If you don't know what you're doing, yes. But

Grandpa does.'

'Okay, but –'

'He has made beds up for us. It would be rude not to.'

She pulled a face – a visual, "Oh really?"

He laughed. 'Don't worry. We have separate rooms. Sex outside of wedlock is a big no-no. Despite what he says, he knows that we are friends, nothing more. Yet.' That cheeky grin again, the raised eyebrows, the twinkle.

'Ha! In that case, sure. That would be really nice.' She paused. 'I think.'

'All is good?' Grandpa asked.

'All is good,' Nadia answered.

They broke into Ukrainian again. Nadia smiled then stopped. It seemed that the conversation had turned serious, but she couldn't follow it. She suddenly felt awkward, intrusive, so she stood up and walked over to the edge of the terrace, put her hands on the railing and looked out at the millions of sunflowers. They stood now like exhausted sentinels, their heavy heads bowed at the setting of the sun.

Chapter 14

December 2001

'Where the hell has she got to?' Sasha whispered. Worry and fear for his little sister were preying on him. 'She knows not to run off without saying anything.'

'Maybe she's hiding. Playing hide and seek from us too?' Dima suggested.

'Shit. Maybe. Look, if you have to go, then go. I need to call her. She'll die out in this.'

'Right.' Dima nodded his head. He was relieved to be getting out of this situation. To be on his own again, for a while at least. To not be responsible for anyone else. Guilt niggled at him, but it was lighter than his need to get away, to do something. 'Right. You okay with that then?'

'It's not like I have a choice right now.'

'Right. Right. I'll be at the *rynok* at midnight, then again at eight. If you don't show I'm gone. Give me a couple of minutes, all right.' He held out his hand. Sasha took it, pulled him close.

'You take care, man.'

'You too. Good luck.'

'Yeah.'

They broke apart, punched fists, no smiles, a shared feeling of trepidation, perhaps a last farewell, and Dima was gone.

Sasha waited for a count of one hundred, each second killing him, then he started calling. 'Alyona? Alyona, where are you? Come out, sweetheart. Please come out. Alyona? Alyona! Alyona!' He was trying so very hard to keep his voice calm, but it was breaking and urgent, and he was worried. So very worried. He didn't know how far to walk. Maybe he should just stay still and keep calling? Yes. If she was hiding, she knew where he was and she would find him. But what if she was lost? What if she had fallen and hurt herself? What if...what if he had caught her? Lezo. There were so many possibilities. For the life of him he couldn't dredge up one that was positive. He focused, tuned in to her. She was alive. The feeling. It was there. The connection. That was all that he needed. She was alive and there was still hope. Still something.

He stood where he was and called then listened. Called then listened. Nothing. He tried to reach her with his thoughts. Tune in tighter. Still nothing. That wasn't good. Something else must be stronger in her head. Stronger than them. Their connection. He would have to start moving. Start looking a bit further away. He tried to imagine that he was her. What would she do if she was hiding? She would be a tree, wouldn't she. She would find a tree thick enough and she would hug it like it was part of her. She was a part of it. In her head she would become it. When they played hide and seek on soft summer days. When the sun beat down on a parched earth. When birds sang. When the trees were heavy with leaf and blossom. A swathe of green stroking the city, cloaking it with life, feeding it with oxygen. That was what she would do. Breath it. Become it. So at one with it that she wouldn't feel him. Nor he her.

He would usually find her quite quickly but would pretend otherwise; pretend that he couldn't see her, mumble, "Where is she?" just loud enough for her to hear. He would walk past the tree she had become and look through her as if she weren't there. Pretend to be surprised when she crept up on him and lightly tapped his shoulder. Tickle her. Chase her. Giggle.

But now it was so cold. She would be so very cold. Surely she couldn't stay like that for long? No. No, she couldn't. He walked from tree to tree, checking, calling, in ever increasing circles. Each one more difficult than the last. A claw at his heart.

*

Leonid stopped. Listened. He heard a voice. A young voice. It was coming from further up the hill. He smiled. It was calling Alyona. His pace quickened. *Got you, you little fuckers. Come to Uncle Leonid.* This would be over in no time at all.

*

'Alyona,' Sasha called again, this time with hope, with excitement. He felt something. He felt her. She was near. Thank God! His voice became a soft whisper again. 'Alyona, you can come out now.

101

You've won. See? Come on.' Trying to be calm, positive, playing a game.

There was a strange noise. A sort of squeal. His heart hurtled all the way down to his stomach. His breath caught. She was hurt. He strained to catch the direction the noise was coming from. Where was she? Oh, Christ. Where was she? Why wasn't she answering?

He was feeling his way along in the direction the noise had come from, tree to tree, checking each one, checking the roots, the trunks, fighting through the shrubs. Calling quietly, softly, soothingly, trying so desperately to keep it together. Keep it together.

At last he saw her, sitting hunched against a tree, her legs pulled up to her chest. Something else was there. A presence. Something was with her. At first he thought it was one of her imaginings, the creatures of her make believe life.

'Alyona, are you okay?'

She was mumbling soft soothing words, as a mother to her child. Her arms were wrapped around some kind of animal. He couldn't see what it was. A small, still, dark shape.

He bent down, took one of his gloves off. The frost snatched at it instantly. A burning cold. He reached his hand out to touch it. His fingers met feather and bone. He flinched at first, wary, unsure. He felt again, this time more firmly. A crow. Lifeless. Cold. 'Oh Alyona, it's dead. I am so sorry. But we have to go. There is nothing you can do for it now.'

'No. Bird is only cold. If we can warm it enough it will live.' She unzipped her jacket and gently placed the bird against the beating of her heart. 'There.' She stroked its head. 'There. You will fly again. I promise that you will fly.' She looked up at her brother as she zipped her jacket back up, cradling the shape of the bird with her arm.

Sasha knew that there would be no changing her mind. She would never give up on an animal. He held out his hand and she took it. They smiled at each other. That soft shared smile that only happened between them.

Chapter 15

August 2001

As the evening progressed and the light faded, shots of *samohon* were downed with pickles and brown bread, fish and tomatoes. Artem explained that this was the only way to drink. With food. A shot, a mouthful of food, a shot, a mouthful of food. It kept the balance in your body. Stopped the alcohol from taking too tight a hold on you.

They moved into the house when the light had gone and the mosquitoes became unbearable. Inside was full of clutter. Old Soviet children's toys sat in rows on bookshelves. She thought there was something spooky, almost frightening about the toys. Their stark, soulless eyes staring with a cold foreboding. Once loved, now redundant. Again, the encyclopedias, the classics, china, glass, so much.

In a corner some old musical instruments stood. They looked used, well worn. Two banduras – a cross between a lute and a harp with thirty, maybe forty strings – a tambourine with ribbons the yellow and blue of Ukraine decorating it.

'Do you play?' Nadia asked Bogdan.

'Yes. We both do,' he replied with a proud smile.

Artem grinned. 'Shall we?'

'Of course!'

Artem and Bogdan took their places on small wooden stools facing each other. Their feet started tapping out a rhythm. They smiled at each other. Heads nodding. The tapping turned to stamping. Their feet drums.

A pure, clear sound rang through the air. Simple notes building into a complex wonderful melody. The feeling so strong that Nadia was moved. A swell in her stomach. She bit back a tear. Everything was just beautiful. The music. The connection between grandfather and grandson. The strength of feeling. And then they started singing. The old man's voice croaky but holding a tune. Artem's strong, clear. Both passionate. Both proud. That's what she could feel. An immense pride. She couldn't help herself. Now she cried.

*

Nadia found herself drawn to some pictures held in wooden frames that were nestled amongst the books. They were all small, sepia and faded colour. History. It was fascinating. She picked one up. A man and a woman standing proud, intense, in national dress, their hands entwined around a small bunch of wild flowers. A wedding ceremony, she surmised. The woman wore an immense headdress of flowers – roses, daisies, sunflowers – at its back a fan of grasses

105

and wheat. Both had matching waistcoats, heavily embroidered, and the full-sleeved shirts like the one Artem's grandpa was wearing now.

'Is this your wedding?' she asked, turning to face Bogdan.

He sighed. 'Yes. Ah, my beautiful Anastasia.' He took the picture down from the shelf and stared at it. Stroking it. A distant watery look in his eyes.

Nadia felt awkward, not knowing what to do. How to respond. She looked across at Artem for help. He signalled her to come and sit down.

Bogdan just stood there, seemingly somewhere else. 'What did they do to you, my love? What did they do?' A tear escaped from his eye. He pulled the photo close to his chest. 'It has been so many years. A lifetime. But I still cry. Forgive me,' he said softly, wiping his damp face with the sleeve of his shirt.

'No! Forgive me for being so thoughtless,' Nadia replied, feeling guilty and intrusive. 'I didn't – I am so sorry.'

'Ah, we had such a love between us. Such plans. But it was not to be. It was 1930 when we married. We were only eighteen. Children ourselves really.' He smiled. 'Such a love. My beautiful Anastasia fell pregnant almost immediately. We were blessed with a daughter. We called her Sofia. A beautiful name, don't you think? And the next year she was expecting another child. I could hardly believe it. Such joy! But it was 1932. Autumn of 1932 and we had no idea of what was to come. How could we? How could anyone? Such–such barbarity. Man's inhumanity to man.' He shook his head and trembled.

'Grandpa...' Artem almost whispered, his voice

was so gentle, so tender. 'Do you think you should?'

'Shh, child. I am an old man and I have stories that must be told. People must remember. I must remember. Always.'

Nadia felt ashamed but intrigued. Such a powerful wave of melancholy mixed with a tired anger had taken over. The pretty little cottage had become something else. She looked to Artem for a clue.

He shrugged. 'Grandpa will tell his story.'

Bogdan made his way across the wooden floor, which creaked with each step, and opened the small door of a cupboard that was under the window. He muttered to himself as he searched through its contents. There were shoeboxes stuffed with papers, bits of material, baby clothes, notebooks. He selected the ones he wanted and brought them over to the chairs where Artem and Nadia were sitting.

'All that is left apart from the stories.' He smiled and turned to face Artem. 'And you my child, and you. It rests with you now.'

Chapter 16

December 2001

Dima heard his friend calling. He felt bad, but he had no choice. He couldn't stop. He couldn't turn back. He had to focus on getting away; on clearing his head so that he could make a plan. Find some answer. Come up with a way to sell this cocaine without getting killed himself.

He had crossed the hill and was scrambling down the slope towards Khoryva. It was heavily wooded here and the going slow, but he knew no-one would be taking this route. There was no path. No easy way down. He lost his footing again and again on the snow, cursed at himself, *fuck's sake man,* tried to make himself slow down, be more careful, but he couldn't. It was like his body was going to do whatever it wanted to, irrespective of what his brain was telling it to do. Two separate entities. Sometimes that was best though, wasn't it? To let your instincts take over, not to overthink, just to be.

He reached the bottom of the hill and stepped out onto the road beside the car park, next to the *rynok*. It was almost deserted. A couple of *bumsh* huddled in a doorway under a stack of cardboard, arguing. Drunken slurs. A *babushka* stooped, laden with layer upon layer of heavy clothing, hobbling towards home, or at least something that served as a home. None of the other kids. Good. No-one he knew. Good. He did a complete circle around the *rynok*. Metal shutters were down. Everything locked up. He checked the clock. Ten thirty. Lezo would know by now that he had betrayed him. That was a death sentence. *Shit!* This whole thing was a death sentence, wasn't it? Or his only chance, he reminded himself. A way out.

He wished he had said eleven to Sasha, not twelve. He wished that he had stuck to his first thought. *Don't get involved.* He had to try and keep warm, keep out of sight, keep safe for another hour and a half. He wouldn't huddle in a doorway. That was only for the very desperate. He wasn't one of them. Wouldn't let himself be one of them. He could try the church, but that was too obvious. No. The bus shelter? He had seen a *bumsh* getting beaten up in one of those. Getting the shit kicked out of him. It was gross but he watched. He couldn't help himself. There was some kind of thrill to it. The soft thud of boot on body, the grunt of pain, the derisive sneers of the attackers, the crumpled heap of someone else's body. Perhaps that was it? The relief that it wasn't him? Him at the receiving end or him putting the boot in.

Of course he had beaten people up, had fights, but not without reason, not just for the hell of it, not on some *bumsh* who would be dead soon enough anyway. No. He wasn't that kind of sicko. He had principles.

There was only one place he could think of to go and that was back into the woods. At least there he could keep moving and keep hidden.

He walked up and down, up and down, staying close to where he thought Sasha would be most likely to pass through, if he had made it out. If. He played over as many scenarios as he could think of as he walked. Half an hour of traipsing, doing nothing when he should be doing everything he could to get himself out of this mess. He had tried to think of people, of places, of favours due. This was too big. He hovered around not knowing. He didn't want to leave, but he felt he had to. Sasha and Alyona? What would happen to them? Would they know to wait? This bag on his shoulder weighed too much. It was stopping him from thinking, from being smart. He didn't know where to go, but he needed to. He needed to know. *Fuck!*

*

Leonid was walking slowly, listening. One step. The crunch of snow beneath his shoes. Listen. Another step. Listen. The calling had stopped. He couldn't hear a god-damned thing apart from the wind. He was on the plateau now. Snow and the odd tree. Beyond that the high rises, the spires, street lights, behind him Andriivs'kyi. He pushed on, scanning, eyes narrowing as he focussed, trying to cut through the blinding snow. This light, the trees, the shrubs, they played tricks with him, made him imagine things. He stopped. Stared straight ahead. Eyes blinking against the snow. No. He was right.

Something was moving ahead of him, maybe fifty metres in front, small, hunched, running. It had to be them.

He didn't want them to know he was near. Not yet. He had to be close enough to get them otherwise they could run again. Disappear again. He knew how easy it was for street-kids to become invisible. To slip out of existence.

*

He had been fourteen or fifteen. He didn't really know. He'd been living on the streets for years, as long as he could remember. And no-one knew. No-one apart from the other homeless people he shared that basement with. He knew he'd had parents somewhere, but no real memory of anyone. Nothing good. Nothing that he missed.

His life had become one of simple survival. Of getting through the winters, staying alive long enough to reach the spring, when the world changed; when there was food and warmth and life was bearable. Sometimes even good. It was the only life he knew until that day he met Igor.

He'd done all right, lifted a wallet. He was going through it, taking out the cash. A few *Rubles*. Not worth shit. Why couldn't he get a big score? A bundle of American Dollars? Real money. At least he had enough for a bit of food, some cigarettes, some vodka and a bit left over for tomorrow. A day off. No begging, no stealing, no rummaging through garbage cans, fighting over scraps with the dogs.

He felt them before he saw them. Shoved the money into the inside pocket of his jacket. Some other people wanting what was his. Creeping up on him. It happened all the time. He felt for a rock. They jumped him.

One of them had leapt onto his back. The other was punching him in the stomach. Leo swung the fist that held the rock. It hit one of them in the face. He went down like a piece of wet fish. Suddenly nothing. The other one was scratching at Leo's face. His fingernails sunk into his eye. He felt the blood. The searing pain.

He screamed, 'You piece of shit! You mother-fucking piece of shit!' He ran backwards, slamming his attacker into a wall. He could feel the crack in his assailant's bones. The man slumped to the ground at the base of the wall. Blood was pouring from his nose. Leo started kicking. Kicking and kicking. He didn't care. He kept kicking until the noises stopped. The pleas, the grunts, the last puff of breath. He stood back and stared at the bloody mess he had made. It left him cold.

'Hey kid?' A voice from behind had said. 'Come on. Let me buy you some food.' It was Igor. He had seen something in the kid. Something that he liked. A hunger. A familiarity. Street-kids made the best soldiers. Not demanding and mean as hell. Give them a bit of luxury and they'll do whatever you want.

He took him in. Cared for him. Taught him how to survive in this new world. How to instil fear in people. How to gain unwavering respect. That was the best thing for Leonid. Respect. He was somebody now. Someone of consequence. Someone to be looked up to. Feared. Someone!

*

Igor had been a KGB officer in Soviet times, moving swiftly, seamlessly, into organised crime with the collapse of the Soviet Union and onset of Ukrainian independence in 1991. It was a time of lawlessness as the old system crumbled and nothing legal took its place. A massive hole was left waiting to be filled by gangsters and thugs. It was easy. Buying Siberian subsidised oil for a dollar and selling it on to the Baltic States for thirty. Tax-less cigarettes, women for prostitution, arms. Everything could be bought and sold. Money flowed.

It had all come so easily to Leonid. He felt like this was what he had been born for. The old Leo left far behind in another world. This was what it was all about. This was life. He watched and he learned. Taking it all in quietly, studiously. He hadn't disappointed and it wasn't long before he was trusted. By the time he was eighteen he was a loyal assassin and body guard. Whatever was needed, he did it. He worked out, spending hours in Igor's gym, pumping iron, boxing, working the equipment, loving that feeling. Adrenalin. Strength. Omnipotence.

But that wasn't enough. He would be better than the others. When they were hanging out, drinking, showing off to women, he studied. He read books, newspapers, learned English. Be better. Be more. Work his brain. He wouldn't be taken in a fight either. His body had grown powerful, as had his mind.

He had travelled to Transnistria with Igor; the lawless state where anything went. It was even dirtier than Ukraine. The black hole for the black market. It was also highly dangerous. Assassinations, gangland killings. A place for dealing weapons, but also for carrying them. Always.

The drug business was now the way to go. Small

packages worth huge sums. Easier to transport than weapons, than women. This was the way forward. Western consumption an insatiable market. Igor had contacts in Odessa from where the drugs would be shipped to Israel: to Europe. Border guards were as greedy as the rest. Decent bribes, and transport would be easy. This deal with the Colombians was crucial. Their trust. Their cooperation. This shit had to be sorted.

Chapter 17

August 2001

Bogdan held a notebook in his hands. Its paper stained by time like the old man's skin. He sat for several uncomfortable minutes just holding it, staring. Nadia didn't know what to do, where to look. Artem had picked up on her discomfort, smiled. *It's okay,* he mouthed.

As the book opened a picture fell from its leaves onto the floor. A baby wrapped tightly in swaddling. A young woman holding it proudly, with that look that only new mothers have. *This is what my life is for. This is my love.*

Bogdan bent down slowly, his body straining, and picked up the photograph with trembling fingers. 'You have heard of the *Holodomor*?' he asked.

'No,' Nadia replied, feeling that this was a monumental thing that she should have known about. Feeling humble. 'No, I haven't.'

Bogdan nodded his head. The need to lessen her discomfort was obvious. 'It is the same with most people. If you were not there you did not know about it. The dirtiest secret of all history and it is my history.' He thumped his chest with his clenched fist. 'My Ukraine. My Anastasia.'

*

The harvest was done. The food stored. The animals fed. Life would carry on as it always had. Winter would come. It would be a struggle, as always, but we had enough and we were strong. We would get through it, as always. We peasants, people of the land, would have it no other way. This was how we had lived for centuries and so it would continue. No directive from Moscow was going to change that!

Stalin had ordered forced collectives; that our land would be taken, controlled by the party. How could they take our land? Have officials from the city, trusted party faithful control us? To tell us how to farm our land. To take it from us. They called us enemies of the people, but we were the people! It didn't make sense. We refused. We would not allow this "collective" thing to happen. But when we refused, demands were made. Demands we could not fulfil. Quotas that were too high. Impossible. Taxes that were too great to pay. Even this could not quell our rebellion. We were strong, yes. But so were they. And they were many.

It began with the seizures. Party activists came. Stormed their way into our farms, our homes. Removed everything. Stories spread from farm to farm, village to village. All we could do was wait. I remember well the night they came to us. The feeling stays with me. Never lets me be.

We heard them first. Their heavy feet. Their shouts. Their arrogance. Party slogans spewing from their mouths. Fools! They kicked in our door. Dozens of them. I tried to stop them, but of course it was useless. One against so many. I was thrown to the ground, a rifle at my head. My Anastasia was heavy with child. One in her belly, the other in her arms. I told her to stay. To let them do what they had been sent to do. She wouldn't be quiet. Not my Anastasia. "What do you think you are you doing?" she had demanded, as they took all of our food from our cupboards: the grain from our barn, the animal fodder, the seed for next year's harvest. Everything. "You are behaving like wild animals. No. Worse than wild animals! How are we to live? How do we feed our children?"

I was praying that she would stop. That she would be quiet. I had heard stories of what they did to people, to women that argued. She heard my thoughts. We were so close, you see. As one. We didn't need words. She knew. She looked at me and stepped back saying, "Okay then, you win", with her body. It was awful to see her defeated like that, submissive, but I was so glad that she had done it. Hidden the thing that I loved most about her. Her strength. Her righteousness. Her bloody mindedness.

He stopped. Smiled at the memory of her.

They didn't stay for long. How easy, how quick it had been for them to remove everything we, and our fathers, and our father's fathers had worked so hard for. When we were sure that they had left we searched the house, the barns, the underground store where we kept our beets, cabbage and potatoes. Gone. Our cow, our chickens too. Everything. We were lucky. At least we had shelter. Our neighbour's house was on fire. Smoke, thick and black and dirty swept across the fields, choking everything. Killing.

We just held each other in silence. Even the baby was silent. It was as if she knew that this was the time that everything would change. That life would become something awful. Something unthinkable.

As the days passed we scavenged for scraps of food, like dogs. We went through our garbage, we picked rotting fallen fruit from the ground; dying grass and weeds, nettles to make into something we could call a soup. It wasn't enough. I decided to go into town. To take our last things of value and try to sell them. Of course, I wasn't the only one. It was all we could do and we got little in return. I exchanged our wedding rings for a few kilos of flour. Imagine...

He fingered the space where his wedding ring should be. Squeezed it. Tears were running down his cheeks. Nadia desperately wanted to wipe them off for him, to hold him, to comfort him. This proud and beautiful old man trying so hard to maintain his dignity in front of her. He swiped at his face as if he were angry with the tears, with himself.

Can you imagine? No, of course you can't. No one could. When everything you value has gone. Your way of earning a living no longer there. Your most precious things bartered, gone. Just gone. All of it.

Returning home to my wife and child with nothing but a couple of bags of flour. I had become less than a man. So much less. My Anastasia did her best by mixing the flour with dry husks and grass. This became our bread. Of course, it didn't last long.

The winter had bitten the land. Nothing lived. The crows, the wild things, had been trapped and eaten. Nothing lived. The worst of silences smothered the earth. All the time hunger gnawed at our bellies. Hunger took the souls out of our eyes. There was no food. Nothing to eat. Anywhere. We tried to travel to Kyiv but we were stopped. You had to have a pass to travel, and only the party faithful had them. Not us. Not us peasants and farmers. The young, the old, and the frail were dying and we could do nothing. We were barely alive ourselves. Shadows. Empty people.

Anastasia's time had come. The baby. May God forgive me but I prayed for a still birth. How could we bring a child into this? And Anastasia? She was a mother. Of course she would die for her child and I couldn't stand that. No. Life without her didn't bear contemplating. It couldn't happen.

The child was born, a girl, Katya. We fed on the afterbirth. Boiled it up. Pretended it was a stew of pig's liver. A new life which we now had to provide for had given us a little bit longer. Sustenance for a few more days. Anastasia made stock of the remains, and more stock from that until we were eating only water. It had become useless.

We couldn't stay where we were. Here. In our home. There was nothing. The snows had come thick and fast. The earth frozen and dead. Not even grass to eat. Nothing. We had heard that the big houses where important people lived, they still had food. But they were in the towns where we couldn't go. It was like a prison. Our home, our land, our neighbourhood had become a prison. And we lived under a death sentence.

Then they closed all of the borders of our country so that nothing could get in or out of Ukraine. No-one could help us. We walked. Not knowing why, not knowing where. Just walking. If we kept walking we might find something. Stay alive somehow.

Chapter 18

December 2001

Sasha felt a stickiness on his hand. He checked. It was blood and it wasn't his. 'Alyona? Are you hurt?' he asked.

'Yes. I fell. It was how I found bird. I fell over the roots and it was there on the ground. Still. Birds shouldn't be still on the ground like that. They should fly. Up there. Up high. Fly.' She looked up at the sky, then back down to her leg. 'My leg hurts.'

'Let me see, sweetheart.' He bent down. There was a gash across her thigh. It was deep. It was nasty. 'We need to get this clean, Alyona. Does it hurt very much?'

'It is not so bad. I don't think it is so bad. See? I can walk.' She limped for a couple of steps, wincing. The smile that she was trying to hold on her face was more like a grimace. The pain obvious.

'Shit,' Sasha mumbled. He took off his scarf and tied it around his sister's leg. 'I need to carry you.'

'No look!' she insisted, 'I can walk.'

'I need to carry you,' he whispered, firmly but gently, like a big brother does. He scooped her up.

'Be careful of bird,' she said, as she wrapped her arms around Sasha's neck. 'We must be careful of bird.'

They moved off slowly. She didn't weigh much, but neither did he. Small and weak and fragile. This was going to be so very difficult. Keeping upright in the snow was problematic enough, without the extra burden of Alyona. They had reached the edge of the trees and had to cross the open ground of the plateau. Sasha glanced back over his shoulder. He thought there was a shadow. A movement. *Shit! I have to run. I have to keep going.*

It was ten metres, less maybe, to the relative shelter on the other side of the hill. They would lose the track, not have a path to follow, but maybe they would lose that person also. If it was a person. He wasn't about to stop and check. Up here, in the cold and the dark it could only be someone bad. Something bad. He was scared. Thank God for the bird because it was keeping all of Alyona's attention, all of her focus. She seemed oblivious to anything else. That suited him fine.

He hurried along the line of the trees, just inside them, hoping that it was cover enough. The plan was to get to the far side then to go down the slope to the *rynok*. He didn't know if he could do it. The weight of his sister was becoming too much. Despite the cold he was sweating. Beads of perspiration had formed on his forehead and were slipping down into his eyes. He couldn't let go of Alyona to wipe them away. They were making him close his eyes, trying to blink them away. The snow was falling almost horizontally in a brutal wind. He stumbled. Fell. Hit his head against a tree. A searing pain. Blackness.

'Sasha?' Alyona crawled over to her brother. 'Sasha!' She turned his head to face her. 'You have to wake up, Sasha. Please! Please wake up! I don't know what to do. Sasha, please tell me what to do.'

The bird had begun moving, its little claws twitching, scratching underneath her jacket. She pulled the zip down far enough to reach her hand in. 'It is okay little bird. It will be okay.' She stroked its head. Its beak nudged slightly at her hand and dropped back against her chest. 'Good bird,' she whispered through tears. 'Good bird.' She zipped her jacket up again and picked up a handful of snow. She wiped it on her brother's face. 'Sasha. Can you hear me Sasha? What do I do now, Sasha?'

*

Leonid couldn't see them any more. Their shadows had disappeared. He could just make out tracks in the snow. They were human. It had to be them. He followed the tracks. The snow was so heavy that he had to be quick. He had to stay close or he would lose this trail as well. It took him across the hill and into the woods on the far side. He had expected the trail to head downhill but it hadn't. Whoever this was they were skirting the tree line. Hiding.

Chapter 19

August 2001

We all just shuffled, barely able to lift our feet. Shadows of people shuffling, not looking at each other. Not looking at anything other than the ground. It was there that we might find something to eat. A stick to chew on. Insects. A rodent. Anything. Time had become nothing. It meant nothing. It was dark, it was light, we were always hungry and it was perpetually cold. Such a cold you couldn't imagine. Things that there had always been an end to were now with us. Unceasingly. A part of us.

We had been walking beside the railway track, but it had become too much. Anastasia's legs had swollen up grotesquely and we knew that death was coming. That was a sign you see? A sign that hunger had won and the body had given up.

In the distance a rumble. A tremor. A train. As it drew close Anastasia looked at me. I could see what she was thinking. I nodded. We had watched it happen before. Mothers and fathers so desperate, so close to death. Now it was us. This is what had become of us. She kissed our baby's head and threw her onto the train. Little Katya, silent, wrapped in her swaddling. Perhaps someone would take pity on her. Would give her life. Perhaps she was already dead. We didn't know. Nothing was said between us. Words had become too difficult. What could we say anyway?

We sat where we were. Anastasia's head on my shoulder, Sofia lying across our laps. And she was gone. Anastasia's life had left her. I didn't even shed a tear. I had nothing left. Nothing.

He cried now though. Silent tears.

'Grandpa,' Artem said, the concern in his voice blatant. 'This is too much for you. You don't need to carry on. Please. It's late. We should go to bed.' He stood up.

Nadia sat silently, her eyes misted, her head not making sense of this. She wanted it to stop, but she was engrossed. The most heartbreaking, devastating story she had ever heard was being told to her. How could she not listen? How could she not want to hear it all to its conclusion?

Bogdan motioned Artem to sit back down. He didn't want to, hesitating, looking intently, pleadingly, at his grandfather. But he knew this was going to happen. Bogdan's story would be told.

We sat there, Sofia and I, the body of the woman we loved, the woman who had been everything to us, lying heavy between us. I didn't know if Sofia knew, if she even understood anything. I had no idea of what to do. How to stay alive. Anastasia's body was still warm, still fresh. I knew what people did. When you are starving, when all that you see is death, you become something else, something not human. I tried to rationalise it. It was meat, nothing more. Meat that could keep the life of our child possible for longer, Maybe save her. But could I?

It was the life of little Sofia that made my mind up. Something of Anastasia still here. I had to do whatever it took to keep her alive. We ate the flesh of her mother. It gave us the strength to move. To carry on. I pulled her body behind us on sticks I had tied together with pieces of her clothes. I made it look as if she were still alive and headed back towards home.

The longer we walked, the more bodies we saw. People collapsed on the roadside, propped up against walls. Body collectors came round with a horse and cart to pick them up and take them to pits that had been dug in the ground. The bodies were thrown in, pile upon pile, corpse upon corpse. Some of them weren't even dead. You could hear a soft groan as they were picked up. It was ignored. None of these people were going to survive anyway. The body collectors were paid for each corpse they delivered. They were desperate too. Each corpse would keep their own families alive – them alive.

I don't know how long it took, how far we had walked. I didn't look at anything. My child on my back, my wife. I didn't stop. Not once. I just walked and walked in the direction I thought was home. My hands clamped around Sofia's ankles, her body heavy on my head. I could feel her breathing and it kept me going. I would have given up otherwise. Laid down beside my Anastasia and given up. Joined her. But I had this life now. This little girl who needed me to keep going, stay alive.

The days were getting longer, the sun started to release the beginnings of warmth, of hope. If we could get home, hang on until spring – until the leaves, the buds, the shoots came back – then we could survive.

At last I saw it. The narrow straight track that took us here, back to this house. It was still standing. No-one had taken it over. The party hadn't burned it to the ground or destroyed it. Our little house was still there. The feelings–the feelings were tiny, so small, so confused. Our home was joy but such an empty, hollow joy. A joy that cut through my stomach, that destroyed me. I opened the door and collapsed on the floor, sobbing and laughing. Insane.

He stopped looked across at Nadia and smiled.

Chapter 20

December 2001

Leonid heard a laugh. An adult sounding one. Then another. *What the hell?* He could see the people he had been following now. A couple. A couple of teenagers leaning against a tree making out. Unbelievable! How much time had he wasted following some fucking, lusty little teenagers? He didn't care if he could be seen now.

They pulled away from each other. The young man shouted, 'What are you? A pervert or something? Piss off man!'

Normally he wouldn't allow that. The boy would be taught some manners. But he had no time to waste and a favour to ask.

'I've lost my kids. You haven't seen them have you?' he called, trying to mask his anger with worry.

'You mad? Bringing kids up here in this? Ain't seen no-one.' They turned back to kissing, to fumbling, to making disgusting noises.

Leonid had let the trail go cold. He seethed. Checked the time. Turned back. Headed down the hill. Cursing. Striding. Hoping his *militsiya* had been having better luck than him, though doubting it. His leather soles weren't designed for these conditions. He lost his footing, slipped, fell, slid into the trees.

'For fuck's sake!' he mumbled.

He got back to his feet using one of the trees for support, dusted the snow off his coat.

'Where the hell are you, you little bastards?' he hissed. 'You are really starting to piss me off!' The tick beating.

*

Sasha came round, sat up, put his hand to his head, checked for blood. Sure enough there was a gash on his forehead and a pain that felt like a knife was chiselling through his skull. What was he going to do now? Both of them hurt. Both of them bleeding. He thought that this was it. After everything that they had been through – everything that had been thrown at them – they were going to die. Here. Alone. In the snow. With nothing.

'Can you walk?' Alyona asked. 'Can you?'

'Yes. I am okay Alyona,' he lied, believing the lie himself so that she couldn't read it. Feel it. 'But maybe you could try and walk a bit yourself. Can you do that for me? Just for a little while. My arms are very tired. You are becoming such a big, grown up girl!' He forced a smile through the pain.

'I can try.' She opened the zip of her jacket and whispered softly to the bird. 'We can try, can't we?'

Sasha and Alyona were leaning on each other.

Numbed by the temperature. Each of them limping. The going so slow. Dangerously slow. The urgency wasn't only to escape that man, Lezo, but also the cold. The cold could beat them if they didn't move quickly enough to stave off its best efforts. They were lurching from tree to tree, so thankful for their presence. Their support. When they lost their footing there was a tree to cling to. To lean against. To gain strength from.

Keep moving. Keep hold of Alyona, Sasha repeated again and again in a silent mantra. He tried to think where this would lead them to, but he couldn't focus, couldn't work out exactly where they were. Just keep heading downhill. Downhill. The cold was beginning to take hold of them. It was creeping through their new clothes, scratching at them. The fingers of the devil. They could do nothing about it. Nothing other than keep moving. Pushing against it. Pushing themselves.

Alyona stopped suddenly, listened, nodded her head. 'This way. We need to go this way.' Her whispered voice was strangely confident, assured.

Sasha could hear nothing but the odd caw. A bird somewhere in a tree. What harm could it do to follow Alyona now? They were lost anyway. Perhaps she knew better than him. It wouldn't be the first time. He went with her, praying that she knew what she was doing. Trusting in her. It felt as though they were heading in the wrong direction, away from the *rynok* where they were meant to meet Dima.

'Where are we going Alyona? Where are you taking us?'

'There is a place. A secret place,' she whispered

conspiratorially. Excitedly. 'It is nearby.'

'Are you sure?'

'Yes!'

She was walking with purpose, as if she knew everything about this wood. No hesitation. A knowing. Her limp had all but disappeared.

They had walked for about half an hour, but their going slow. Little distance had been covered. She stopped beside a thicket of bushes sharp with thorns. A scattering of bricks, old stone. The foundations of a collapsed building – now covered in a tangle of branches and wild plants – hid amongst the bushes.

She hunkered down on all fours and crept through the overgrowth. Sasha crawled in after her. Concealed by the outer ring of bushes a small clearing stood. He watched, in disbelief, as she swept away some of the snow, kicked back the plants. They revealed an arch of stone draped in ivy, still green and alive, and brambles, almost fallen back for the winter but clinging on.

'Help me Sasha. Come,' she whispered, as she began pulling aside the plants.

There was a door. Small, ancient, wooden. They tugged at it. It creaked open. A tunnel opened itself up to them with a belch of stale air. Alyona crawled in, seemingly unperturbed, like this was the most natural thing in the world to be doing. Sasha could do nothing but follow, albeit with trepidation.

The tunnel was short, more of an extended archway. It led to a chamber high enough for them to stand up in. They couldn't see, but it felt large and empty. Sasha fumbled in his pocket for his lighter. He flicked it on and held it at arm's length. Indistinct walls of earth. Nothing clear.

'What is this place? How come you knew it was here? I don't understand Alyona.'

She simply smiled and said, 'It is a safe place. We will be safe here.'

He didn't pursue it. Sometimes questions were best left alone. Things just were, that was all. He needed to rest. They both did. This just was.

*

Dima knew that time was his enemy. He had to shift the cocaine and he had to shift it fast. If he left it too long word would have spread like a virus. Everyone would have been warned. No-one would touch it. Perhaps that had happened already and this was all futile. All worthless. He had to try. Giving up was never an option for him. His life had been a constant battle. This was just one more.

He decided to go back to the dealers at Darnytsa. They were the only people he knew that he thought would help. They had contacts. They had money. But most importantly, they were trying to make their mark. To get known. To move in. That could only help.

He didn't want to use a tram, or a bus. They were slow and open and dangerous, and he was in a hurry. He had money. If his luck was in there would be a taxi idling on Kontraktova. He ran down, focussing only on his destination. Not scanning for Lezo, for *militsiya,* for anything.

When he reached the square, sure enough a taxi was sitting there, waiting for a pick-up. Perfect! Something going his way at last. He opened the back door and jumped in. The driver had turned around and was staring at him. Sniffing at him. His face was one of contempt.

'Really kid? Scarper!' he growled dismissively, gesturing to the outside with his thumb.

Dima was ready for this. 'I have money. See?' He held up a bundle of notes.

The driver paused, weighing up the annoyance of a stinking kid in his car against some much needed cash – dollars spoke. 'Okay, but you pay me first. Where to?'

'Across the river. Darnytsa.'

Dima handed the agreed amount over – a rip-off but he wasn't about to haggle – and they drove off. The fan heater was on. It was almost too much. Almost painful. The blast of heated air uncomfortably hot. Sticky. Hard to breathe in. The temptation to just close his eyes and doze was so strong. He fought against it. The driver was playing loud music. Russian rock songs. That was good. A rhythm to nod his tired head to. To push the drowsiness away. Force his eyes to stay open. It left no space for awkward conversation. Questions to answer with lies.

He got the driver to drop him at the wrong apartment block and pretended to make his way into the stairwell, until he was sure that the taxi was far enough away, out of sight. He turned back, ran across the road and round the corner. Just as he was approaching the building a *militsiya* car pulled up, then a black Mercedes. *Shit! Militsiya* were always dangerous, but together with a black Mercedes with blacked-out windows. That was more than trouble. That was something you didn't mess with. Ever! He froze and pushed himself hard against the wall of the building, as if it could somehow absorb him. Make him invisible.

He tried to rationalise it. Think it through. They could be after someone else. There were always dodgy dealings going on over here. Shootings, killings, all kinds of shit. But he couldn't take that chance. His face might have been plastered all over the place by Lezo and his cronies. This was really bad.

He could wait. See what happens. Maybe they'll be out soon enough with some poor bastard in cuffs? Maybe.

Chapter 21

August 2001

I don't know why God chose us. How we survived. But we did. When the snows began to melt and the shoots forced their way through the black soil, and the buds sprouted from the branches of the trees and shrubs, we ate. Picking at them as soon as we saw them. We should have waited long enough for them to grow but how could we? We were starving and we didn't know how many days, hours we had left. Thinking. Thinking about anything had stopped long ago. We had no room for thoughts. If we thought about anything it would be of death. And what then? Then it would take us. Like all of the others we would be gone.

He made a strange, heavy sigh and paused. Caught in something. Not just a memory. A feeling. A feeling he had to fight through so that he could carry on. He stared into the distance. Nodded. Swallowed hard.

It is a terrible thing, a hunger like that. When you see food you want to eat. Of course you do. Your body is screaming for it. Aching for it. But you must be careful. Once your feet start to swell and death is close you can only eat morsels. Tiny morsels. People died because they ate more than the tiniest scrap. Your body can't deal with it you see? It kills you. The tiny shoots, the buds. They were just enough to keep us alive.

We stayed in our house and only went out to gather food. Only close by. Our garden. Our land. Staying hidden. If soldiers came, or patrols, or scavengers, we would hide in the darkness of our underground cellar, sometimes for days. Hiding. Praying.

He walked across to the window and looked out at the black night. The sky was clear and full of stars that looked as if they had been thrown up there in a random act of beauty. He nodded his head.

This. This is what kept us alive when all around people were dying. This earth is magic. It is powerful. It is ours.

Well, there was spring, there was summer, but not like before. Not plentiful. Not happy. It was only about survival now. One day after the next. Survival– Yes. Survival.

He smiled weakly, shook his head, and left the room.

There was a silence. A heavy silence that lingered

in the room after he had left it. Artem softly stroked Nadia's arm.

'We should go to bed too,' he said. His voice hushed and distant.

'I had no idea. My God. No idea at all.' She felt ignorant and confused. How could something so monumental not be common knowledge?

She had so many questions, but now wasn't the time. That night, as she lay in her bed, she couldn't help but imagine what it must have been like. What it must have been like for Bogdan and his daughter. Awful. Just awful. How do you live with that? The knowledge that you ate the person you loved. That her death brought you life. Images filled her head. Awful sickening images. She glanced across at the window; at the black sky and the stars. Things of beauty. Always, there are things of beauty.

*

The next morning it was as if last night hadn't happened. Everything was normal. Grandpa smiling and chatty, eyes sparkly and warm. Artem likewise. They had breakfast on the terrace. Watermelon, home made bread, coffee. Soft, casual conversation. The sunflowers, the weather, the deep sleep offered by the countryside.

Firm hugs and kisses were shared as they took their leave. As the car pulled away, Nadia looked back to see Bogdan standing proudly in front of his little house. He was waving. She leaned out of the window and waved back, blowing a kiss with the final wave.

'So?' Artem asked.

'I don't know what to say. That was just incredible. The place, your grandfather, his story, everything.

Incredible.'

'Yes. My grandpa is a very special man.'

'I can see that.'

'And his story? One of history's best kept secrets. No-one knows how many for sure, but millions died. Some say two, others say ten. I would guess somewhere in the middle. You know, it's probable that more Ukrainians were killed by the *Holodomor* than Jews by the Nazis. And yet–' He shrugged. 'When the local school opened again two thirds of the seats were left empty. Two thirds of all the children had died.'

'And yet, you don't hate. You speak Russian. You have Russian friends.'

'Of course. The *Holodomor* was our famine. The Russians had theirs, but history knows of that. It wasn't the Russians, it was Stalin. He killed millions of his own people too. Anyway. It is done. We are here. And I have you beside me.' He turned to her and smiled. 'One day you will see that we are more than friends.'

She laughed softly. 'You think?'

'I know.'

Chapter 22

December 2001

Nadia and Maggie were walking back from their regular midweek night out. They had been up Andriivs'kyi in one of their favourite local bars. It was small and intimate and when there was live music, like tonight, it left barely enough room for customers. The drink was ludicrously cheap and they had become known. Smiles and warm welcomes.

The snow had made the hill treacherous and they were sliding rather than walking. It was easier to stay upright that way. Plus it was a lot of fun, especially when you've had a healthy amount to drink. A slide, a stumble, a giggle. It was like being a child again, taking aim across a frozen puddle, sliding, feeling free, reckless, and slightly brave.

They reached the bottom of Andriivs'kyi and turned into Borichyv Tik Street, then Frolivska Street, and towards home.

'Oh my God,' Nadia said, suddenly stopping, pulling her hand over her mouth. 'Look.' She tugged at Maggie's sleeve. 'I can't imagine a life like that.' She pointed at a pile of clothing under which there was obviously a person.

'Pretty shit, eh?' Maggie shook her head. 'What can you do? It's just the way of things here, isn't it?'

'Let's at least give him, or her, some money. A few *Hryvnia*. You got anything on you?'

'Should have. Let me see.'

They came up with fifty *Hryvnia* between them and were bending down to find a hand. A place to leave the money where it would be found. The hand, grossly swollen, purple from the cold, from the way of life, snatched; clung on to Nadia's wrist. She tried not to pull away, not to show her feeling of repulsion. The stench, the filth.

'Thank you. Thank you so much,' crept out in a hoarse whisper. The bundle of clothes shifted, sat up, sobbed. Fifty *Hryvnia* – about ten dollars – was a lot of money to her. An awful lot. The hand let go. The money was stuffed into her pocket. Their eyes met. Both sad. Both frightened. She hobbled off, almost running, and disappeared into the night. A smell of stale urine trailed in her wake.

'Jesus!' Nadia exclaimed. 'Sometimes I feel so–so bloody privileged. An accident of birth and that could be me, you know? A different roll of the dice. But here I am, in their country, making what to them is an obscene amount of money, and doing what? Fifty *Hryvnia* here and there. It's not enough, is it?'

'Hey. Don't beat yourself up. At least you do something. And there's those street-kids you help all the time. You ain't so bad.' Maggie squeezed Nadia's arm, smiled at her. 'And that shit's way too philosophical for a boozy Wednesday night!'

Nadia allowed herself a soft laugh. 'Yeah. I guess so. You have to wonder though. Alyona and Sasha on a night like this? How do they get through, keep going? What a shitty life.'

'But they do. They get through it. They're tougher than you give them credit for, you know?'

'Maybe, but still...'

'One more before we go home?'

'I could be persuaded.'

'A bottle from a kiosk like a local, a posh drink in a bar like an expat?'

'It's too bloody cold to play at being local but...'

Her friend could read that Nadia's thoughts had drifted back to life on the streets. The homeless. 'You know you have to leave it behind you. Toughen up a bit.'

'Maybe.' She forced a smile. 'How about a compromise? A bottle from a kiosk but we'll take it home?'

'Sounds good to me.'

They were walking past an alleyway, a square opening that led into a dank, dingy courtyard where a car workshop stood. Some rusty shells, piles of tyres, padlocked gates, a smell of diesel that caught in your throat. Maggie glanced up and lost her footing on a patch of ice under the snow, slipped, screeched, grabbed onto a drain pipe, fell. Nadia landed on top of her. They were laughing, lying on their backs in the snow, unable to control the fit of giggles that had taken over them. Nadia eased herself up, leaning on the wall for support.

'You okay?' she managed in between giggles, holding her hand out for her friend.

'Um, yeah. Just a dented ego is all. She took the hand and got to her feet, almost losing her footing again as she did so. A slide, a screech. 'No-one saw did they?'

They looked around, wiping the snow off themselves. A smartly dressed man called from across the road. 'You need to be careful. It's slippery!'

'No shit!' Maggie called back. She turned to Nadia. 'How do they know we speak English?'

'It's the curse of the expat! You don't see locals slipping and falling, do you? They have this weirdly difficult grace-on-ice-and-snow-thing going on – so unfair! Plus we were being kind of noisy!'

'We were, weren't we!'

Chapter 23

September 2001

It had been a week since Nadia's visit to Artem's granddad and she had been putting off talking about it, neglecting her friend. So much had happened and she was struggling to process it herself. The story was so personal, so beyond comprehension. How could she tell someone else that? Do it justice? But how could she not? She had kept to the trivial, the expected, when she had bumped into Maggie at work. Now they were meeting up. She knew she'd be questioned. Probing was a Maggie speciality. Now she had one more thing to keep hidden.

'So? How did it all go? Have you done it yet? Taken the plunge? Admitted you really like him?' Maggie asked excitedly, nudging Nadia in the ribs. 'At least shagged him. Come on. You can't waste a cutie like that!'

'Sorry to disappoint you but we're just friends.

Good friends. And you know I'm not in the market for anything else right now.'

'I know but, well, that's half the fun of being an expat, isn't it? You can reinvent yourself. Just have fun.'

'And I can't have fun without a man in tow? Is that what you're saying?'

Maggie threw her head back and laughed. 'No, no, not at all, but a girl has needs after all, and he's as cute as get out. Really! I sure as hell wouldn't say no.'

Nadia laughed in return. 'You are awful!'

'Would you mind if I did?'

Nadia left too long a pause before she began to reply.

Maggie cast a knowing look. 'And there you have it. No way are you two just friends and the sooner you do something about it the better, my friend. You see, I'm a friend.' She put her hand on her chest. 'He is not.'

Nadia pulled a face. 'Maybe,' she acknowledged. 'Maybe. But not right now.' She drifted off into her own personal thoughts. Would she ever be ready? That leap of faith to trust someone like that. Trust a man to share her life with. It seemed very far away. As a friend? Sure, she trusted him. But more then that? Not yet.

Maggie was watching her. 'I'm offended, you know. You've got this big, dark, secret thing lurking around and you're not sharing.'

Nadia sighed. 'Well, to quote you – reinventing yourself,' she cocked her head, raised her eyebrows. 'In expat land...'

'Ah. But there's also a problem shared and all that

stuff. Sometimes it's good to offload. I reckon there's something to do with children. Your obsession with those little street-kids.'

'Maybe I just care. It's heartbreaking, you know?'

'Yeah. Yeah it is, but what can you do? It's life and it happens everywhere. You have to get on with yours. It'll kill you if you let them get under your skin too much.'

'So what? Ignore them? Turn that blind eye like most people around here seem to. Is that what you're saying?'

'No. What I'm saying is be kind, be sweet Nadia, but don't get sucked too far in. That's all. Anyway, nice try at avoiding talking about you.'

'Oh, don't be a pain. There's nothing to tell. We all have histories but they're just that. I'm sure you've got some decent stories as well. I'm not pushing.'

'Fair dinkums. Time for drinkies?'

'That sounds like a very good idea.'

The mood lifted. The atmosphere flitted off on the breeze of a warm, late summer's evening.

'Beer in the park followed by some music? Busker hunting?'

'Sounds about right!'

They linked arms, picked up some beers from the kiosk and headed towards the park on Kontraktova. The street-kids were there again. The brother and sister. There was a gravity about them which didn't fit with their ages. It bothered Nadia. She had talked to them a few times now, bought them an ice cream, a burger, some chocolate. Tried to find out about their lives, but the subject was always flipped back to her and the West. This magical place where everything seemed to be wonderful, dreams achievable. Who was she to snatch that away from them? It wasn't as if they were going to leave Ukraine, was it? That took money and contacts and visas. Exit visas for Ukraine and entry ones for pretty much everywhere else. No. They would be staying here.

Alyona wanted to hear about the Loch Ness monster, about folk tales and mythical creatures. Nadia was only too happy to share them, putting on silly voices like her own mother had done for her. It was comforting, familiar. And she loved the look on Alyona's face. The wonder and excitement.

Nadia tried to ask about them. To find out about their lives. How they existed, what they did to get by, to survive. Nothing was forthcoming. A shrug of the shoulders from Sasha, a smile from Alyona. How did she always manage to smile like that? It was as if nothing could break through. Nothing could take away her outward innocence. But Nadia was sure there was nothing innocent about that black Mercedes that she had seen picking Alyona up and taking her away for a couple of hours, while Sasha waited quietly, nervously.

Chapter 24

December 2001

Leonid had met his *militsiya* in the cafe as agreed. They didn't have any good news for him. He picked up his Mercedes and drove to Voloska. Enough of freezing his balls off! The English woman lived here. She was the last person who had been seen with the kids. Word had it that she spent quite a lot of time with them, bought them food, even let them into her apartment. Maybe she would know where they were. He was sure it wouldn't take much to make her talk. A weak little Western woman. Easy enough. It might even be fun.

His *militsiya* opened the apartment block door and climbed the stairs to the top floor, banged on the door to shouts of, '*Militsiya!* Open up!'

There was no reply. They listened at the door. No noises. No lights escaping. The neighbour's door cracked open.

'Nothing to see here. Go back inside,' Leonid said, leaving no room for doubt. Pointing at the door to their apartment without bothering to look at them.

The door shut, locks bolted, metal slipped into metal.

'I need you two to wait here. She'll come back. When she does take her inside and keep her there until I can get back. You got that?'

*

Dima waited at the tower block in Darnytsa, watching from a safe vantage point. It looked grimmer, starker in the dark. The feeble orange glow from the street-light only accentuating its foreboding presence towering above him. Most of the apartment windows were dark. It was late. People wrapped up in their beds, sleeping. Oblivious.

The *militsiya* weren't inside for long. They came out of the building with three men in handcuffs, heads bent down, backs arched, curses spewing. The men wrestled against the open door of the car, were hit with the butt of a gun, and pushed inside.

Dima couldn't be sure. Not from this distance, and in the dark. The murky aura leeching from the street-light was no help at all. It could have been them. It could have been anybody.

He watched the cars pull away along the desolate side street and turn onto the main road. Anonymous trails of headlights. His heart was thumping, breath heavy, frosted. A quick glance around, just to make sure, then he skipped across the concrete, and into the building.

The doors squeaked open then clunked shut behind him. He stood and listened. Nothing. He hurried up

148

the stairs, not wanting to use the lift. Too risky. Small spaces, confinement. There was no way out. By the time he got to the tenth floor he was winded, breathless, but warm. His heart was hammering, his mouth dry. He checked the corridor in both directions. Peeling paint, reinforced doors.

'Fuck's sake. Be in!' he muttered to himself.

He knocked on the door. It swung open to an empty silence. There was no need to go any further. His worst fears confirmed. The apartment empty; turned over. His contacts gone, along with his hope. His way out was a place he couldn't see any more. A thing intangible. He turned back and ran.

He flew down the stairs with the panic of a rabbit caught in the stare of a hawk. This hawk had eyes everywhere, and he knew that. He also knew that he had been sloppy. Foolish. But he hadn't known what else to do. Thinking blurred by danger, by something so unknown, so totally out there. Ridiculous. Him. A street-kid. A bag stuffed full of thousands of dollars worth of cocaine. The Mafia. He laughed to himself. The fucking Mafia on his trail! Of course he didn't know what to do. Of course he was going to die!

Everyone he knew spun through his mind, sifting for possibilities. Did he know anyone at all who could deal with this? There wasn't anyone, was there? The realisation weighed heavy. It had all gone to shit again. Why was there never a break for him? A piece of good fortune. Just once. Something to go his way. No. His life was just this. Shit. He knew that and he should accept it, get on with it, like normal. No dreams. No thoughts of anything different than shit. He reached the bottom of the stairs, scarf over his mouth, hat pulled low. He was just a kid in a hurry. That was all.

When he opened the external door the cold punched him, almost winding him. He hunched his shoulders, pulled everything close, and walked briskly into the night. The bag was heavy on his shoulders digging a pain into his flesh. A deeper one into his mind. *Shit!* He hurried towards the train station. The anonymity, the warmth, the movement. The exposure wasn't wanted – wasn't good – but he could keep himself hidden amongst the people. Slunk down like a moody teenager. Shrink into someone else, someone of no consequence. Huh! Like that would be a problem!

The trains were regular and his wait a short one. It shouted its arrival, clattering and humming into the station. He allowed himself a quick glance up and down the platform, as he stepped forward and into the hiss of the opening doors. There were empty seats at this time of night, but he wasn't taking one. He stood in a corner, next to the doors, from where he could see everything and make a run for it, if necessary. The difficult part was trying to look casual, unperturbed, normal. He wanted a cigarette, a drink, a bag of glue, a way to disappear.

He glanced up at the clock in the train. Half past eleven. He had wanted to ditch the bag somewhere; stash it safely away, but there wasn't time to do anything other than head back to the *rynok* to meet up with Sasha and Alyona. He could get back there for midnight, at a push.

It would have been safer to get off at a different station; somewhere he wasn't known; somewhere they wouldn't think he would show up at, whoever "they" might be. Leonid, for sure; his Brigade? More than likely; the *militsiya?* It seemed that way. How many though? What line had they been fed? Had it gone official – some story made up about him – an APB put out? No. He didn't think so. This would be kept small, tight. They wanted this bag, they wanted Alyona, and now him too. Lessons to be taught, money to be made. Officialdom wouldn't be high up there. Not yet. That would be too messy. Too public.

Right now there was no choice. He jumped off at Kontraktova, keeping himself as inconspicuous as possible. Along the platform, bright with strip lights, up the steps, and out into the night. He blew out a plume of misty breath as he turned away from the station and headed towards the *rynok*. The streets quiet, the traffic hushed by the falling snow. The people who were out hunched, staring at the ground. That was good.

PART II
Slipping

Chapter 25

October 2001

Nadia had been in Kyiv for almost five months now. It had become familiar, strangely normal. The honeymoon phase was beginning to fade as the excitement of life in another culture slipped into ordinariness. Early summer had slipped into late autumn. The city was awash with golds and reds, now more on the ground, a slowly rotting carpet rather than the beauteous aura of a few weeks ago. The parks had begun to empty, frequented more by old men playing chess than young people having fun. The fountains were ignored, somehow now an irrelevance. A coldness was creeping in. A seriousness had swept across people's faces; their demeanour changed, as if they knew something, and it was ominous, dangerous. Shoulders hunched, bodies tensed. Smiles were rare.

She was coming back from work. It had been her evening shift. Not one she liked. The students were tired, not so enthusiastic about studying, paying attention. And honestly, neither was she too keen on the teaching. The darkness outside didn't help. Darkness and work weren't a good combination. The body didn't appreciate it, neither the mind.

In the summer she had preferred to walk home, the gentle surrender from central Kyiv down to Podil. It was pleasant. A switching off walk. She had taken detours, wandered off behind the building of the National Philharmonic, up the steps and across to the park where the Arch of Friendship stood, huge and impressive, like so many things in this place. Beneath it the bronze statue of two workers, Ukrainian and Russian, holding aloft the Soviet Order of Friendship of Peoples. Cold and metal.

At the edge of the hill a concrete wall, a viewing point. The panorama from here was spectacular. The Dnieper river sweeping through, alive with history and stories, hopes and fears. It branched open, on one side twisting through forests, along beaches, around islands. The other past huge housing schemes, docks, rusted metal bridges, gigantic cranes. A city of such contrasts.

But now that it was cold and dark, she took the metro to Kontraktova, stopped off at the kiosk for a bottle of beer, which Tatiana – the lady behind the counter – would open for her with a smile and an acknowledging nod.

As she was taking a slug from the bottle, enjoying the taste, the bubbles, the slip into relaxation mode, she caught a figure in the corner of her eye. She turned towards it. On the wall where Sasha usually sat was Alyona. That was strange. She didn't think that she had ever seen Alyona without her brother. Alone. No. She hadn't. Alyona was sitting in the glow of a street light, watching the crows in the skeletal trees above her. They waved at each other. Nadia joined her on the wall that was so often Sasha and Alyona's place.

'No Sasha tonight?' Nadia asked.

'No. He has gone tonight. Sometimes they take me. Sometimes Sasha.' She shrugged nonchalantly.

'Where do they take you?'

She smiled that strangely vacant smile. That smile that meant she wasn't going to carry on with this conversation and there was no point in forcing the issue.

Nadia took her hand. It was so delicate, so pale, and so very cold.

'You're freezing Alyona. Look at you.'

Alyona shrugged again, smiled.

Nadia didn't know what to do. She wanted to get something for her, some warm clothes. Something. It was too late for the *rynok* or the shops to be open. She couldn't just sit here, all wrapped up in her down jacket, her wool and comfort, and do nothing. She undid her scarf and wrapped it around Alyona's neck. There were marks. Bruises.

Alyona smiled, ran her fingers over the softness of the wool. 'Thank you Nadia. It is very beautiful.' She stroked it across her face. 'It smells like you.' A soft smile.

'You are very welcome Alyona.' She spread the scarf over Alyona's shoulders. 'There, that should help a little bit.'

'Do you have some food? Something for the birds?

I think they are hungry.'

'I do. I've just bought some bread.' She took the loaf out of her bag. 'Here.'

'Thank you.' Alyona tore the bread into small pieces and threw them high in the air. Crows cawed, starlings chattered, both flew down. The noise became louder as word got round. The odd brave sparrow flitted in and out with its prize, before eating in safety on the opposite pavement. Alyona smiled, watching the birds swooping and snatching, fighting each other for crumbs, flapping wings in aggression, heads jerking, warnings screeched.

A woman and her two children walked past, kicking at the crows. 'Tsk! Shoo!' The children shrieked and laughed, chasing them. Stamping their noisy little feet. Flapping their arms. The mother smiled at them encouragingly.

Alyona's nose wrinkled disapprovingly. 'They are like us, the crows,' she whispered, not taking her eyes off the birds. 'People don't like them. Don't see the beauty inside. Dirty pests they think. But I know. I know they are smart and beautiful and wise.' She turned to Nadia. 'When the sunlight strokes their feathers you can see all of the colours they hide in there. Not black. All of the colours, shining like a rainbow. They are my friends.'

As if to order one of them landed on the wall beside her and shuffled along in awkward little skips, its head tilted to one side, its sharp, beady eyes staring. Alyona smiled and held her hand out. The bird hopped up and cawed, bobbing up and down, up and down. She slowly reached her other hand out, lifted it above the bird's head and stroked it with the lightest of touches. 'Hello beautiful crow.'

The birds scattered. The Mercedes pulled up and Sasha got out. His look was one of embarrassment. A quick hello. No smile. An outstretched hand for Alyona and they were gone.

As Nadia stood, watching them disappear towards Kontraktova, she resolved to do something. To do more than just pass some of her excess on to them. Walking home she felt guilty knowing that warmth and security were waiting for her. She would open the door to her apartment, be welcomed by the constant pumping of the centralised heating system, which meant that even in this cold she left a window open to prevent the place from overheating. She would eat well – choose from a generous selection in her fridge, her cupboards – sink into the settee, have a beer or two, perhaps decide against having a snack (she had to watch her weight, didn't she?) watch a movie, have a hot bath, snuggle up in her bed. It was all easy. Comfortable and easy. She had nothing to complain about. Her only problems were historical. Things that she had no power over at the time but now? Now it was her choice whether or not to allow her past to tangle up, twist her present. Her gift. All she had to do was live for now. Be now.

Chapter 26

December 2001

Leonid jumped into his Mercedes and drove back towards the underground at Poshtova. His *militsiya* had already checked, but he wanted to be sure. You can't leave anything to chance. Risk your future on someone else's say-so. He pulled up on the pavement, hurried down the steps. The place was empty – Of course it was! He wasn't expecting anything different – The concrete awash with dirty brown puddles of slush. The smell of a cold night. Stale cigarettes, stale alcohol, stale bodies, and a strange metallic smell that clung to these places when they were empty.

Back out. Back in the car. A slow cruise along Petra Sahaidachnoho Street. Quiet. The odd drunk. Down towards Kontraktova. The usual sprinkling of late night revellers, lonely people, solitary drinkers. Staggers and mumbles. The cry of a startled bird shrieking through the night air. The baleful howl of a dog.

As he was driving, scanning the pavements, the doorways, shadows, his mind was spinning events around. Who knew about this? The Colombians, sure, but they wouldn't be risking future deals by doing something stupid like this. This was their first deal with Ukraine. A tester. The quantity was relatively small – enough to confirm that they could handle it, the quality was as expected – It had to go well. Millions would be made from this if it all worked out. Millions for both sides. How had it all gone so very wrong?

He should have been there. It would have been a different story then. He was smarter than Gregor. Much smarter. Nothing would have got past him. And now, here he was, cleaning up that ass-hole's mess. Well, trying to. He had been given the basics from Igor, but there was more, surely? And he should have been told. How was he supposed to do the job right if he didn't have all of the information? He knew that someone had opened up on the cars just after the deal had been done. Some people were dead. People on both sides, apparently. He didn't know who. He didn't even know if Gregor had survived. He hoped that he hadn't. The creep didn't deserve space on this earth.

The cocaine was gone. The money too. This didn't make sense. Who knew? Who would have had the balls to try and take the drugs and the money? That was suicide, surely. Igor loses his coke, the Colombians their money. Both sides totally pissed off. And what about that? The money? The street kid, Alyona, she took the coke, apparently. How the hell did that happen anyway? Some little street kid is in

Gregor's car when he's doing a deal as big as this. What a dickhead. He'd never had time for him. The man was dirty. Obnoxious and dirty. Fat stomach, fat cigar, fat wallet brigade. Chunks of gold hanging distastefully around his oversized neck. Leonid had always steered clear as much as possible.

The man had a big mouth too. How can you trust someone with a big mouth? Why did Igor trust someone with a big mouth? And, it would appear, stupid. Jesus! But the money? Who has that? One of the Colombians doing a con of some kind? Some foot soldier gone over the edge? Had to be. The deal had been done. They had their money. We had our coke. It had to be one of them, didn't it? No-one on Igor's side would dare. But on their side? He didn't know. These Colombians were an unknown entity. How they did things. Maybe one of them was just plain stupid.

He didn't feel good about any of this at all. His twitch was going off again and he could feel it. That nasty little thing, that was beyond his control, was ticking away in his cheek. Tick fucking tick.

He slapped the steering wheel in frustration, in anger, out of control. That was bad. In this situation that was bad. *Get it together Leonid. Get it together and sort this out!* He would find Dima. He was sure the kid was in on the whole thing. Should never have let him out of his sight. Careless! What was he doing making a mistake like that? Not like him. Not like him at all. Of course Dima knew the girl, Alyona. They all knew each other – the street-kids. He knew that, and yet he had made such an obvious mistake. He had to fix this. More than just his reputation was at stake here.

Keep moving, keep searching, keep thinking, keep it sharp. He drove up and down the main streets, the side streets, crawling along, scanning. In his rear-view mirror he kept seeing headlights. There, then gone. There, then gone. It could be nothing, but he had a feeling of something not right, and those sorts of feelings were best acted upon.

He didn't want to have to get out and walk again, but that would be a sure way of finding out if he had a tail. It was also the next thing he would have been doing anyway. There were too many places around here where cars can't go and you can hide. He had already checked the Andriivs'kyi side of the hill. Now he would check this side, the *rynok* and its nooks and crannies, doorways, car parks, garbage bins, woods. *Fuck it!* He pulled up next to an alleyway, stretched into the back seat for his fur hat, his winter coat, his gloves. *Fuck it!*

He locked the car and stepped into the shadow of a basement that stood next to the alleyway. From here he had a clear view of the road in both directions, his car, and the entrance to the alley. He would wait long enough to be sure that there wasn't a tail.

*

Maggie was limping. She stopped, leaned against a wall. 'Sod it. I reckon I've only gone and sprained it.'

'Can you make it home?'

'Here. Gimme your shoulder. Let's see.' She held her arm out, gesturing for support. Took it. 'Okay.'

Nadia secured Maggie's arm around her neck and held her wrist, her other arm around her waist.

Maggie tried to hop but the ground was too slippery. Each step too precarious. This wasn't going to work.

'I'm going nowhere right now,' she complained.

Their outlines were lit up by headlights. Long distended shadows cast on the snow. Unnatural. Something not human.

Nadia turned around to face the oncoming car, stuck her hand out, waved it up and down, like the locals do, hoping it would stop, gypsy-cab style. The car drove on by, splattering her with slush that spewed out from under its wheels. She screeched in exasperation. 'Well screw you too,' she called in its wake.

Maggie laughed at her, not used to seeing Nadia lose her cool, get angry, use phrases like, "screw you".

'What? I'm cold and covered in slush!' she responded, realising where the amusement had come from.

The car stopped, reversed back up towards them. Nadia panicked for a minute, thinking that they had seen her shouting, had heard, and were coming back for a confrontation. She had seen it before. Some hapless person getting pulled up by the driver of a big, black car for showing frustration; for getting angry, for just being there. Big, black cars did what they wanted over here and it was best left that way. She had learned to ignore if at all possible. Right now she wished that she had managed to keep control. To ignore.

The window opened. Nadia stepped back. Braced herself for something uncomfortable. The driver leaned across, a smile on his face. *Phew!* Nadia stepped closer, bent down to the driver's level, smiled sheepishly in return, explained what had happened. Her friend was hurt. It was cold and late and they wanted to get home. Could he help?

The driver grinned back. 'No problems,' he said, in heavily accented English. 'I take you. Come!' It seemed that no matter how hard she tried to disguise it, to use her Russian and be local, she was blatantly an English speaker. It annoyed and amused her, depending on the time, the mood. Right now it didn't matter. They were getting home.

She gave directions to the stranger who was all smiles and helpfulness and questions. Who were they? What were they doing in his beautiful Kyiv? Did they like it here? Why didn't Nadia speak Ukrainian? They should learn. He would be happy to teach them. English lessons for Ukrainian lessons. A good arrangement. He didn't stop. It was only a five minute drive, but it seemed so much longer.

He insisted on helping them to their building. Him on one side of a wincing Maggie, Nadia on the other. This was all too worrying. All too intrusive. Both of the women were trying to work out how to get rid of him without causing offence.

'We're fine now. Thank you so much,' Nadia said, turning to face him.

'No, I help you!'

He moved forward with intent. Nadia stepped across his path. 'It is very late. Thank you. Goodnight,' she said purposefully, pleased with her strength. Her attitude. The friendliness was still there but the intent, the denial, not up for negotiation. 'It is the first floor. No steps. We are good now. Thank you.'

He shrugged, disappointed but resigned to his fate. 'We shall drink tomorrow, like we agreed, yes?'

'Of course,' she replied with a smile, knowing that there was no way that would happen. 'Tomorrow! Goodnight and thank you again.' Her voice lightened.

'Please,' he replied, as he headed back through the alleyway, a smile on his face.

They waited until they heard his car door slam, the engine turn, the car pull away, before opening the stair door. Once inside Nadia lowered Maggie onto the cold, concrete stairs and switched the light on. It flickered and buzzed, threatening to fail them, before it settled into a dim, depressing light which only heightened the bleakness of the stairwell. The smell of old dust. The peeling paint. The broken railings. Somehow its quaintness had disappeared with the summer.

Nadia sat down beside Maggie.

'Why did I have to live on the third floor?' Maggie complained.

'Could be worse. You could be in a high rise with a broken lift.'

'True.'

'You could be being carried up the stair by a rather too friendly and slightly creepy stranger.'

'True again! Okay. Let's do this. I can hop up holding onto the handrail. You come up behind me in case I fall. Okay?'

'Oh, excellent! So I get squashed if you fall.'

Their voices echoed up the stairwell, the sound amplified. It made them giggle. Progress was slow. The lights went out. 'Shit.'

Chapter 27

October 2001

Nadia had finally convinced Sasha and Alyona to come back to her apartment, to relax, to have something to eat, to have a bath. They were in the bathroom now. She could hear giggles, water splashing, whispers. It made her smile. Made her feel warm inside.

She was in the kitchen cooking some dinner for them. Roast chicken with all the trimmings. It had been a while since she'd actually cooked a proper meal like this. A meal for more than one. When it was just her she made do with snacking – easy quick food – bread and cheese, soup, sandwiches, or if she felt the need for more, a take-away. There didn't seem much point in spending hours in the kitchen if there wasn't anyone to share the result with, to accept compliments from, or laugh at failures with. But it hadn't always been like that.

Snippets of unwelcome memories crept up. Her making a meal, him shouting. 'You don't expect me to eat this muck do you?' Throwing it at her. Storming out. Coming back drunk and angry. They hadn't been living together for very long before the veil began to slip. The charade of the happy couple. She thought it was only a phase. He was struggling with adjusting to this new life; that was it. It was her fault. She was expecting too much from him. If she was more patient, more understanding, more loving, more like his mother, more. Always more.

A squeal snapped her back to now. A happy, normal, child's squeal of enjoyment. The bathroom door squeaked open and the two of them, Sasha and Alyona, came padding out, wrapped in towels and laughter. Nadia smiled at the scene. Condensation dripped down the tiled walls, covered the mirror. The steamy air was thick with the scent of bubble bath. Pine and freshness.

'Run into the bedroom. I've put some clothes there for you,' she said, pointing to the door at the far end of the hall.

There was a pile of new clothes on the bed for each of them. She had shopped for them in secret, guessing at their sizes, their tastes. Nothing flashy but practical, warm, comfortable. She hoped that they would like them.

A deep intake of breath. 'Look!'

*

Sasha was edgy, not wanting to sit, pacing up and down, looking out of the window. Alyona perched like a little bird on the edge of the settee, then slipped down to the floor where she felt more comfortable.

Both not being the children she knew on the street. It was as if they didn't want to be here.

Nadia felt awkward. This wasn't what she had imagined, expected, wanted. And she felt guiltily relieved when daylight began to fade and Sasha used that as the reason to leave. As she closed the door behind them she questioned who that had all been for. What use was a meal, a bath, a momentary lapse from the harshness of their everyday lives? Had it done more harm than good? Made them feel less worthy, less human? Perhaps. At least they had decent clothes. That had to be a good thing.

It wasn't. The clothes were soon spotted. Stolen by some other kids. A gang of them. Dima would give them a doing if he knew who they were. Sasha didn't tell. Best to leave it. Trouble only bred trouble.

*

Nadia was left feeling miserable, in need of picking up. Maggie was busy, working the late shift, so she called Artem, invited him round. He arrived with a smile, a bottle of wine, and a bunch of flowers. Very Ukrainian, sunflowers and grasses. Very much what she needed. She told him about the children.

He shook his head.

'Don't say I told you so,' she said disconsolately.

'Well?' he smiled, shrugged, 'I did. You are a beautiful, kind woman, but you don't know the way of things here. This,' he waved his arm around the space between them. 'This is not their life. It is yours.'

'But –'

He put his finger on her mouth, pulled her close, kissed her. First gently, like a friend, like the way they had always kissed. This time he needed more. The wanting had been there from that very first day but he knew where he stood. He knew she wasn't ready. She wasn't looking for anything more. But now it felt different and he took his chance.

They locked mouths, locked tongues, breathed each other, tasted each other. She twirled her leg around his. They staggered towards the bedroom, removing each other's clothing as they went, tearing at it, desperate. Hands grabbing, stroking, clutching, searching.

'Are you sure?' he managed to puff out.

'Yes,' she replied, her hands reaching down inside his boxers. 'Oh yes...'

The love making was fierce, wild, immense. And short.

'Okay. Sorry. I–shit–I. That was just too...shit,' he mumbled in her ear, his dead weight on top of her, their bodies wet, sticky. This wasn't what he had planned, what he had wanted. What must she think of him?

She laughed.

'I wanted it to be slow and beautiful and – can we go again?'

This time he asked her to lie still. He started at her toes, kissing every bit of her, running his tongue up her calf, the inside of her thigh, around her groin.

'Oh my God,' she mumbled, clutching his hair, wanting to reciprocate but enjoying this so much.

He licked her stomach, pausing at her belly button, nibbling at it. His hands reached for her breasts, caressing, stroking. She began slipping her fingers down his back, over his buttocks, round his hip bone.

'Stop, stop, stop,' he whispered. 'Not yet.'

He explored the most secret of places until he felt her body explode in a multitude of spasms. He couldn't wait any longer. This time he entered her slowly. The heat, the beautiful caress of her flesh. Each centimetre felt, as he crept deeper and deeper inside her. He held himself back slowly, slowly. He took her face in his hands, looked in her eyes, exploded inside her, collapsed.

*

'Oh. Look at you! Big cheesy grin on your face, squirmy swagger. You've only gone and done it, haven't you?' Maggie sang at her friend.

Nadia laughed. 'It's that obvious is it?'

'Uh-huh!'

It was a lazy Saturday afternoon and they were walking along Khreschatyk, all of its eight lanes closed to traffic and dotted with street performers, musicians, story-tellers. One of the roadside kiosks supplied electricity to a band, allowing them to be wired up. Crowds stood around watching, listening, dropping coins and notes into guitar cases, upturned hats, plastic cups. The sun was shining and it was still just strong enough to lift the temperature, to push away the frost, to allow people to stand and watch, unhurried by the need to escape to a place of warmth. One of those autumn days that offered a last glimpse of carelessness before the winter took hold.

The band was the one from Podil. Maggie grabbed Nadia by the hand.'Cool!' she said, a grin on her face, excitement in her voice. 'I could do with a bit of what you've been getting!' She pulled her to the front of the small crowd. The singer nodded and smiled at them. The guitarist was lost in his music, his foot pumping out the rhythm, his fingers dancing over his fretboard.

'Tell me that isn't sexy!' Maggie whispered.

'You're so bad!'

'I know,' she grinned, eyebrows raised, her tongue on her upper lip.

They stood watching. Maggie in blatant lust mode, Nadia enjoying the music, but her attention wandering into the people. There were some scruffy little street-kids, as always, flitting around, working out how to scam a few *kopeks,* a bite to eat. Men in suits and leather, women in boots and fur, young people less edgy, looking almost Western, almost casual. Hovering in the background the ever-present *militsiya.* Weapons and intimidation. They were talking to a man. Tall, dark, dressed in black. There was something about him. An intensity. It made her feel uncomfortable. He caught her eye. Stared. It wasn't friendly. Cold, arrogant, intimidatory. She moved her gaze slightly, trying to pretend she had been looking at something else. Turned back to the band.

'Creep,' she muttered.

'What?' Maggie replied, surprised.

'Ah, nothing. Just some creepy guy behind us.'

Maggie turned around. 'Who? Where?...Oh. The stereotypical tall, dark, handsome, all dressed in black guy with the *militsiya?'*

'Yep. Well spotted. Still staring, is he?'

'Yeah. A looker though.' She smiled at him.

'What are you doing?'

'Just being nice. You know me.' She nudged Nadia

in the side, raised her eyebrows, bit her lip.

'You're going to get us in so much trouble one of these days.'

'You think?'

Nadia shook her head and laughed.

Maggie turned her attention back to the band who had started playing Hotel California. The words were cutely wrong, the accent strong. The crowd sang along, smiled, clapped. The band were finishing up. Unplugging. Maggie began to saunter towards the guitarist, hopeful. A pretty young blond beat her to it, put her arms around him in a territorial kind of a way. Planted a kiss on his cheek.

'Bollocks. That'll be me scuppered then,' Maggie complained.

Nadia laughed.

'Or I could go and chat up mister tall, dark, and handsome.' She grinned and looked back at where he had been standing.

'Don't you dare! Come on. A drink. The Basement Bar?'

Maggie sighed exaggeratedly, like a reprimanded teenager. 'Okay then my sensible friend.'

The Basement Bar was nestled in the back of a courtyard off Kreschatyk. It was smoky, small, and intimate with an ethnic, liberal, arty feel. Musical instruments, posters, and prints hung on the walls. The furniture was thick and wooden, matching the heavy beams that supported the roof. Candles sat on the tables. It was frequented by a mix of locals and expats, more the former than the latter. A gentle mix of cultures. Journalists, musicians, writers, politicians.

They ordered two beers at the bar and went to sit at

a table in the corner.

'In you go,' Maggie said, offering the seat with a view of the door to Nadia. 'We cant have you nervous and twitchy now, can we?'

'Thank you!'

'Have you always had this, "must sit with my back to the wall," thing going on?'

'Pretty much, yes.' She shrugged sheepishly.

'Why? I mean it's kind of restrictive, isn't it? I mean, what do you do if there isn't an appropriate space free?'

She laughed softly, slightly embarrassed, knowing her foible was irrational, foolish, but unable to cast it off. 'I'll sit if I have to, but I really don't like it. It makes me feel vulnerable – nasty and uncomfortable. And you never know do you? Who might sneak up on you. Like creepy friend of the *militsiya* guy!'

'He's not here, is he?' Maggie swung her head around and back again. 'Ooh, things just got interesting.'

'If you were a man I'd tell you to keep it in your trousers!'

'Can't blame a girl for trying.'

He was standing at the bar, apparently waiting for someone.

'Oh look. I'm out of ciggies,' Maggie announced with a cheeky grin and a wink. 'Won't be a sec.'

'No. Don't do that,' Nadia replied, to no effect. She had learned by now that when Maggie gets an idea planted in her head it will be seen through. But you had to try. Sometimes her ideas were out there. Risky. Plain foolish! There were times when Nadia wondered how Maggie had survived for so long in dodgy places where life was cheap.

Maggie walked across to the bar. She ordered her cigarettes, then, accidentally-on-purpose nudged the stranger's arm as she turned around. 'Oh, sorry,' she said with her best smile, her hand gently touching his arm.

He glanced at her with a look of distaste, a snarl almost. No words, no smile in return, barely a glimmer of acknowledgement that she was even there.

She felt distinctly uncomfortable and stepped away, turning back towards her table, towards the friendly face of Nadia.

'God, you were right. Creepy guy indeed. Wow!'

Nadia laughed lightly. 'What happened?'

'Nothing. He just made me feel like–like an insect that he would happily squash!' She wasn't used to being treated like that. Her affect on men had always been positive, lust inducing. It had got her jobs she wasn't the best qualified for, apartments she wasn't first in line for, a life easier than most. Sometimes it annoyed her. How easy it all was. How bloody transparent most men were. How her looks were the most important thing about her. It pissed her off, but when necessary she used it to her advantage. Needs must.

An envelope was passed from behind the bar to the man and he left. No smiles, no handshakes. The chill he carried on him was exchanged for the cold draft of the closing door.

Maggie looked back, watched his figure stride up the basement steps, and disappear. She raised her glass to the window.

'And to you mate. And to you.'

Chapter 28

December 2001

Dima had reached the *rynok,* but there was no sign of Sasha and Alyona. He had told Sasha midnight. They should be here by now. He walked around the concrete and glass, the shuttered stalls, one eye on places of safety, hiding places, the other on the road, the danger of passing cars, passing strangers. They were few and far between and he felt strangely alone in this vast city. He called out a few times in a loud whisper, 'Sasha?' Nothing. Hanging around here wasn't wise. It was ten past midnight. He would come back in the morning, as agreed.

His priority now was to stash the bag again. It was flash, expensive, and it made him too obvious. Kids like him didn't saunter around with designer workout bags slung over their shoulders. He decided on a quick sprint along Zhytnotorzka, heading away from Podil centre. A hasty glance down one side of the dual carriageway of Verkhnii Val Street and he ran; traffic lights flashing amber, tram tracks, skeletal trees, shuttered kiosks, the path of the central reservation; across the other side.

Too much space. He felt like a target. Nowhere to hide. Better further along on the other side. Derelict buildings, a fence to twist through, one more carriageway to cross.

Behind the back of the bus station, the car park. Up towards the hill, through the break in the fence, another derelict building. This one unused by street-people. Hidden. It was small, too broken, too cold. No doors, no windows. Nothing. He had used it in the summer when he wanted to be alone. To be quiet and peaceful and something else, somewhere else. But in winter? In winter it was a place you would die in.

There was a broken fireplace. Too broken to use but the bend of its chimney perfect for his purpose. He felt around in the dark, checking first for any bodies. No light reached in here. The darkness total. Solid. The scurry of a street-dog. A snarl. More of them. He stamped his feet at them. 'Tchh!' They slunk off, eyeing him with suspicion, tails tucked tight between retreating legs, hovering in the shadows just beyond him. Shivering. They wanted him gone. They wanted their shelter back. He felt bad, kicking them out of their hiding place into the freezing snow. It wouldn't be for long, then they would come back and huddle together in the corner. One body keeping the next warm, alive.

*

Dima didn't show his soft side. It wasn't a good idea. You can't show weaknesses. Can't expose yourself. But it was him who had encouraged the street-dog into their basement when he had found her outside, heavily pregnant. Her stomach huge and bloated. Everything else emaciated, scarred and dirty. Him who had made a safe area for her. Him who had sneaked bits of food to her. Someone else's excess he had found in the garbage cans at McDonald's. Always a good place for picking up something edible.

He dismissed her when the others were there. 'Fucking dog. Fucking stinks!' But when it was just him he stroked her, rubbed her head, made her feel at least a little bit welcome. Loved? No. Not that. But welcome. And when the puppies came he sat with her. Calmed her. Smiled at the squirmy little bursts of new life. Thought about giving them names. Decided against it.

*

He felt for the fireplace. Found it. Slipped the bag off his shoulders and stuffed it up as far as he could. It had to be out of reach of the dogs when they returned, curious. Otherwise they would drag it down, tear the speck of what was left of his alternative future to pieces. He wedged the bag in with a piece of metal and some sticks, some bricks. Tugged at it; it was secure. More than just the physical weight had been lifted from his shoulders. He breathed out heavily. *What now Dima?*

*

Leonid had waited long enough. There was no tail, just his paranoia. Sometimes it was a good thing to have. Kept you safe in his line of work. You can never be too careful. There was always someone. Something. Now it was time to get on with business.

He walked up and down Frolivska Street, on to Mykilska, around the church, pristine, softness and swirls, ornate fencing set in turrets of bricks. An odd building, he always thought. Designed for beauty, not functionality. Something from somewhere else. Not belonging.

He carried on past the buildings of the university, elegant places of learning. He would love to have done that. Been a student in one of these places. He had managed to learn so much by himself, ploughing through books, studying off his own volition. Given the chance he could have done well. He was sure of that. A life different. No time to wonder now. Focus. Keep searching.

Blanks. All blanks. A few drunks, people in a hurry, nothing of any use to him. He turned up Khoryva Street. The area around the *rynok* was always worth a look. Kiosks, nooks and crannies, places to hide in, sneak under, slip through. And it backed onto the hill where he had lost the kids. They could easily have ended up here.

It was a strange place to walk past at this time of night; vast, cavernous spaces, which, in the daytime, are a bustle of traders selling their wares. Fresh fruit and vegetables from the south, slabs of meat lain across blood stained trestle tables, chickens still with their heads on, dead eyes staring, salo, cheeses, cream. Upstairs furniture, clothes, shoes, handmade shawls, lace. Now it echoed with emptiness. Too silent to be called silence. An eeriness that might disconcert some. Not him.

He checked its perimeter thoroughly. Nothing. He stood on the concrete steps by the entrance to the *rynok* looking around, slowly breathing in the night air, calculating. What would his next move be? He stood at a cross-roads. What would he have done? In their shoes, what would his choice have been? Behind him the foot of Castle Hill, the place where he had last actually seen them, streets he had already checked. To his left the main thoroughfare of Verkhnii Val Street: busy, exposed, heading out of their area. Unlikely. The opposite direction, back to the main drag of Podil. Familiarity, perhaps security, perhaps danger. Or head away along Zhytnotorzka and its quiet residential side streets?

He knew they were street-kids. He knew where they lived, but apart from that he really didn't know very much about them at all. That was the problem. When he had a mark, he knew their history, their routines. He had time to follow, to watch, to prepare. That was what made it interesting. Learning about them. What they did. What made them tick. The excitement of knowing that, once he knew all that he needed to know, their lives were his for the taking.

But these little bastards, they were something else. Something unknown. Something unpredictable. That wasn't good.

He was about to turn towards the hill, double check the trees at the bottom, when a shadowy shape caught his eye, slipping along Zhytnotorzka. Leonid moved off, quickened his step, staring through the snow which was making everything blurry, surreal.

The figure skulking along the road ahead of him looked very like Dima. He couldn't be sure. The kid wasn't really known to him. Not that well. And it was dark, snowing, but there was something about him. A hunch. A feeling. But Dima on his own? Why?

They had been together. He was sure that he had been on the trail of all three of them across that Godforsaken hill. If they had split up that would make this all so much more difficult. Whatever, he, if it was Dima, had to be followed, cornered, questioned. Right now it was all that he had.

The figure was nervous, looking over his shoulder, but trying not to look as though he was. Trying too hard to be casual. Leonid knew that act. He had lived like that for long enough himself. Pretending. Getting by. He was weighing up what might be his best next move as he strode after him, gaining on him, keeping his eyes trained on him, despite the snow beating against his face, making him blink constantly. The kid was wily, streetwise. He would notice a tail soon enough. And he would run, disappear again.

Leonid kept at a safe distance, pretending as well. The irony wasn't lost on him. Ex street-kid pursues current street-kid. Both playing games. But how much had he changed? How much had really changed? Stupid thinking! A lot. A hell of a lot. They were worlds apart.

As he watched the lonely little figure in the distance – hunched, probably frightened – he remembered the cold of nights like this; of winters like this. Once it started you knew that the cold would creep into your bones and stay there, digging at you, hacking at your resolve, your ability to hang on, until at last spring showed up, lazy and unreliable. The pain, the misery, would slip away for a few months. Life would be bearable. Sometimes even good.

*

Dima decided to turn off into Yaroslavska. Keeping to the smaller, quieter streets would be safer. He could twist and turn, double back around blocks. A pain, but this was all a pain. As he turned the corner he allowed himself a glance back. The blur of a man could just be made out through the relentlessly falling snow. It was too far away to tell but the gait, the build, looked worryingly familiar. Could be nothing, could be Lezo. He would have to be careful. Just in case. He didn't want to quicken his pace too much; just enough so as not to raise suspicion, but to begin to draw more of a distance between him and the figure. As soon as he hit the junction with Yaroslavska Street he turned the corner and bolted.

A quick sprint and he cut into Kyrylivska Street. Windows with bars on them. That would be nice, something to protect – funny, the things that flash through your mind – another turn, a break in a fence, maybe an open gate, he couldn't be sure, didn't check. Running and twisting, and again. Not looking back, just running. A sprint across some open ground. Gardens. Now he checked. No-one in sight. Footprints in the snow. *Fucking snow!* If he was being followed he hoped that his prints had mingled with others along the way. A chance at confusion. He stepped off the pavement and walked heavily across the road to the other side, doubled back, tiptoeing in his footsteps. Leapt as far as he could. Ducked into an archway and waited. If the figure passed by here he would know for sure that it was after him. His route had been so convoluted. He would know for sure if it was Lezo.

He stood as far away from the street as possible,

while making sure he could still see who passed by. His back was to a small garden with a low fence. If he had to, he could jump it and make his escape.

He kept his breathing shallow – barely a breath at all – as he waited, thinking it made him less visible, less of a target. It also heightened his ability to hear what was happening all around. The distant hum of traffic from Nyzhnii, a car crawling along the street in front of him, a dog growling not far enough away. *Please keep quiet. Please don't fucking bark. Shit!* Footsteps. Running footsteps. Heavy breath. A curse.

Dima was caught between wanting to run, but needing to make sure. To see. He stood prepared for flight, his body already around the back of the building, his muscles tensed; only the top of his head showing in the alleyway. The figure stopped. Dima didn't need to wait any longer. It was Lezo all right. Dima took off, crashing over fences, through discarded rubbish. The dog barked, yanked at its chain. It sounded big, fierce. He didn't look, just kept focussed on his path; on his exit.

Something caught at his leg. Metal. A sharp pain. He stumbled, hands in the snow stopping his fall. Scrambled to his feet again.

'I wouldn't,' Lezo's voice threatened, slowly, the words lingering, slipping through the night air. A knife in the dark.

He felt the shape of the barrel of a gun in his back. 'You stay right where you are.'

Fuck! Dima stood still, his hands up. His heart thumped. He tried to breathe. Slowly, deeply, calm down. Get through this somehow. *Think Dima, think!*

'Turn around.'

The gun was flicked under his chin, lifting it skywards. His neck stretched.

Leonid sighed. 'You and I have some talking to do.'

'Fuck's sake. I didn't mean anything. I was just scared, man. I don't know anything. I swear. I don't know a fucking thing.' He held on to the control of his bladder this time, pushing fear aside with anger. Anger at his whole fucking situation. Everything stank. Everything was rotten. All he wanted was a break. Just one chance. And if this was it, if his future lay in that bag, he had to keep his head. Be strong. Be smart.

'Oh come now. You know that I know different. You were seen with Alyona, with Sasha, with the bag. The bag on *your* shoulders. Just tell me where it is and you can go.'

'Oh yeah, right. You're gonna let me go,' Dima sneered. 'Sure. Just kill me now. I don't know anything.'

'Dima, Dima, Dima.' He lowered the gun, put his arm around Dima's shoulders, smiled patronisingly. 'We're not so different, you and I. Only I smartened up. You should do the same.' He pulled at Dima's jacket. 'New? Nice. You steal it?' He went through Dima's pockets. The jacket first. A pack of Prima cigarettes. A lighter. He twirled the lighter around in his fingers, raised his eyebrows at Dima. A whole pack of cigarettes and a lighter – that meant money. He checked his trouser pockets. Nothing. 'Shoes off.'

Dima's resolve began to shrink. He began to shrink. Time was up. Leonid checked inside Dima's socks and found too many notes for a street-kid to have. There was no talking his way out of this one and he knew it.

'Same place I used to hide anything of value. You see, we really are very alike, Dima. Nice little windfall. But you know you're not going to be able to shift any more of it. Even if you did know where to take it you'd be dead as soon as you handed it over. You know I'm speaking the truth here kid. Hand it over. Let me deal with this and I'll give you and your friends a break. How about that, eh?'

'Like I said, I don't know nothing! It was Alyona and Sasha who had the bag, not me. I just got my cut. That's all.'

'Dima, Dima. I thought you were smarter than that. I'm going to lose my patience very soon. It was you who took the coke to those slime-balls in Darnytsa. Me who got them turned over. Come on now. Cut the crap.'

'How the fuck?...'

'Kyiv is really quite a small city, when you get right down to it, Dima. Down to the nuts and bolts of what makes the place tick. Do us both a favour. Cut the crap, okay?'

*

Igor had told him he wanted scalps for this one. The message had to be put out that no-one messed with his Brigade. No-one. Especially not some mangy little street-kids. Leonid had two choices. Get the goods back and kill the kids or get the goods and get the hell out himself. Whatever, the bag was central. And he was in a hurry. His next update to Igor had to be a positive one. This had to be sorted, one way or the other.

He didn't think a streetwise kid like Dima would let something so valuable slip out of his hands, so he knew. He knew where the bag was and/or where the other two kids were.

'You and me,' he smiled. 'We're going to get very cosy.' He took a tight hold of Dima's arm. 'You got that?'

Dima winced.

'I said, you got that?'

'Yes,' Dima mumbled, accepting his fate. He told him about the meeting that was supposed to happen at the *rynok* at eight that morning. It would buy him some time, maybe some trust. The bag was still his. It was still safe. There was a chance. But what Lezo had said about him not being able to shift it had hit home. He knew that anyway. He knew it as soon as he'd seen what had happened to the dealers at Darnytsa. He needed time to work out his options, if there were any. Now, at least, he had tonight.

Chapter 29

October 2001

'Have you got a favourite place then? All of these countries you've lived in,' Nadia asked, as they walked across Volodymyrska Hill. The day no longer pretended that it had any relation to summer. With the sinking of the sun the wind was picking up and the temperature had fallen dramatically, hinting at a frosty night to come. She blew on her fingers – regretting not having brought gloves – and stuffed them into her pockets.

They paused at the little bandstand that stood on the corner of the hill, rusting silver metal with a moss encrusted wooden roof, red-brick floor surrounded by crazy paving. An odd mix of something trying to be beautiful and functional despite being aged and decrepit. It clung on to quaint. They leaned against the metal railing in front of the bandstand that separated the park from the dangerously steep hill below. The view from here was quite spectacular, as it was from most of Kyiv's hills. From any city's hills. The distance, the height, offering a disguise. Hiding indiscretions. Washing dirty places. Housing schemes blended with trees, the twist and turn of old and new. Lives in the distance, nothing personal, nothing revealing. Make of it what you will.

Maggie lit them both a cigarette and handed one to Nadia, who took a deep draw, enjoying the rush.

'No. No I don't,' Maggie answered, her gaze on the vista before them stretching out far into the disappearing horizon. 'They all have good and bad. Good and bad people. Good and bad traditions. Good and bad places. I think you have to keep an open mind. Keep a distance, but get close enough to taste everything, not necessarily to eat it. Spitting out again distance.' She pointed across the river. 'The trees, the pink sky, the mist rising from the water, it's all very pretty. I mean who doesn't like the tree-coated islands, the beaches, the smell of shashlik?' She swung her arm over to the high rises in the distance, a trail of cigarette smoke drifting behind it. 'But over there. Over there it's not so good. Not so pretty. You ever been?'

'No. I've never ventured into any of the schemes.'

'Probably wise to keep it like that. Some of them are scary as shit! And as for that place over there.' She gestured towards Mykhaila Hrushevskoho Street, where the parliament buildings stood. 'There it's impressive and stately on the outside – grand pillars and arches and shit, designed to intimidate. And it does that so effectively. As for the inside, well, that's really ugly. President Kuchma and his ministers.

Corrupt as hell, you know? I've lived in some dodgy places, but here? Wow! Corruption at its finest. And so blatant. Like they don't give a shit. They just don't care. The dividing line between politics and the Mafia is, well, it isn't there! Then again, it's all screwed up, isn't it? Everywhere! Not just here.'

'You think so?'

'I do. To greater or lesser degrees. Anyway, enough of that.' She beamed her best smile. 'Shall we do the funicular or trail through the woods?'

'The woods I think. They'll be nice and quiet. I like dusk in the woods. Always have.'

'You're weird, but I like you!' she said with a laugh, linking arms with Nadia.

They walked along the edge of the park, then down into the woods. They were on one of the high paths. Below them more trails, the tops of trees sliding down to the roofs of the buildings of Podil, far below. Amongst the trees the chatter of birdsong rose above everything else. It was like the birds were all competing, all trying to out-caw, out sing each other. Standing in amongst the trees, staring across at the birds, her arms raised high in a V, stood Alyona. Sasha was leaning against a tree, smiling, watching her. Both of them seemingly elsewhere.

'Hi you two,' Nadia called as they drew close.

Sasha lifted a hand in casual recognition.

Alyona stopped. Waved. Put her finger to her lips. 'Shh. You will disturb them,' she whispered. 'See. They dance.'

Nadia and Maggie turned their faces to where Alyona was pointing. The crows were twirling, spinning, lifting up in great, collaborative flumes and swooping down again, then repeating it over and over. Their cawing swelling and quieting with each rise and fall of their bodies. It was indeed quite mesmerising. The choreography. The ability to fly like that and not collide. The birds began to settle, to take their places on the branches they had chosen to roost upon. The sounds began to lessen, as if someone were turning the volume down ever so slowly, until there was almost silence. The odd plaintive "*caa.*"

'Wow. That was quite special,' Maggie admitted in a hushed tone. 'I've never noticed it before. Strange. I've heard them, you know? But never really looked. Strange.' She turned to Alyona and smiled. 'Thank you!'

The smile was returned. 'I watch them every night. Watch their dance and listen to their stories. It makes me happy. They are so free and beautiful and clever. They will wait, making their own special noises, until each bird has chosen its place. Until they are all settled and happy. Then they will all quieten down. It's like they're whispering stories before they fall asleep. Night time stories like me and Sasha. They all care. They look after each other. I like to fly with them.' She lifted her arms and spread them wide, her fingers opened like the tips of the birds' wings, twirling and dancing again. That smile.

*

'I see what you mean,' Maggie said, as they carried on down the hill towards home. 'There really is something a bit special–different about them.'

'Isn't there! It's like they're ethereal but their world is so very not.'

'My, we've been having a deep and meaningful old

day, haven't we? Time for a drink, I think.'

'Wee music bar place?'

'They don't have music on a Saturday, do they?'

'I don't think so, no. But small and intimate and warm, is good right now.'

They followed the path through the trees to Andriivskyi, stopping off in their favourite local bar where the beer was cheaper than a Twix and the welcome as warm as a log fire on a cold and stormy night.

After a couple of drinks they headed back out. It was dark and frosty. The pavements sparkled. Each tiny speck of frost glinting in a sea of silver. The scene almost magical. In front of them two figures drifted into an alleyway. Nadia quickened her pace.

'What's the hurry?'

'It's them. The kids!' she said excitedly. 'I want to see where they live. It's always this big secret.'

'Maybe there's a reason for that. You have no idea what goes on in their world, who they shack up with. There could be some Fagin-type figure, some really bad guys who wouldn't want you nosing around. You should leave it. It could be dangerous.'

'We've come this far. Just a wee peek. Are you coming, or not?'

She sighed, 'I guess, but under protestation.'

'Noted!'

They followed at a discreet distance, through the alleyway – wrinkling their noses at the smell – across the wasteland, over the wall, and stopped at the track that led to the derelict house. The shadows of the children slipped into the building.

'Jesus. It's as creepy as hell,' Nadia whispered.

'What did you expect?'

'I don't know. Something a bit more habitable. You know? Standing up. Safe.'

'They're street-kids. This is probably quite a good little number. Quiet. Nice part of town. Hidden. We should go. Leave them to it.'

'Yeah.' She felt queasy and it wasn't just the alcohol. 'Yeah, we should.' As they turned and headed away Nadia glanced back at the desolate figure of the decrepit old house. She was caught between wanting to know more but not wanting to know anything at all. Her imagination threw up all kinds of scenarios. None of them good.

*

Sasha and Alyona crept into their sleeping bags and whispered stories to each other. Alyona wanted to hear about animals and magic and fairies. Sasha didn't mind. It kept their thoughts away from the glue induced giggles, and moans, and unpredictable rantings of their compatriots. It kept them separate. It held them together.

Chapter 30

December 2001

Sasha and Alyona huddled together, arms around each other, in the relative safety of the cavern. It was incredibly quiet, the air dank and heavy. A smell of earth, humid and musty, enveloped them. They drifted in and out of sleep. Sasha's waking thoughts were of "what ifs". What if they met up with Dima? What if he had managed to swap the bag for a decent amount of money? They could escape this life. Live. He imagined sunshine and warmth and safety. What if they had a home? A place of their own where the cupboards were full; where they could choose what clothes they wanted to wear. They could sleep behind locked doors in a warm, comfortable bed.

Sleep allowed the darkness to creep back in. The fear. The people who were after them. Unseen but felt, heard, imagined. He didn't even know this Lezo person. He had seen him – had him pointed out with a nudge and a whisper. He had heard stories, but they all told stories. It was one of the things that helped time to pass, kept them feeling. Fear at the scary ones – the tales of evil people, evil things. Laughter at the mistakes, the misfortunes, the near misses of a day on the street. Loving the camaraderie, the closeness, the collective understanding. Of course they made things up. They all knew it, but that was fine. It was a part of them. Pretending.

Sasha was woken up by a sliver of sunlight sneaking through the crack of the door. 'Shit! It's light out. Must be at least eight!' he exclaimed in a panic. He jumped up, brushed his legs and arms, rubbed his head to clear any bits of dirt that had got stuck in his hair, winced at the thumping pain in his head. He tried to ignore it. 'I need to meet Dima. You wait here Alyona. Don't go anywhere. I'll be back as quickly as I can.'

'I want to come with you.'

'No! You stay.' His voice was firm. 'Look after the bird. I'll bring back food, okay? Stay here.'

He could tell that she was fighting back tears and he hated what he was doing, but he had no choice. She was too much of a liability out there. She had proven that last night on the hill. Sometimes she had to be left behind. This was one of those times.

'Okay. I will stay. You will come back for me?'

'Of course.' He stroked her face. 'You know I will. I always do.'

'Yes...' she whispered, looking at the ground.

Once outside he pulled the door to and tugged at the plants, trying to cover the entrance as best he could. 'That'll have to do,' he mumbled, not satisfied, but in too much of a hurry to do any more. The air around him was full of crow-song. Cawing, replying. Cawing, replying. A cacophony of the sounds that filled Alyona's heart with joy. He allowed himself a smile. Once out of the thicket he stood tall, searched for familiar landmarks. The crows swooped and dove, flying off in search of food and whatever else crows do.

The churches were the best way to get your bearings here. They were so plentiful, so obvious with their domes and swirls and colour. But today they were all white. Everything was white, as if something magical had happened. The blanket of snow was transforming all that was dark and dirty into a clean, bright vista. As if the world had become a place of beauty and safety and goodness. Momentarily he allowed himself to drink in this Kyiv.

He pulled himself back to the now. Yes, he knew where he was. He wanted to run down the hill but that would be foolish, dangerous. His fingers ran over the scabby crust on his forehead, the tender bump beneath it, just to reinforce the point. A slip, a fall, was all it would take to change their fate. He controlled his step, keeping it at a decent pace, but steady, using the trees for support again.

It took only a few minutes to reach the *rynok*, already busy with stall holders and early shoppers. He checked the clock. Ten past eight. Dima would wait, wouldn't he? He would still be here somewhere. They had been through a lot together and Dima had never let him down. Never said he would do something and not do it. This had to be the biggest thing they had ever faced together. Dima wouldn't let him down. Not now. Surely?

They had met that second autumn in Kyiv, when Alyona and he were begging, sat on the pavement, a plastic cup in front of them. They weren't doing so well. A few *kopeks* tossed as they chatted, looked around nervously, unsure. Across the street a kid was watching them. He looked like a street-kid. Messy, dirty, hungry. He skipped across the road, dodging the traffic with a laugh.

'Name's Dima. You?'

'Um, Sasha. This is Alyona.'

Alyona looked up at him, her eyes trying to read him. She smiled. He was okay.

'You're begging in all the wrong places, man. Doing it all wrong. We should team up. Work together. Looks like hers,' he pointed at Alyona. 'And brains like mine we could do well, you know? You got a house? A place to stay?'

'Um, sort of.'

'You start every thing you say off with um? What kind of answer's that? Shit man. You either have or you haven't.'

Sasha laughed. There was something he liked about this kid. He felt honest somehow. Real. 'We live with our father and his girlfriend. It's not so good.'

'Ah. Like that, eh? A few of us have that problem. Or had.'

He told them about his basement, the others who had been thrown out of their homes, or left voluntarily, because of girlfriends or boyfriends, drink or drugs. Some sort of abuse. Some sort of desperation.

As they walked towards Kontraktova he told them

196

how to beg more efficiently. Who to approach with smiles and tugs. Who to pull the sad face for, the cheeky face. Who to be chatty with, who to force a tear for. Most important of all, he'd said, was to let Alyona do the begging. They would stand far enough away so as not to be noticed, but close enough to be there if she got into trouble. He and Sasha would be like her bodyguards. Sasha took some convincing but it worked. They made more money. They were a team.

Dima warned them about the old drunks that fought over their cardboard and bottles. Stay away from them! When winter came he took them to the metro, the underpass, places where you could grab a bit of warmth. Not freeze to death on the open streets. He knew how to survive.

Sasha heard a familiar, unwelcome refrain. The voice slurred and drunk. 'Alyona! Come to Papa. Alyona! Papa needs you honey.'

'Oh no,' Sasha mumbled to Dima. 'Shh Alyona. Hide and seek, okay?' He put his finger to his lips.

'Okay.' She copied. Their well-worn gesture of secrecy. Time to hide.

'You need to get out of here?' Dima asked.

'Yeah.'

Dima led them away, kept them out of sight until their father had gone again, staggering from wall to wall, swearing at strangers.

'What was that all about?' Dima asked.

'He wants money,' Sasha replied with a raise of his eyebrows and a sinking of his pride – what was left of it. 'Must have run out of whatever he needs today. Sick of it. So sick of it.' His head hung low, shoulders stooped, eyes on the ground.

'You mean what we've been making. Your share. It goes to him?'

'Something like that. Yes,' he mumbled, lifted his head up. 'We either cough up or get beaten.'

'That's fucked up, man. You should leave.'

'Yes. That's what I'm thinking.'

'Come stay with us. You almost do anyway.'

They did and they had had each other's backs ever since.

*

As Sasha ran around the building, towards the entrance where they had agreed to meet, thoughts of what could have happened nagged at him. Dima could have been caught by the *militsiya,* by Lezo. He could have run into trouble with the dealers, he could have simply done a runner. Taken what he could get and run. Sasha wouldn't blame him if he had. Everything was so messed up. Their lives were such a struggle. If he had the chance he would probably take it too. Who wouldn't?

He had just turned the corner to the main entrance when he saw Dima. He was standing with his back to the wall, stock still, staring ahead, across the main road. Cars, trams, a line of women on the pavement, heavy coats, thick boots, hats and layers of headscarves. Those that didn't have a stall were sitting beside bags of their goods, chattering. Vapour escaping with their breath, drifting up into the icy air. A normal day.

But nothing was normal for them. Dima standing still? That wasn't right. He was always twitchy, nervous looking, skipping from foot to foot as if he couldn't stay still. Sasha stopped behind a billboard, craned his neck around. A man was standing beside Dima. With Dima. He focussed in on the man. It was Lezo all right.

Chapter 31

October 2001

Artem had called. His grandfather had decided that it was time to say goodbye. He didn't have long left. No, no doctor. He just wanted Artem and his Nadia.

'Of course I'll come. I'm so sorry, he's such a lovely old man,' Nadia had answered, without hesitation.

In the old man's mind they were as good as married. They were meant to be together. She was family now and he was glad of it. The line could continue. Something of the love he shared with his Anastasia would breathe on in this world. Of that he was sure. He pictured them with children, perhaps taking on the farm, carrying on the traditions he held so dear. Growing his beloved sunflowers. Being surrounded by beauty.

When they pulled up at the little wooden house he wasn't there to greet them. The place felt so different.

An emptiness hung over it. The sunflowers had died back. Around them nothing but black earth. Trees in the distance clinging on to their few, remaining leaves, almost bare. The ruins of the neighbouring building was now visible. A mound of rubble, sticks and rock only just holding on to their shape amongst the onslaught of weeds and wild grass, now brown and withered.

Artem blew out a heavy breath as he climbed the wooden steps. His hand was shaking as he reached out towards the cast iron handle, paused, inhaled, twisted it open. The house felt cold despite there being the smell of a recently burned log fire, embers glinting from beneath the ash. Someone had been in since Artem's last visit a week ago.

He had made the journey every weekend, checking on his grandpa, bringing supplies to which Bogdan always muttered, "Oh, you shouldn't have. I don't need such things, my child." Of course he did and inwardly he was so grateful for his kind young grandson, for the gifts he brought, but mostly for his company. The best visits were when Nadia came too. To be in the company of a young love like theirs was such a special thing. It swelled his heart.

There were neighbours, people who had also lived here for generations. They would drop in for a drink, for a chat about politics, about history, about their families, their farms, the weather. The usual things old men and women talk about. But not the *Holodomor*. It was a thing unspoken. A history no-one wanted to linger on, talk about. It had been forbidden in Soviet times because it hadn't happened. It was a lie. To talk about it risked your being reported, being sent to a labour camp in Siberia. A life so harsh, if you survived at all. Or being killed. That was the way of it. And now it was a deep, dark space hidden in the souls of those left.

Bogdan was lying in his bed; the simple single bed he had built for himself. He had destroyed the beautiful ornate marital one that he had lovingly made for Anastasia, in preparation for their wedding. He had chosen the tree carefully, selecting the wood for its scent as well as its beauty. He cut it down, sawed the lengths he needed, sanded them over and over, his fingers checking and checking again for splinters, rough edges. It had to be perfect. Each piece interlocked with an assortment of joints that he had been taught to make by his father: dovetail, dado, and rabbet. All handmade and natural. He meticulously carved the curls of leaves and petals as if they were an oil painting – sunflowers of course. Always sunflowers.

The excuse for taking an axe to it had been that it was needed to make a fire with when he and his daughter had finally returned home that awful winter. But in truth he couldn't bear the sight of it, the thought of it. He hacked at it with a fury that echoed the pain he felt inside. As it burned he watched the flames disappear up the chimney, the scent now somehow pungent, unworldly. The smoke dissipated in the sky with the essence of his wife. His Anastasia.

*

Now his face was so pale, his eyes sunken in dark circles. The sparkle gone. There was so little left of *him*. Skin, transparent, wrapped itself around bones and rivers of bulbous blue veins. Nadia swallowed hard, forced a smile through her sadness, and held tightly onto Artem's hand. She tried to pull back the memory of the last time she had seen Bogdan, to transpose the broken figure lying before her with the beautiful, proud old man she had come to know. It had only been a month. She wished it had been less; that she had got to know him better; made the journey more often.

They pulled up two wooden chairs and sat beside him. Artem took Bogdan's hand and stroked it. 'Hello Grandpa.' There was the slightest of smiles in return. Bogdan beckoned him closer. Artem leaned in, his ear against the old man's pale lips.

Something inaudible to Nadia's ears was whispered. She felt awkward and intrusive, despite Artem having told her that Bogdan had asked specifically that she be here. It was such a compliment, but horribly difficult nonetheless.

'I'll just be a minute,' Artem said, leaving the room.

Bogdan stretched his hand towards Nadia asking for it to be held. Of course she took it. It was cold. Horribly cold. As if his blood wasn't pumping any more. He smiled at her. Squeezed her fingers so weakly it was barely felt. Nodded. Their eyes locked. She couldn't look away, no matter how uncomfortable it felt. She knew she couldn't break this.

Artem came back with the box that Bogdan had taken from the cupboard all those weeks ago. There was a large, brown paper parcel as well. 'He wants you to have this,' he said softly, handing her the package.

It was surprisingly heavy. The paper so old that it

had become fragile, crumbly. A piece broke off and fell to the floor as she took hold of it, mingling with the dust at her feet. She ignored it, pretending it hadn't happened.

'For An-as-tas-ia,' Bogdan managed to whisper so slowly, a raspy breath in between each syllable. 'You– you.' His head dropped. Silence. It seemed he had gone, but another breath struggled in and out again. Then there was nothing.

'Grandpa? Grandpa!' Artem gently placed the box on the bed, stroked his grandfather's head, kissed it, closed his eyelids. 'I will always love you Grandpa. Goodnight. Rest with the angels.'

He fetched a bowl of water and a cloth and carefully washed his grandfather's body, redressing it in the traditional outfit he had been wearing that first day. Nadia stayed in the other room, giving them peace and dignity. She stood at the window, her face tear-stained, her thoughts with that story, with all that she had been told. All that Bogdan had been through. All that he was, despite it all. Such a beautiful soul.

'I have to stay with him for three days. It is our tradition to protect the departing soul until it has left. Do you have to be somewhere?'

'No. No, I can stay. I want to stay. He found a way into my heart.'

Artem smiled. 'He would like that. I know you did the same to him. I must light some candles for him. You should too.'

They found five candles in the kitchen and took them into the bedroom. Nadia was shocked, taken aback. She was expecting his body, his face to be covered with a sheet or something. His torso and face were uncovered, exposed. Despite having witnessed him die this was a shock. She gasped, feeling stupid, feeling ignorant.

They lit the candles and placed them ceremoniously around his body. Artem was quietly reciting something with each lighting; with each placing of a candle. She presumed prayers, holy words. The door was left open as they returned to the sitting room.

Artem was carrying the bundle in brown paper. 'Do you know what he gave you?' he asked, his arms outstretched offering it to her.

'No–no, I haven't looked. I–I'm not sure if I want to.'

'You should look.'

She placed the package on the table and carefully untied the string that was wrapped around it. As she peeled back the paper, little by little, it opened up to reveal Anastasia's wedding dress. She pulled her hand to her mouth. 'Oh my God! That is the most precious, the most beautiful thing I have ever been given. I can't possibly. He barely knew me.'

'It's not time that matters. It's the person. You can feel for a person from that very first moment you meet them. Special heart friends. He called you his special heart friend.'

Chapter 32

December 2001

Alyona opened her jacket and put the crow on the ground. It wobbled slightly then stretched its wings, staring up at her, its head cocking from side to side as if trying to make sense of her. Was she something to take flight from? It shook, tucked its wings back in and hopped around, exploring this space it had woken up in with Alyona. She smiled at it, clapped her hands quietly, bent down beside it. 'You see little bird? You see? You are well again.' She checked her own leg. It was healing nicely. Not too painful. 'I am well too. We are both well now!'

The rays of sun that broke through the entrance lit up enough of the chamber for her to make out its perimeter. The floor was earth, but packed as if feet, many feet, had trodden it down. The walls and ceiling were one, arched like a cave, not much taller than a man. She jumped, trying to touch the ceiling but couldn't; it was just out of reach.

The crow tagged along at her heels as she walked all the way around, feeling the walls. Her fingertips flitted along the bumpy surface, hardened straw, dry mud, something different. A shape, a picture. There wasn't enough light to make it out, but she could definitely feel it. She pressed her palms against it, leaned her forehead there too. Felt pictures in her mind. Words. She couldn't make out the meaning.

'What is this place, bird?'

She listened. The voice in her head told her it was a safe place.

'I want Sasha to come back. I want him to be safe too.'

*

'Your friend had better be here, and soon,' Leonid threatened. 'Or this is all going to end very badly for you.'

'We agreed, man. We said eight. It's not my fault if something's gone wrong, is it?' He knew he was just stalling for time. Time to work out how to get away. To wait for a moment to appear that might somehow allow his escape. The type of moment that didn't come to people like him. A chance. It was so much more than a long shot. It was a fucking ridiculous stretch shot. But maybe...

*

When Dima caught sight of Sasha the look on his face was one of fear, not the hope he had been anticipating. Not the "Hey man. Let's go!" he had imagined, longed for.

'Go,' Dima mouthed. Eyes staring. He really wanted Sasha to stay. There was that extra chance of something happening if there was more than just him. But his mouth overruled. 'Go,' it mouthed. *Help me,* his brain whispered.

Sasha hesitated, not knowing, trying to work out what to do, where to go. Lezo wasn't doing anything. He didn't think he had noticed him, recognised him – maybe he didn't even know him. He turned, slid behind a truck that was being unloaded. Cabbages, dozens and dozens of cabbages. The smell almost overpowering. He and Dima had stolen one not that long ago, just as the driver had jumped into his truck. A quick snatch, a sprint up the road. Food was food. They had laughed. Thrown it back and forth to each other. Alyona unaware, tagging along, whispering to the things she whispered to.

He stuck his hands in his pockets, cursing at having lost his gloves on the hill. They were so cold that it hurt. The pressure of material on skin burned. It felt as though they had been sliced with rows of tiny razor blades, raw and bleeding. He swaggered, pretended, walked around the corner of the building. He still didn't know whether to leave Dima, hurry back, hide or–or what? Hang around, wait and see. Hope?

He could see that neither of them had the bag. That was good, right? He guessed that Dima had stashed it or else why would they be here? They had to be looking for him and Alyona. *Christ...* Then it sank in. He was an assassin, Lezo. Of course they would have to be killed. Certainly Alyona would. You don't do things like that, steal from the Mafia, and get away with it. They all knew that. Everyone knew that. He would keep Dima alive until he had all of them and they would die. It would be messy and public and awful.

*

Nadia had stayed the night at Maggie's. They had carried on drinking. 'Helps with the pain,' Maggie kept saying. 'Medicinal.' They had moved from beer to vodka, which was a definite no-no when there was work the next day.

'Oh my God. Hangover from hell city,' Maggie complained. 'I feel like shit. You?'

'Not so bad. I stopped before you, remember? I drank gallons of water too. How's your ankle?'

'No idea. Everything hurts. Shit!' She lifted her hand to her head and winced.

'Coffee, toast and you'll be fine.'

Maggie just groaned, stood up to go to the bathroom, sat down again. 'Okay. No. It hurts. It hurts like hell.'

'Hospital hurts?'

'Maybe. Chuck me some pain killers, will you? I'll see if they do the trick.'

'Sure.' She rummaged in the kitchen cupboards. Found some Aspirin. Filled a glass with water and handed them over. 'There you go. Do you want me to call in sick for you?'

'Oh cheers.' She said, accepting the glass and pills with trembling hands. 'Shit,' she whispered. 'The state of me.' She swallowed the tablets gingerly, struggling, anticipating the gag. Thankful they went down and felt like they would stay there. 'I'm on the late shift. I'll wait and see how I feel.'

'Right. Look, I'd better run. Call me if you need anything, okay? See you.'

209

Nadia had just enough time to make it to the *rynok* to pick up some supplies for her class, before heading on to work. Her head was down, watching where she was placing her feet, trying not to slip, to fall. Her thoughts drifted to the kids. How the hell did they survive when the weather was as vicious as this? It was so very cold. A cold she had never experienced before. The snow was relentless, but she was quite enjoying the novelty of it, wrapped up, prepared. She felt guilty. Privileged and guilty.

She looked up when she reached the kerb at Zhytnotorzka, checking for traffic before crossing. There, on the other side, she saw Sasha. There was something odd about him, like he was hiding, nervous, hesitating. She hurried across to him.

'Sasha?'

He jumped. 'Shit!'

'Are you okay? You look...strange.'

He shook his head, not knowing what to do, what to say. Should he say anything? Tell her? Hell, what harm could it do? She was a foreigner. A good person. 'Everything is very bad. We have big problems. Don't look, but up on the steps over there is Dima. He is with a man. A bad man. He is in danger.'

'What do you mean? What kind of danger?'

'He must get away. We must get away.'

She stole a quick glance. 'Uh-huh. And Alyona?'

'She is safe. Hiding.'

'Right! Wait, okay?'

She hurried off towards Dima and the man, not looking at them, pretending that she hadn't seen them. She was just a woman in a hurry to get out of the snow. None of this had been thought through. She had no idea of what she was going to do. Trusting it to instinct. To karma. To something good. Her father's voice crept into her head. 'Think lass, think. Take your time. Nothing good ever comes of rushing into things.' She wasn't so sure that she agreed. Sometimes the actions taken on the spur of the moment were the most honest. The most trustworthy. Instinctive. This could be the most stupid thing she has ever done, but it didn't really matter right now. She was doing it regardless.

She had honed in on their feet. No need to look up. Head down. A slip as she climbed the first step. A slight stumble. That would do it! Just as she reached the step they were on she feigned another slip, a stumble, landing against Leonid, almost knocking him over.

'Oi! I am so sorry,' she said, with the best accent she could muster, grabbing his arms, sliding, not looking at him.

Dima saw his chance and bolted. Back through the stall holders, back to where Sasha was waiting. They took off. Both of them running, dodging, running.

'You little fuckers! Shit!' He glanced back to the woman. *Her! I knew it. I damned well knew it!* She was hurrying off into the *rynok* apparently oblivious. 'Fucking, fucking, fuck!'

So. She was obviously in on it. Obviously up to her neck in it, but he couldn't lose the kids again. There was no option. They had to be followed. The woman would have to wait. He knew where she lived. His *militsiya*...wait. Why weren't they on her tail? What the hell was he paying them for?

He could still see them. The street-kids. Just. Or

211

rather he could see people moving out of their way, cursing at them, the inconvenience of them. They were not getting away again. They were not! He stared, not letting go of the trail of them, the sight of them. There they were. Out of the crowd, turning up to the hill again. He smiled. That was foolish of them. It was daylight. The snow had stopped falling. Their tracks would be fresh. No, they were not getting away again.

*

Alyona stood as still as a rock, listening. 'No, no, no, no. Something is wrong bird. Something is very wrong.' She picked the crow up, stroked its head, stared at its unblinking, shiny black eyes, searching for something. It flew off and sat in the darkest space at the far end of the cavern, cawing, stamping its feet. On another day, a different situation, it would have made her smile. She would have copied it, bird-dancing. It pecked at a piece of the straw that was sticking out of the wall. Pecked and pulled, pecked and pulled. Alyona walked over to it.

'I am sorry bird. You are hungry, aren't you? Of course you are.'

She pulled at the straw, scratched at it. Pieces of the wall began to fall. The cladding was thin, barely there at all. She chipped and scratched and pulled away at it. Her fingers felt wood, hinges, the outline of a small door, a handle, metal.

'It's a secret place, bird,' she whispered in awe. 'A special, secret place.'

She held her breath. Her heart racing with excitement. She pulled on the cold, rusted handle. Nothing. Twisted it. A creak. A slim gap between door and wall. A sigh of escaping air. A smell dank and dark and dirty. It made her pause, double think. No. She would do this. It felt right. She pulled hard on the door. It opened with a baleful groan. Beyond, nothing but black. From behind her the sound of the outside door opening.

Chapter 33

October 2001

Over those three days a steady trail of neighbours came to offer their condolences – to say farewell. They brought flowers and soft words and memories. Loaves of home-made *Kolach* were brought to share. The body was never left alone. After the three days, at which time the soul is said to have finally left its former body, Bogdan was buried.

Nadia was guiltily relieved to be heading back to *Kyiv*. Everyone had spoken Ukrainian, the customs and conversations were so very foreign to her. She felt like an intruder. An intruder who now sat with the most precious gift on her lap.

'Thank you,' Artem said, as they pulled away from the little house. 'I was so glad to have you there. It made it all...easier.' His eyes were filling with tears. He blinked them away. 'Thank you.' His voice cracking.

She reached for his hand. 'It was the least I could do. Are you okay?'

'I will be. The first layer of gauze has been wrapped around the pain.'

'Gauze?'

'Grandpa said that grief was like a wound. Time was like a dressing. A piece of gauze. At first the blood, the pain, flows through. Then, as the dressing gets thicker and stronger the flow stems, until it can no longer be seen. Sometimes a scab breaks. The blood seeps through again with a memory, but the dressing holds. With time.'

She sat quietly, thinking about that. Such a typically wise thing for Bogdan to have said. The vision helped. Layer upon layer of bandaging. It spoke to her as well.

The drive back to Kyiv was a slow, contemplative one for both of them.

He dropped her off at her building. As always he insisted on getting out of the car first, opening her door for her, offering his hand to help her to her feet. At home it would have annoyed her, but over here it was somehow endearing.

'Will you meet me tomorrow?' he asked. 'I'd like to show you something.'

'Yes. Of course. I'd arranged to meet up with Maggie but I can cancel.'

He smiled. 'No, no. Bring her. I'm sure she'll appreciate it. I'll pick you up here at seven.'

'Dressed for what?'

'Normal.' He pulled a face. 'Casual.'

When she got into her apartment she lay the package on the little padded chair in her bedroom.

Stroked it gently. 'Wow,' she said to herself. She couldn't bring herself to open it up. Not yet. It somehow felt right to leave it wrapped. Intact. The way Bogdan had left it for so very many years.

*

Maggie was full of questions. Her usual effervescent self. She had this ability to lift any situation. To sweep everything up in a warm, soft breeze. A *life is beautiful*, breeze. 'So what is this big secret?'

'No idea. So you're coming then?'

'Too right! You know me. Always up for an adventure.' She grinned. 'You've really got no idea?'

'Nope. Could be anything. The man is full of surprises.'

The next night Maggie was casually gorgeous. She had a way of making it look as if she had made no effort at all, but everything was perfect. Perfect hair, perfect smile, perfect jeans that were just the right amount of tight. She looked polished.

Artem took them to an old college-type building which had a large hall on the top floor. There were monkey bars on the walls, the markings for a basketball court on the ground. A gym hall. The floor was highly polished and squeaky. The air smelled of beeswax. Artem placed Nadia and Maggie in collapsible wooden chairs and disappeared.

'Well, this is totally bizarre!' Maggie exclaimed.

Nadia laughed and shrugged. 'As I said, no idea!'

'Is he going to come out and give us some mind-blowing gymnastics display?'

'I doubt it. He's not that type.'

'But he has the physique.'

'He does!'

Traditional Ukrainian music started up behind them. They turned around. Three men, looking very serious – one playing the *bandura*, another an accordion, the last keeping the rhythm with a *bukhalo* – were at the back of the hall, stamping their feet, swaying. The music filled every space, reached every corner. The swing doors opened and a troop of male dancers strode in. Steps choreographed, pronounced, hands proudly on hips, heads high, like haughty dressage horses.

They were all dressed in tight black T-shirts, black leggings, red pumps. They formed a circle, feet stomping, hands clapping, pride written on their faces, voices shouting, 'Hoi!' Artem was amongst them.

'Oh my God!' Maggie squealed, squeezing Nadia's arm.

The men began dancing, doing ridiculously difficult leaps and leg-kicks, thrusts and jumps. Ukrainian Cossack dancing. It was full of emotion and vibrancy and fantastic showing off.

'Well this all puts your standard break dancing to shame now, doesn't it!' Maggie whispered in Nadia's ear.

'It does indeed. Now I know where the muscles come from.'

'You didn't know your boyfriend was this super talented dancer dude then?'

'Not at all.'

'Tell me you're not totally turned on.'

'Totally!'

The dancers took a break and Artem came across, a big smile on his face, his breathing heavy.

'Aren't you the sneaky one,' Nadia said, a gentle nudge to his ribs. 'That was just brilliant!'

'Seconded. Wow! Like wow!'

'Thank you.'

'You must have been doing that like...forever,' Maggie said.

'I have. Since I was a little boy. My grandpa–' He hesitated. Swallowed hard. Forced back a tear. 'My grandpa taught me. This,' he gestured to the other dancers. 'This is for him.'

'Ooh, that is just beautiful,' Nadia added, taking Artem's hand, choking up. 'He would have loved it.'

'Yes.' He smiled. 'He is here.' Artem thumped his chest with his fist like his grandpa used to do. 'Always here. He came to watch us dance sometimes, when we put on performances, before he got too old, too frail. Always the best seat for Grandpa. Come, meet some of my friends.'

'Oh, yes please,' Maggie answered. She turned to Nadia and raised her eyebrows her tongue panting like a needy puppy.

'Shameless,' Nadia mumbled with a smile and shook her head. 'There is no hope for you.'

Chapter 34

December 2001

Leonid hustled past the street sellers, the early morning shoppers, his eyes fixed on the two figures disappearing into the woods. His attention was snapped by a murder of crows as they took off, cawing loudly, shouting, swirling above the black trees like dervishes. A mist of madness. He shook his head, pulled himself back to the chase, tried to think of what the kids might do. Prepare for all eventualities. Not let them outwit him. Again! In their situation what would he have done? He sure as hell wouldn't have gone up the hill again. That was plain stupid.

Of course he had run from people, from danger, plenty of times when he had lived on the streets. He had run with what he had managed to pick from pockets. Cigarettes, change, or if the pickings were good a wallet or a purse. They were rare. People held onto things of value, kept them in inside pockets. He could fleece a coat pocket, the back pocket of a pair of jeans, a carelessly open bag, on his own, but inside pockets, they needed two of you or more and he had never hooked up with someone; never trusted anyone else. It didn't do to trust. They always let you down. People always let you down.

*

Nadia rushed through the *rynok,* skipping around stalls and counters, past tutting shoppers and stall-holders, thankful for the familiarity of the market. She had been determined to avoid the supermarkets as much as possible. To shop like the locals did. That meant learning how to manipulate the *rynok* and to stand her ground with unscrupulous stall-holders who, on realising that she was a Westerner, would attempt to grossly overcharge her. At first she had been disheartened, disappointed by the blatant racism. Foreigner! Then she had stood her ground. Argued back.

'I may be foreign but I am not stupid!' said nicely, with a smile. A brief barter. Grumbles. A throwing back of the head in disgust at her impudence. Hands on hips. What did she know? Westerner... Finally, a 'Tch!' Acceptance. A reasonable price paid. Still above the cost to a local, but that was okay. She was being taken for a ride, but a short one. One she could afford.

The *rynok* was a place where people took their time, inspected produce, haggled, gossiped. No-one else was in a hurry and she felt so noticeable. So obvious. The smell of flesh, of meat, of fish and poultry was unpleasant, making her feel slightly sick.

Or perhaps it was nerves. Adrenalin. No time to think. The chaos of the place. People, stalls. So many of them. Why did people always stand and block your way when you were in a hurry? It was as if they knew and they weren't on her side. Foolish thinking. Dismiss it.

After what seemed like far too long she reached the exit on Zhytnorzka Street, along which Dima and Sasha would have run. She couldn't see either of them. That wasn't a surprise. She knew how tricky and illusive they could be. But she could see the man. He was tall and stood high, like he had more of a right to be here than anyone else. There was a feeling he gave off. A tangible badness. Like something was rotten deep inside of him. There was a familiarity too. She didn't ponder on it. Despite the trepidation he instilled in her she followed. Artem's warning was nagging at her. "Don't get involved." It was way too late for that. Of course she was involved.

The man had turned up towards the hill. She waited at the corner, hiding behind the huge concrete bollard that stood between the road to the hill and whatever lay underground, beneath the *rynok*. There was nowhere to hide between there and the hill. It was devoid of people, empty of traffic. She would have to wait until he was well into the woods, skeletal and bare but still thick enough to hide a body, disguise a person. Confuse.

She could call someone. Maggie? Artem? And say what? That she was heading up into Castle Hill in pursuit of a scary man and a couple of kids. Of course they would talk her out of it. No. She would wait and follow. She wasn't actually DOING anything was she?

*

Sasha pulled at the plants and bent down to crawl through the gap he had made.

'Look man,' Dima whispered urgently, pointing at the prints they had left behind. 'The tracks. He'll find us straight away.'

Sasha looked back over the snow, the trail. 'Shit. I need to get her out anyway.'

'This is fucking suicide, man,' Dima mumbled, more to himself than anyone else. He couldn't see the point. It was over. Lezo was so close that he could hear his footsteps crunching their way through the snow. Slow, strong, and regular. But he followed anyway, hoping for a miracle. Yeah, right!

The sun was now hidden behind a thick bank of cloud, heavy with the promise of more snow. The glimmer of light that had been offered through the flash of sunlight, gone. The chamber gloomy, grey fading to black.

'Alyona?' Sasha called through the darkness in an urgent whisper.

Dima flicked his lighter on and moved it in a circle around the cavern. 'What the fuck?' He thought he knew the area, this hill, but he had no idea that this place even existed. No time to think. Only time to be.

Neither of them could see her.

'Not again. Jesus, Alyona.' Sasha's voice had fallen in disbelief.

'Psst.' She giggled quietly, conspiratorially. 'Over here,' in a tone so unfitting, so wrong for their circumstances. It was as if she were playing; they were in a game. Of course they were. That perpetual game of hide and seek.

Dima held the lighter towards where her voice was coming from. Her head was peering out from behind a strange, little door, set in the middle of the wall. They hurried across, clambered in, pulled the door closed behind them. Dima found a bolt, slipped it across. Not much of a deterrent but something. Little things mattered.

They were in a small room, about two metres square. Hard packed mud walls. Stretching away from it a tunnel, supported by wooden posts not unlike an old mine shaft. It was narrow enough for them to touch both sides with outstretched arms, and too low to stand up in.

'What is this place? Is there a way out Alyona? Is there another way out?' Sasha asked quietly, trying to remain calm. Trying not to frighten her. Confuse her.

'I don't know. It goes a long way back.' She dramatically stretched out long. 'It was too scary.' She shivered to emphasize the point. 'I didn't go. And you said wait so I did. I waited.'

'Okay. Good girl.'

'Shall we go now?' she asked

The bird suddenly hopped into view, made a strange grating chirrup, dipped its head up and down, up and down.

'What the fuck?' Dima muttered.

'It's just bird. She's my friend. See?' She stroked its head and smiled.

Dima shook his head and shuffled forward on his elbows. Things were never normal when Alyona was around. Her world different from theirs. He had wondered if it was a better world. Probably.

He shuffled forward, lizard like, flicked the lighter, shuffled, flicked the lighter, shuffled. Frustrated at the slowness of it all, of the unknowing, but also just a little bit hopeful. It felt as if the tunnel was beginning to slope downhill. That would mean an exit, wouldn't it. But he had no idea to where, to what. The Dnieper river? A monastery? A church? The government buildings? Some fucking Mafia bosses house? Shit. It could be anywhere. Anything.

From when he had entered the cavern he had lost his bearings completely. No sounds, no smell other than the heavy dankness of the earth, but somehow dead. There was nothing of any familiarity, nothing to cling to.

His life had been full of not knowing. Of not knowing when he would next eat, what nasty surprises each new day might bring. A lost friend. A body to drag away from his basement. A visit from some other street people wanting to take over his place. He would fight. It didn't matter who it was, how hard they were, how many of them. He would fight. Broken bottles, bricks. It didn't matter as long as it could do damage. Enough damage for word to get round. This was his place and he wasn't giving it up.

He kept an iron bar at the top of the steps in case someone had sneaked down in the daytime when they were out. Always on the alert. Ready. A voice he didn't know. The familiar feel of the iron bar in his hand. 'Get the fuck out of here!' They would leave soon enough, one way or another. Sometimes he would get it wrong and some poor sod who had come down with one of his "family" would get a doing.

That was okay. That made people think he was crazy. Word got round. "Don't mess with Dima. He's crazy!" Yeah. That was okay.

But the man who was after him now? Lezo. He really was crazy. Stories told and retold of fingers being snapped, sliced off, legs being broken, limbs removed, scars being carved, and that was if you were lucky. If you weren't meant to die. Mostly you were a body dumped into the Dnieper river. Fish food drifting down in ever diminishing pieces to the Black Sea.

He flicked his lighter. Nothing. Again. And again. He shook it. Flicked. Still nothing. 'Shit! You got a light, man? Mine's only gone and died,' he mumbled over his shoulder.

Sasha fumbled in his pocket. 'Uh-uh. I must have dropped it somewhere. Sorry.'

'Just keep going,' Alyona piped up. 'We need to keep going. Bird. She wants to fly. In the sky. She knows. We must follow.'

Dima raised his eyebrows. A sarcy comment caught on his lips. Instead he kept still and listened. There was nothing. Absolutely nothing but the sound of their breathing. That was good, right? But sure enough, the bird had taken the lead and was fluttering, jumping, flapping its wings, almost flying, just ahead of them. Dima couldn't see it, but he could hear the flapping, feel the welcome movement of the air it left in its wake. It made sense that it would smell or feel an exit, didn't it.

The tunnel took a slight turn, then split into two of equal size. Dima felt each with his fingers, padding at the hardened dirt, trying to gauge size, suitability. One sloped down slightly, then became quickly steeper. The other stayed level, then appeared to head upwards. Both ways blind – nothing to chose between them. He pulled his lighter from his pocket again. Enough fuel might have gathered for a moment's light. The warmth from his body might have spurred it on to work again. Who knew?

You never gave up because sometimes, just sometimes, things worked out and good shit happened. The end of a night hanging around at McDonald's, hoping. About to head home hungry but you wait. Just one more minute. Just hoping. And someone chucks an almost whole burger into the garbage can and it doesn't spill out of the wrapper. It doesn't get covered in cigarette ash, or cola, or some other shit. It just sits there looking like a real burger. And you grab it – it's still warm, fresh. And you eat it and ketchup drips onto your fingers and you love it and you lick them and feel almost real. A proper person. Yeah.

'Come on,' he whispered to himself, as he flicked the wheel of the lighter. A spark. A momentary flicker of flame, enough to catch the shadow of the bird as it took off along the downward turn. Dima and the others followed. *Fuck's sake. Following a fucking bird! Madness!* He almost laughed, but he couldn't.

Most things you could laugh your way out of. Laugh above. This wasn't one of those things. He knew that somewhere, not too far behind, Lezo was still on their trail. Men like him didn't give up. Unless, of course, he knew more than they did. This place. This tunnel. He knew where they were heading to and he was waiting. Christ, they were going to die.

No matter what, they were going to die.

Time, distance had become immeasurable. The volatility of this tunnel could also only be guessed at. Darkness and dirt, and God knows what else. Keep going, keep going, keep going.

Sasha imagined a collapse of earth, a crack in one of the wooden supports finally giving way, a burden too heavy, and it would all be over. An awful, slow death. Dirt invading his mouth, his nose, his lungs. Fingers clawing at the suffocating mass around him having no effect. The weight of it. Life squeezed out of him.

In front of him Dima and Alyona pushed on. He could hear them. Their struggle along the earth, their breath, panting at the exertion. It gave him the strength he needed. Alyona was being so brave. So very brave. He wanted to tell her. To say, "You're a star, Alyona. I am so proud of you." But he couldn't. It might bring her out of whatever it was that was keeping her going, keeping her calm. He would tell her when they got out. When it was safe.

He thought he could see them. He blinked. Was he imagining this? Their shapes now outlined in front of him, crawling along like strange creatures. Different from the black of the mud, the dark of the air. He stared, blinked again. No. He could see. Light was getting in from somewhere, and they were heading towards it. A faint light, barely more than a shadow, but it was there, and it was getting bolder.

'You see?' Alyona whispered excitedly.

He could see her head turned back towards him. Make out her smile. 'Yes. I see,' Sasha whispered back, almost breaking into tears. He choked them back. He would be strong. They would make it out of here.

The sound of water. The rank stink of sewage. Dima's fingers had found iron railings. A round grill. A padlock. He pulled at it. The sound of metal on metal slipped back along the tunnel. 'Fuck!'

'What's up?'

'The end of the fucking road is up. It's locked. There's a gate, a way out, but it's locked.'

'No!' Sasha protested. 'There must be a way.'

The tunnel had broadened into a semi-circle, large enough for all three of them to kneel together, peering out in disbelief through the bars that blocked their exit. Out there it was broader, higher. They could almost have stood up. Walked. Breathed. The walls were made of brick, not mud. Safer. Much safer. It only served to reinforce the perilous journey that they had just taken.

'We can't go back,' Sasha whispered, his voice unusually high pitched, frightened. 'He's following us. We're trapped.'

The bird hopped through the iron railings and flew off.

'Fucking great. Yeah. Off you go,' Dima moaned, dismissing the crow with a dejected flick of his hand. 'Fuck's sake!'

'We need to follow him. We need to follow bird!' Alyona squeaked, panicking, pushing through to the gate. Her fingers felt all around. She gouged at the earth, scratching and scratching, breaking her nails. Her fingertips bleeding. Little insignificant pieces of mud fell off. 'Come on. You need to help!'

Chapter 35

October 2001

'Shit day, man,' Dima grumbled. 'Nothing but empty pockets. Christ I hate this fucking place. I had to scrape around for fucking bottles and cardboard. *Kopeks* man. Fucking *kopeks*! Picking cigarettes butts up off the ground. Christ I've had it! Any of you lot done any better?'

'No man. Shit too! Got some glue, though.' The kid sniffed, wiped his nose with his sleeve, handed Dima the bag.

'Nah. Not wanting that shit either. Some fucking food. Some vodka. Not that shit. Had enough of that shit.'

'Suit yourself, man.' He put the bag around his mouth and nose and breathed, slumped back with a groan. Breathed out the heaviest of sighs, as if his breath were separate from his body, escaping.

Dima paced up and down the basement. He wanted

something else. Not this. There must be something else. Bury that thought. Thinking like that doesn't do any good. But sometimes, Christ sometimes... He aimed a kick at a bottle, missed it. 'Fuck's sake!'

He heard Sasha and Alyona coming down the stairs. He always knew when it was them. Their footsteps were lighter, different from all of the others. Sometimes he wouldn't hear them at all. They arrived with a feeling, not a sound.

'Hey bro!' Sasha called out, his hand raised. They high-fived.

'Yeah,' Dima replied heavily. 'Hey!'

'What's up?'

'Nothing's up. That's the fucking problem. Nothing.'

'We brought some food and it's from the shop, not a bin,' Sasha said, trying to lift his friend's mood.

'Yeah?'

'Come on, let's eat.'

They sat cross-legged on their sleeping bags, tore at chunks of black bread, its yeasty smell temporarily overpowering the nastiness of their normality. They had sausage and cheese and *kefir*. Even some chocolate.

'I dunno what's worse man, being hungry or doing what you two have to do for this,' Dima stated, his mouth full, his belly expectant.

Alyona smiled, Sasha shrugged. 'You aren't pretty enough anyway.' He grinned across at Dima. 'Ugly bastard.'

Dima grinned back. 'Yeah, yeah, pretty boy. At least my arse is intact!' He was grateful for the easy chat, for being able to say anything and it was okay;

for the friend that managed to pull him up when he didn't feel like it. For the laughter.

Alyona's thoughts had drifted off to her birds. She stuffed some of the bread into the pocket of her jacket.

'You bring me any vodka?' Dima asked, knowing the answer, but it had become a regular piece of banter between them. It passed the time.

'You know I'll never do that. You want that shit you do what you need to do to get it. I ain't helping. No sir.'

'You should, you know. It helps. Makes it easier. Makes things better.'

'Yeah? Not what I see. *Kefir* or nothing.'

'Shit, you're no fun. But I love you anyway.'

They knocked shoulders and laughed.

Alyona had crept back up the stairs and walked around the side of the house to where the trees began. The ground was heavy with fallen leaves, the soft squelch of them under her feet whispered her presence. She looked up at the trees, held her arms high in a V, imitated the sound of the birds. 'Caa, caa,' she called. Then soft sounds. Chirrups, clicks. Black shapes flitted from the trees in a swirl, twisting away from the branches, making them look suddenly thinner. They flew above her head. She threw small pieces of bread up into the sky for them. They swooped and snatched and cawed. She was lost in them. Flying with them. The smile broke into a laugh. A gentle joyous laugh. Everything else had disappeared. Flying high in the sky.

Inside Dima and Sasha could hear the cawing.

'Doesn't that bother you? I mean, I know she's

your sister, but that's good food she's wasting.'

'That's what makes it all okay for her,' he shrugged. 'Why not? They take glue.' He nodded towards the other children who had settled down for the night, wrapped in their sleeping bags and a glue induced fugue. 'You drink vodka, she feeds the birds.'

'And you?'

He smiled. 'I have her.'

Dima shook his head. He wouldn't admit it to anyone, not even to himself, but sometimes, sometimes he was a little bit jealous of what Sasha and Alyona had.

Chapter 36

December 2001

Leonid muttered under his breath as he bent down to crawl through the little door behind the shrubs. 'Fuck's sake. What the hell is this place?' He shone his torch around looking for the kids. They were nowhere to be seen. The beam picked up odd markings. Something that looked like words but illegible to him. Some strange language. An eye in a triangle. A five pointed star enclosed in a circle. He knew the significance of the symbols but didn't ponder over them. No time. No need. He didn't believe in any of that shit. Ghosts and witches and otherworldly nonsense.

At the far side of the room he saw the small door, through which the children had scrambled, now clearly visible. He strode across and pulled at the handle. It wasn't budging. He kicked at it. Again. Again. It didn't take much to splinter it. The wood old and rotten.

'I don't believe it,' he mumbled. He shone the torch in. There was no end in sight, just a long, dark, narrow tunnel and if he went in...

The one thing. The one and only thing that truly frightened him was small enclosed spaces. No way out spaces. There wasn't a memory, just a feeling. A feeling of being locked up in a very small space. Dirty pitch black. Him curled up in the tightest of balls. Terrified.

He had been young, a toddler, but even at that age he knew he just had to be quiet. To wait. Noise meant more angry words, more pain. In the morning it would be okay again, for a while. He didn't understand but he didn't know any different either. Life was pain and hunger and darkness and cold. Until he was old enough to sneak out of the door, of the building, of that life.

The day of his seventh birthday had started off with smiles and "happy birthdays". A cuddle. A present. A football. His parents had a drink, clinking glasses, to celebrate. He knew it was best to get out of their way before the second and third but he wanted the feeling to last. It was summer. Hot and sticky. It was his day.

'Come on, Papa. Can we play?' he asked hopefully, excitedly. He tossed the ball towards his father, laughing. It bounced away from him and knocked over one of the glasses, the bottle of vodka. Drink spilled across the lacquered wooden table, dripped onto the floor. Drip, drip, drip. It was like time had stopped. He couldn't move.

'You stupid little bastard!' his mother shrieked, her

face red and fierce, as she snatched at the bottle and stared at its contents. 'Look what you've gone and done!' She raised her hand.

He knew what was coming. She swung at him. Missed as he ducked. That would only make it worse. Anger to fury. He ran. Just ran. Until his legs were too tired to run any further. He walked along streets he didn't know. People. Strangers. No-one noticing. He felt invisible. Just him and his ball. Hunger didn't make him turn back, didn't bother him. It was normal. Darkness came and he curled himself up under some bushes. It was okay. It was better than the dark cupboard. He wasn't blocking his ears to shouting and screaming, threats and counter threats. Humming songs in his head trying to change it all. Make it different. Imagining he was somewhere else. He didn't fear a beating. Yes, he was scared, but it was a soft scared. An easy scared. A scared he could deal with. He was soon asleep.

He woke up to the sound of birds, the brightness of the summer sun, his eyes squinting at the strangeness around him. It didn't take him long to spot other children living on the streets. He saw them taking food out of garbage cans. He copied. He followed them to parks and basements and secret places. A few nights here, a few nights there. It was soon his life too. He could deal with it.

*

Nadia had watched him disappear and decided it was safe enough to follow. She hurried up the hill, following the tracks made by the children and Leonid. When she reached the copse she paused. Stared through the twigs and branches. Focussed. She could just make out what looked like a doorway. The tracks she had been following stopped there. They must have gone through the door.

What was she going to do now? She could call Artem on her mobile. Ask him about the tunnels, the passageways. That summer day flashed back into her mind. The two of them up here, him telling stories about them. It seemed so very long ago. Were the stories real? Did he know this place? He worked for local government. Maybe there were maps. Plans of some sort. He could give her an idea of what lay ahead. She tried her phone. No battery. *Shit!*

She crouched down, her hands in front of her face, pushing aside the worst of the twigs and branches, and pulled at the door.

*

All three children scratched and gouged at the mud around the gate, until finally it felt like it was loosening. Noise didn't matter now. Only escape did. Dima lay on his back and kicked and kicked. The gate was moving. The force of each kick throwing out mud and stones. The metal eventually clattered down the brick of the next tunnel. He didn't wait to check what was there. There was no point. He pushed off and slid down. Old brick. Slime. Not too far. He whistled quietly. Gestured, "come on". Sasha and Alyona followed.

They were in a long tunnel. This one entirely brick. It was small, so they had to stoop to walk along it, but at least there was no more crawling. Their elbows and knees were bruised and sore. This was much better. Much easier. And there was light.

The path twisted and turned before eventually

opening out into a cavernous tunnel, as wide as a man and as high as two. They walked along, their eyes looking all around, trying to take in this place. Trying to make sense of it. Every few metres there were more tributaries, like the one they had just crawled along. Drains of some sort. Old and dank with a wetness that crept under your skin. The constant drip, drip of fetid water. It wasn't frozen down here, the water strangely warm, but the dampness made it feel colder than the snow and ice of outside.

The bird appeared to have waited for them. It was flying up and down in front of them, stopping every so often to inspect something on the ground. A morsel. It pecked at things slimy and foul, finding nourishment in the dregs and dross that floated on the shallow trickle of water, as it flowed along the floor.

Alyona's heart had lifted again at the sight of it. 'You are the best bird!' she exclaimed warmly. A lightness radiating from her.

Sound echoed. The splash of their footsteps, their breathing, drifted back along the old brickwork, ricocheting far off, to wherever these tunnels led to. They were on alert for other sounds, sifting through the noises that they knew, they recognised. There would soon be something else, something heavier, something menacing. They were anticipating that.

They couldn't hear Lezo yet, but assumed he was there. He could have taken a wrong turn, back where the tunnel split. Would he realise that he wasn't on their tail any more? They didn't know. But there was all that noise they had just made. Of course he would have heard; would know where they were. They kept on running, following the bird. Trusting in something, but they didn't know what. Each other? Fate? A conspiring universe? A bird? Anything would do.

The ground was slippery and treacherous, but somehow they managed to stay upright, to keep their balance, despite the pains of last night's injuries and today's exertions. They rose above them and kept going.

They came to intersections, hesitated, looked up and down what was in front of them, to the side of them. Sniffed for air, for something that might give them a clue as to the way out. Nothing showed itself to them. It was all down to the bird, trusting that it too was looking for a way out.

Dima stopped. 'I'm sure we've been here before. Look. The markings, the letters. We saw them ages ago. We're going around in fucking circles man. Fucking circles.'

'So what? We turn back? Veer off down there?' Sasha pointed to another tunnel that looked exactly the same as the one they were on.'

'No. We follow bird,' Alyona cut in confidently. 'That way.' She pointed towards the bird. 'These markings could be all over the place. We don't know.'

'We'll mark it. Make a scratch under the letters. Then if we come back we'll know.'

'Okay. Good idea, Dima.'

A pause as they made a little discreet scratch through the slime on the wall. A sound. It was echoing all around them. There was no way of telling where it was coming from. But it was definitely footsteps. Heavy footsteps. Footsteps in a hurry. They exchanged frightened stares and moved on, following the bird. *Following the bird! Jesus!*

Chapter 37

November 2001

'Your parents?' Nadia asked. It had been nagging at her for ages. She had met Artem's grandfather, but there had never been any mention of his parents. And now that she knew he was the only beneficiary she felt that she was justified in asking. 'You never talk about them.'

They were lying in bed enjoying a post-coital cigarette, her head on his shoulder. He was playing with a strand of her hair. She felt him take a deep draw on his Pryluk – she had tried them but preferred sticking to a brand she knew. The familiarity of a Marlboro would do nicely. He had laughed at her. "You know they make those just along the road, don't you? It's all the same shit. It all kills you. It just costs you more to die young than it does me." She heard the crackle of chemicals as he inhaled and the grey tip of his cigarette turned a fiery red. He blew the smoke out slowly. Deep in thought. An uncomfortably long pause.

'Hmm. They died when I was a child. A long time ago now. I went to live with my grandpa. I grew up there. In his house. In the fields of sunflowers.'

'Ah, that explains a lot.' She turned to face him. 'I'm sorry. I didn't mean to bring up painful memories.'

He smiled. 'That's okay. I had a very special childhood. I was loved and cared for. What can I say?'

'What happened? How did they...?'

'It was an accident. Nothing unusual. No KGB conspiracy. A car crash. They died. I lived.' He pulled a face.

'You were in the car?'

'Yes. I don't remember it at all. I was six. Apparently the car drove into a tree. The front end caved in completely. I was thrown free. My parents were trapped. The car exploded. That's all.'

'And your brother?'

'Brother?' His brow asked a question.

'Yes. The one whose car you borrow.'

'Ah. No,' he replied with a laugh. 'He's not a blood brother. A brother in arms from my army days.'

'I see. I just assumed – Did you sign up then?'

'No, no. We all have to do conscription here. I did my year. Hated it, but made some good friends. When you're all thrown together like that bonds are made. Brothers – '

'Yeah, I can imagine. So what was it like? Being a soldier?'

'I learned so many useful things. How to make a

bomb. How to kill silently. Things I might need for everyday life. You know.'

She craned her neck to check that he was smiling. That this was a joke. He was.

'Your face!' he chuckled softly. 'That was so funny.'

She poked him in that ticklish spot on his side that made him giggle like a little boy.

'Oh now, that's not fair.'

Her cigarette had reached its end. She stretched across him and stubbed it out in the saucer that was making do as an ashtray. 'Time to get up.' She made to get to her feet.

He pulled her back down beside him. Nuzzled into her neck. 'Let's just stay here.' He nibbled her ear. Stroked her back, tracing the length of her spine with his fingers.

'You are insatiable!'

'When it comes to you, yes I am.'

She didn't resist. The day drifted into lovemaking and chat, lovemaking and chat. Exploring each others' bodies and minds.

'Did your grandpa ever find out what happened to his other daughter, the baby?'

'No. There was no way of knowing. He didn't even know what train it was, the day, anything. It happened to many children. Not just Katya. She could have ended up anywhere, assuming she survived at all. I think perhaps it was easier as well, not knowing. He could pretend, imagine.'

'Did he talk about it much?'

'No, not at all. Not until I was an adult. It isn't something people talk about.'

'No. I can understand that.'

'I found the journal and asked him about it. When he told you, that was only the second time he had told his story. To me anyway.'

'I can't imagine. It's just–I can't imagine.'

'Maybe we should read it, the journal? I could translate for you.'

'I would love that. You haven't read it yourself then?'

'No. It was something too private. If he had wanted me to read it he would have given it to me.' He turned to face her. Smiled softly. 'And now he has. This would be for him. He wanted the story to live on. That's why you got the dress and I got the notebooks, the little pieces of his memories. We should respect that, shouldn't we? Pass his story on, like he wanted.'

'I think so.'

Everything had become serious between them. There was an intensity, a strength of feeling, something she hadn't experienced before. Part of her loved it, another was petrified. She hadn't expected any of this. This was meant to be a break, an adventure, a chance to find herself again. Falling in love, becoming a part of someone else's life, their family, no, that had never been on the cards. She wasn't sure how she felt about it all. It was unnerving.

'Enough of this seriousness,' he said, swinging his legs off the bed, gently tapping her head. 'Come on, let's eat! I'll cook you something.'

'Are you serious?'

'Yes, I am a very good cook, you know?'

'Don't tell me, your grandpa taught you.'

'Of course!' He beamed his best smile at her.

She stood in the shower enjoying the force of the water; the feel of it trickling down her back. Her body and mind awash with warm, sensual feelings. From the kitchen she could hear him singing, the clatter of pans. She was caught in a mix of emotions. This was all lovely, but serious, relationship stuff – domesticity. She wasn't sure if she wanted to go there. Despite it all. Despite having this gorgeous man wanting her, in the room next door cooking for her, talking about translating his grandfather's most personal diary for her. It was a lot. No, it was immense. Perhaps it was all too much.

Chapter 38

December 2001

Dima, Sasha, and Alyona had come across nothing living but rats and insects. Spider's webs with the remains of tiny carcasses caught in them. None of which bothered them. They were always nearby in their house, in places they hid, in the piles of rubbish they rummaged about in for food, bottles and cardboard.

Sasha and Alyona didn't have to do that so often. Not like the other kids. The man in the Mercedes gave them just enough. Enough to withstand the pain, the degradation when their bodies became tools for someone else's amusement, gratification. It was all dirty but it was what they had, what they did. It kept them that little bit less hungry, less desperate. It was their life. They had no choice anyway. Once it had started there was no way out. The introduction from Vika. The exchange of notes. That first drive in the black Mercedes with darkened windows.

*

There was more water now, a channel cutting its way down the centre of the tunnel. The brickwork to the sides was sloped and too slippery to safely keep their balance on. They were forced to make their way through the water. Their pace was now a quick walk. Running had become too dangerous, too difficult, too noisy.

*

Leonid's progress had been slow. Crawling his way through the first tunnel had been so very difficult. Partly because of his size, but also the fear. It had been terrifying. Black, tight, crushing. Once he had started there was no going back. He had to focus on the prize. On knowing that there was a way out. There was an exit. Somewhere along here there was an exit.

When he reached the space where the gate had been, the widening of the tunnels, the bricks, he blew out a heavy exhalation. The kids had been here. A gasp of relief. This was better. This was doable. That nasty piece of blackness had lifted. He was Leonid again. He would catch the kids. Get the coke. Then? He began playing things around in his mind. He could simply do his job. Carry on. Or get his cash. Disappear. Yeah. He could disappear. Igor's rogue. *Quit it Leonid. Focus. Focus on catching them. All that matters right now is catching them.*

He had to keep stopping, listening, trying to follow the sounds he could hear, pretty sure it was them. But the tunnels echoed, confused. Sound travelled in a peculiar way, crawling along the walls, slipping around corners. He couldn't be sure.

He knew about this place. The many rivers, perhaps fifty of them, that ran under the city; the adit systems built to drain the excess water out of the hills; the canalisation systems, the sewerage systems, some of them hundreds of years old. It was a warren of tunnels. Kilometre after kilometre of them. A place you could easily get lost in. Die in.

He had heard tales of the people that stayed down here. Quasi rooms dug out of the brick and the mud where people actually lived. People of the dark, venturing out at night to feed and then scurrying back in before daylight struck. It might all be made up. He didn't know and it wasn't about to deter him. People weren't frightening. The only issue was that the human footsteps he was trying to follow might not belong to his quarry. He was confident enough, though. They were travelling together, their footsteps light, childlike and they were in a hurry. People in flight not residents, he surmised.

*

Nadia had stopped in the cavern. Unsure. She would rather know what she was about to crawl into. Be at least a little bit prepared. She had no idea of what she was dealing with here other than a "bad man". It was Ukraine. He would be armed. Despite warning bells going off in every direction she carried on.

Chapter 39

November 2001

Leonid sat at the rickety little wooden table in his kitchen. Outside the wind sent tired, brown leaves clattering against the window, hammering out a rhythm with the relentless rain. He looked up at the scene, peering through the streams of water that gave the outside an indistinct blurriness. Two crows sat in the tree's branches, their bodies hunched, their claws gripping.

He swung back on the wooden chair, nodded his head and picked up one of the six knives that were lying on a piece of leather on the table. He stroked it back and forth on a whetstone. It was like a caress. Back and forth, back and forth, until he was sure it was just right. Beautifully sharp. This was when he did his best thinking. There was nothing to distract him. Just the rhythmic scrape of blade on stone. It settled him, focussed his thoughts.

Igor had some new deals going down soon. He had been talking to some strangers. Leonid had seen them all leaving the Hotel Dnipro. Igor, some dark-skinned men. Jumpy looking guys. Taking up the rear, Gregor and his cronies. Leonid was pissed. Excluded. Not impressed. He wasn't getting anywhere. Not moving up to the decent jobs, the ones above just killing.

He wasn't trusted despite everything. Despite years of doing Igor's bidding. Protecting him. Countless bodies. Yes, it had felt good. Very good! He could walk down the street with his head held high. The respect he commanded. People were frightened of him. His reputation had spread. Lezo. Leonid Lezo. The Blade.

"I trust you for this," Igor had said. Right! I trust you to hunt down street-kids, to knock off some idiot who's overstepped the mark, done something stupid. I trust you to risk your life for the Brigade but not to *be* the Brigade. Sidelined again. Left out of the decent scores. It was tedious. He had never screwed up. Never not killed when he'd been told to. Never said the wrong thing, let something slip. Hell, he hardly ever spoke to anyone else. He just wasn't going to get anywhere, was he? It was wrong! He was worth more than a fancy suit and a nice car.

Gregor. Always Gregor. The man was dirty. Something not right about him. But he and Igor had history. Back in Soviet days they had been colleagues. Some big secret they shared, apparently.

Igor had made noises. "You are like a son to me, Leonid." The firm arm across the shoulder. The patriarchal smile. Really? No. He was a tool. A trusted assassin. A man who gets things done. Kept close because that's best. That's safest.

*

He ran his fingers over the handles of his knives. Some wooden, some bone, all smooth and beautiful. None of them fake or plastic. Natural. That's what he preferred. The feel of it. How it wore down to become a part of you. Intimate.

He had been collecting knives for years now, searching out the very best match for himself. Knives were such a personal thing. The weight in your hand, the fit of your fingers, the curl of the blade. They all had to be just right, marrying up into a thing of exquisite perfection. These he looked after. These he loved. He rolled the leather back up, each knife in its place, and the one he would take out tonight in its sheath. Ready.

He heard Andrei come in. He couldn't be trusted either. None of them could. No-one could. That was a fact of his life. Trust no-one and don't get let down. He was getting sick of it, though. Of constantly being on edge. Of listening out for secret conversations, a dropped word, a mistake. It had become monotonous, tedious.

'Leonid!' Andrei slapped his back.

Leonid wished he wouldn't. *Fuck's sake!*

'How goes it?' Andrei asked.

'Yeah. All good,' he lied.

Chapter 40

December 2001

Dima, Sasha, and Alyona had walked past several of the peculiar junctions now and none of them had borne the scratch that they had made. At least they knew that they hadnt doubled back on themselves. Strange whispers, sounds they didn't know made them pause, listen. They came from different places, different parts of the tunnels. It made the hairs on the backs of their necks prickle.

'It's nothing. Water, that's all. Come on.'

They carried on, all trying to be brave for each other. Stopping, looking back, checking at each junction. Listening, straining, staring. Shadows dripped. Unearthly, ghostly. Just the water. Just the water. They didn't know what to make of anything – just keep going. Clinging on to the hope that they were heading in the right direction. In any direction that was going to get them safely out of here and away from Lezo.

The crow had disappeared. They had all been so intent on watching where they were putting their feet, on checking behind them, that they hadn't noticed where it had gone. Dima shrugged, Sasha wasn't overly concerned, but Alyona was becoming frantic. She started to cry.

'We have to find bird. We have to!' Her voice was rising, in danger of screeching.

'Be quiet. You need to be quiet,' Dima whispered as gently, but as purposefully as he could, without appearing too angry. A hysterical Alyona was the last thing they needed.

She lifted her nose, inhaled, tilted her head, listened. Hurried off.

'What the–?' Dima muttered.

He pulled a questioning face at Sasha who shrugged and gestured that they should follow. They hurried after her. Followed her around a corner. She had stopped, was standing in the water and was smiling, her eyebrows raised excitedly. Her fingers pointing upwards. 'You see?'

They heard it first. A whistle of wind. Then a trickle of fresh air. Not the dank, hard to breathe air that they had fought through. Outside air. There was an exit! Somewhere very close to where they stood was an exit, the outside, escape.

Sasha gave Alyona a hug. 'You are so clever.'

She beamed at him. It was like she was glowing. Both of them wrapped in that special light that was theirs alone.

'Come on, man!' Dima grumbled, feeling distant, left out. Jealous. 'We still need to get out of here.'

There were some steps. Some rusted, metal steps that climbed up the side of the tunnel and disappeared into a hole. The children looked up. There was nothing. Only darkness. They couldn't see how far up the steps went – where they led to – but they had to take the chance. This had to be the way out. The contraption felt dangerous, like it might detach itself from the wall with the slightest of tugs. Rust flaked off in their hands, rungs protested under their weight, but they inched up. One rung after the next. One rung after the next. Closer.

'Okay, okay, we will keep going,' Alyona was whispering.

Dima had realised soon enough that it would have been smarter to have Alyona in between them, like usual. She was a liability. What if she stopped and wouldn't move any further? What if those voices in her head gave her some stupid idea? What if they came to the end and she couldn't open whatever was there?

It would be something heavy and metal. Some kind of manhole cover. How the hell was she going to shift a manhole cover? How were any of them going to without some tool or other? Dima had never paid much attention to the workings of a manhole cover, other than watching the steam escaping in great plumes in the winter time – Kuchma gasses, he had heard some people say with a laugh. A drug that kept people at bay. Maybe not so funny – He was pretty sure that some kind of key, or some such thing, would be needed. This was all going to end so badly. They were dogs in a cage. No way out. Their captors prodding them with sticks, tormenting, laughing.

*

Leonid stopped, listened. There was nothing. He couldn't hear a goddamned thing any more. No footsteps. Nothing. Where the hell had they gone? Focus. He had to focus. What direction had the last sound come from?

It had felt like he was closing in on them. He was sure that they had been just ahead of him. So close that he had held back. But now? He tried to tune his ears into the sounds of the tunnel. Just the interminable drip, drip, drip, of the sodden walls. The slight hum of the effluence around his feet. Something else. Something behind him. He checked. Yes. Something behind him; footsteps, and they were getting closer. Had he got ahead of the kids somehow? No. There was a different quality to these steps. Adult. And it sounded like there was only one person making them. Someone else following them?

There wasn't time to think. To wait. He could see another of those junctions up ahead. He had to move swiftly. He had to hide. Find out what was going on. Moving as quickly as he could without making too much noise he turned into one of the smaller passageways and waited.

This wasn't a gun situation. Silence. He drew his blade. Ready. A few feet away was an odd, ladder-type thing, that led up into the dark. He thought he heard something from up there too. *Shit*! Who or what the hell was behind him? Were they following him? Working with whoever was up those steps? No. That was the kids. Had to be. They had reached these steps and scurried up. He wanted to follow. To keep the trail hot. But he had to check who else was down here first. Maybe someone he had to get rid of. He would climb the first few steps until he couldn't be seen. Whoever it was would be here in a matter of seconds.

*

Nadia had no idea of where she was, what this place was, where it was leading her to. But she was sure the man had passed this way. She wasn't relying on anything other than her sense of smell. Amongst the noxious, damp, and dirty odours that the tunnels were exuding there was a trail of aftershave. It was the smell that had engulfed the man when she had bumped into him at the *rynok*. It was uncomfortably familiar, *Eau Sauvage*, the same as her partner used to wear, but slightly off. Probably a knock off – counterfeit – like so many things here. She knew that she was at least on his trail and the smell was strong enough to let her know it was fairly fresh. Yes, this was recent.

If his scent disappeared she doubled back until she caught it again. It had happened several times at the junctions she had come across, but the detour had been brief. It had happened again now. She turned back, caught the smell, but it was where she had just come from. *Damn!* She looked all around. Two other tunnels she hadn't walked along, but they were considerably smaller and she didn't like the look of them. She would have to clamber up the slimy wall to reach them. It was one thing having her feet in the effluence, in the slime, another having her hands in it.

Instead she leaned her head in, took tentative broken inhalations, only breathing in just enough to tell her what she needed to know. No, she didn't think he had gone along either of these tunnels. Where had she gone wrong?

Now that she had stopped moving she felt cold and damp and miserable. 'What the hell have I got myself into?' she muttered to herself. Her hands were shaking as she reached inside her jacket for her mobile, just in case it had magically charged itself – given her one little bar. Of course there was nothing. What would she have done anyway? She had no idea of where she was. Help me, I'm somewhere underground. Yeah. That was going to work.

Her ex-partner had thrown her phone on the ground that night. Stamped on it and laughed at her. He had dragged her into a back-alley and raped her. A smile on his face. "I can have you any time I want. Remember this." He had been following her, stalking her for weeks. She could always feel it; feel his presence, the nasty essence of him. She had gone to the police but they were so patronising. "Are you sure you're not just imagining it? Has anything actually been done? What can we do about a feeling?"

Whispers of, *I'll never let you go. I'm watching you, bitch.* No sighting of him. Nothing concrete. It wasn't enough.

She didn't report the rape because she couldn't bear the thought of it. Of reliving it. Going through it all over and over again. And if it made it to court, she would have to do it all again in front of him with a defence lawyer. That night, her history, her lifestyle would be trawled through, regurgitated in some twisted bitter way. She could imagine him smiling, charming the jury, the judge. Everyone. That was what he did. And he did it so well. It had worked on her for long enough.

No. She didn't tell anyone. Not her friends. Not her father. She decided to disappear for a while. Take a transient job, in a transient place, where no-one would ask anything of her other than she put in her shift. Pulled her weight.

She settled on a hotel in Cornwall. Far away. Tourists and surfers. Something different. But it hadn't gone to plan. She soon found out that she was pregnant. The bastard had got her pregnant! She couldn't believe the irony. The baby that she had hoped might "mend their marriage," make it all right, make him all right, had never happened. And now it had come along. A rape baby that would grow into a rape child. A constant reminder that she was supposed to love.

Perhaps she would love it? That instant connection that people are always talking about. That bond. That mother-child love.

She worked for as long as she could. Phone calls to her dad, to her friends. Yes, she was having a ball. It was great down here. She wasn't sure when she'd be back. Sometime in the autumn, after the busy season. Maybe even winter. Definitely by Christmas, she promised.

She worked for as long as she could, putting all of her tips aside – enough to get by for a while – and rented a cottage in the middle of nowhere, where she would be left alone. Her days were spent brushing up on her Russian. Focussing on something else. Something very different. Something that took her away; that could open up another world for her, if it came to that.

When the baby came she looked at its little face

256

and saw him. Her rapist. The only feeling that swept over her was one of revulsion. No magic. No, "I didn't know you could love something so much." None of the expected clichés. She couldn't keep the child. Despite the kind words of encouragement from the staff at the hospital – the repeated stock phrases – "Give it time." "It's not uncommon." "You'll grow to love him." She handed him over for adoption. It was best for everyone. It was done. That part of her life was over.

Chapter 41

November 2001

'I don't know what to do,' Nadia said quietly to Maggie, as she sat in the boxroom that was an excuse for a staffroom. A spider plant sat forlornly on the top of a small bookcase, doing little to cheer the place up. The bookcase was packed with outdated text books and workbooks, their edges curled, paper yellowed and stained. Replacements were nigh on impossible to get a hold of and photocopying the norm.

'Isn't that illegal?' Nadia had asked.

A shrug in reply from Maggie. 'Not over here. Counterfeit is normal, right? Copyright? What's that all about?'

The coffee machine gurgled and hissed in the background. Maggie took two mugs from the draining board and filled them with coffee, adding two spoons of sugar to hers and none to Nadia's. Both took it black. She put the mugs on the wooden coffee table. It looked like something out of the sixties, angular, awkward. She sat opposite her friend.

'What's up?'

'It's Artem.'

'Oh, the mask has slipped has it?'

'No no. Not at all. Quite the opposite. I really like him, but that's the problem. It's all too serious, too quickly and–'

'And you're not looking for that.'

'Exactly. But, I mean, I REALLY like him. You know?'

'You're talking to the wrong woman here. I never get in that deep. A few weeks and I'm off.' She shrugged. 'What can I say? A fling is plenty for me. I mean, is it an actual proper love thing you're talking about?'

'Yes. I really think it is. I've never come close to feeling what I feel for him, and he's so special and– Damn it!'

'Yeah, that whole funeral thing sounded a bit, well, that's serious shit, isn't it? I never got invited to any of my boyfriends' granddaddies' funerals.' She put her hand up in stop mode. 'Not that I'd want to.'

Nadia laughed. Lightening the mood. Maggie's speciality.

'You should see this present that his grandpa gave me. It's the wedding dress of his departed wife. I mean! It's the most beautiful thing, and the meaning behind it is, well, it has to have been one of his most treasured possessions and he gave it to me! How can I accept that and finish with Artem?'

'Do you want to dump him?'

'No. Oh God. Maybe.' She grimaced, pulling a sad

face. 'Just because it would be for the best. I can't see me settling down to life in Kyiv, can you? I mean, God, it's Ukraine. It's–well, it is. I mean, would you stay?'

'No.' She shook her head. 'No I wouldn't. I'll do my time, finish my contract, then I'm off. It's been an experience. I'm glad I came, but–'

'Exactly!'

'And he wouldn't leave?'

'No! He's so very Ukrainian. His soul's Ukrainian. He can trace his family back through Cossacks and battles fought and all kinds of amazing stuff.'

'Hmm. Figures. All the dancing and shit.'

'No. He'd never leave and it would be wrong to expect it of him.'

'Sometimes you just have to go with things, you know? Not overthink. Right now, you're having fun. Enjoying it all. Perhaps you should just let it be. Who knows what tomorrow might bring? Live life. Go for it!' She checked her watch. 'On that note! Time to go. Eager students awaiting.'

Nadia stared at the ground, arms folded, shoulders heavy.

'Come on. It'll all be fine. Shit works itself out. Trust me!' Maggie added, rubbing her friend's arm encouragingly.

'Hmm. I hope so.'

When Nadia got home that night she had been pacing up and down wondering what to do, what to say. She'd picked her phone up a dozen times or more, ready to call Artem, and then decided against it. She called her dad instead. He called her straight back, not wanting her to waste her credit. His phone bill didn't matter as long as he got to talk to his wee girl. An hour of easy chat, of stories from him about what the neighbours were doing, how the Sainties were playing, what the government was doing, or rather not doing.

He asked about sending a package across to her; things she might miss, oatcakes, Marmite, Cheddar cheese, Tunnocks Caramel Wafers. It made her smile. The thought. But the actuality was that there was no point. The chances of it getting through customs and on to her were pretty much nil.

'I do worry about you over there. You're sure you're okay?'

'I'm sure Dad. It's fine. Different but fine.'

'You sound a bit...down is all.'

He always could tell when there was something preying on her mind. Always been that shoulder. He had probed and probed when the whole rape thing had happened, but no, she wouldn't tell him about Artem either. She had to work this one out for herself as well.

When she hung up she was left with a tinge of homesickness. She shrugged it off and settled down with a bottle of beer and Ukrainian television.

In the background she thought she heard something. Something out in the stairwell. The faintest of knocks on her door. She tip-toed along the hall and listened. Another faint knock.

It was late; too late for unexpected visitors. She had been advised never to open her door unless she knew who was there. The *militsiya* had been known to barge in and demand money, make life difficult. Foreigners were assumed to be wealthy. Certainly worthy of intimidation. You just never knew. Best to be very careful.

She left the hall light off, checked that the security chain was on, slipped the cover of the spyhole across. A slight squeak. *Shit*! Nothing but blackness. *Damn it. The stair light must have gone again.* It was a pain, but a regular one. There had been plenty of times when she had had to fumble her way up the stairs in total darkness. What to do? She wasn't expecting anyone. Probably best to tiptoe back along the hall. Pretend she's not in.

Chapter 42

December 2001

The children could see some light now. A gap above them. At last they had reached the top of the steps. There was a manhole cover. It was heavy metal, but it was tilted, loose. A space like the crescent of the youngest moon. A sliver of hope. Alyona stretched up and pushed as hard as she could, trying to move the cover to the side, making the gap to the outside larger. Something more tangible. It moved a whisper with a harsh grating noise. Metal on concrete.

It sounded like they were under a street, or a car park, but it was quiet. No traffic. At least none that she could hear. She tried again, and again. Her best efforts were having little impact. She squealed. Air, light, noises from the real world. From out there. But she couldn't reach them.

'Sasha?' she whispered. 'It is too heavy for me. I can't–'

Sasha squeezed in beside her and pushed as well. Centimetre by centimetre it moved until there was a wide enough gap for one of them to struggle through.

Sasha stretched his head up, almost forgetting their predicament with the joy of that first deep breath of clean, fresh air. The invigorating nip of frozen air in his nostrils. He closed his eyes. Held the breath. Relished it.

Dima's whispered voice snapped him back. 'Where are we, man?'

He glanced around. They were behind an old stone wall. The ground was covered with snow. He hoisted himself up onto his stomach, then clambered out, scanning the area with a quick spin of his head. A quiet piece of waste ground, large buildings, nothing he recognised. It was quiet with no-one in sight. He reached down for Alyona and hoisted her up, then Dima.

'Any idea where we are?' he asked Dima.

'None. Dunno where we are man.' He was jumpy and twitchy, his eyes darting from wall to wall, unknown building to unknown building. 'Could be any fucking place. Let's move.'

A crow hopped up onto the wall a few metres away from them and flew off into the sky, which was now heavy with snow clouds. The type that promised a thumping great downfall. Alyona twirled her hand at the bird, following its course. 'Thank you bird,' she called, jumping and waving.

Dima shook his head, though he was beginning to wonder if she had something – some weird connection with birds, with something unseen, unknown to anyone but her. He laughed to himself.

'Crazy man,' he whispered. He began walking uphill so that he could find a decent view of the city and get his bearings.

Sasha whistled to Alyona and held out his hand. She smiled and took it, breathing out a heavy sigh of satisfaction. They hurried after Dima. None of them were looking at the open manhole.

*

Leonid waited until whoever was following him was right there, right below him. It was her all right. That fucking interfering Westerner. She had a lot of payback coming her way. If it hadn't been for her this would all have been wrapped up by now. No-one messes with him like that. No-one! Bitch! He jumped down on her, straddled her, pulled her hair back so that her head lifted up, twisted it around making sure that their eyes met; that she understood. He put his hand over her mouth, poked at her back with the tip of his blade. 'You will say nothing and do nothing unless I tell you. Got that?'

'Mm-hmm,' she managed to mumble, fighting against the awful deja vu that had leapt into her head. This couldn't happen to her again. But no. The feeling was different. Completely different. This man was just angry. And familiar. She had seen him before. Felt that presence before. Not just with Dima at the *rynok*. Of course! The man with the *militsiya* that day on Khreshchatyk.

He stood up, pulling her with him, and gestured to the steps. 'Up.'

She did as she was told. The tunnel was tight and the steps felt dangerous, unstable. Each footstep precarious. At least if she fell she would land on him.

An unintentional laugh slipped out of her at the image of it.

'What the hell have you got to laugh about?' he sneered. 'Move it!'

It wasn't long before she could see light ahead of her. At the top of the steps a circular opening. Above it daylight. She had never been so relieved to see a dark threatening sky before. Pictures, possibilities, suggested themselves to her. She could kick him in the face. One strong determined kick. She could stamp on his fingers, probably break them. She could run up the steps. She was lighter, probably more agile, maybe faster. But the what ifs? There were too many bad consequences. He had a knife. Probably a gun as well. That was all she needed to focus on right now. He was armed and she was disposable.

When they reached the top of the stairs he held her ankle with a viciously tight grip. 'Wait right there!' he commanded. He squeezed up beside her. It was so tight, so disgustingly personal. She could taste his breath, feel it on her face. She started to turn her face away. He lifted her chin up with his blade. 'I get out, I pull you out. Don't piss me about,' he hissed.

He was true to his word. Just kicking her, letting her fall back down crossed his mind, as had finishing her off when he had first caught her – a flick of the knife; her body lying down there for God knows how long, decaying in the effluence, being nibbled at by rats and insects – but he had dismissed it. He wasn't sure if she knew much, but she just might. And if she did, she could be important. He would let her live, for now.

Again, there was the snow. His constant helper

right now. Not too heavy yet, a gentle flutter. Leaving trails but not covering, not disguising, not hiding. He could see their little tell-tale footsteps traipsing up the hill towards the steep cobbles of Shovkovychna Street. This place was dangerously close to Igor's building. He didn't want to be seen right now. No bag, no street-kid. It was all bad. He could talk his way out of most things if he had done the job. But he hadn't. Not yet.

There were a few people around, wrapped in heavy clothes, walking purposefully, not looking at anything other than where their next step would be placed. The children's footprints were mingling with a few others. Thankfully theirs were noticeable. The prints of three children in a hurry were fairly easy to pick out from the squashed, packed snow of heavy booted, adult feet. The occasional streak of a slipped foot, an arrow in the snow.

This was always a quiet street, today, due to the weather, it was even more-so. The hill was so steep that it was treacherous. The metal handrail travelling its whole length, there for a very good reason.

The English woman was being compliant. That was good. Easier than a bolshier Ukrainian who would fight back, argue, spit words of fire at him. Make a scene.

'So what do you know, English woman?'

'Scottish,' she replied coldly, pleased with the fake confidence flowing with her tone of voice.

'What?' he questioned scornfully.

'I'm not English, I'm Scottish.'

'Same thing.'

'Nowhere near.'

'Okay,' he sighed patronisingly, '*Scottish* lady. What do you know?'

They were walking side by side, arms linked, outwardly looking like a normal couple. Inwardly she felt sick. This was foul. His hold was like a vice, the grip on her arm painful. A constant reminder of the superior power he held.

Her free hand was gripping onto the handrail which sucked painfully at her skin, threatening to burn it to its icy coating. She had no option but to let go, manage without it. Instead she had to rely on the support of this man to keep her upright.

She stared at the ground, focussing on where she was putting her feet. Throwing off the intimidation he was exuding. The hill was slippery, standing upright a challenge. She wasn't used to this and it made their progress slower than her captor wanted.

'I don't know anything,' she answered. 'The street-kid told me his friend was in trouble, that he had to get away from you. I thought I could help. I saw you following him so I tagged along. What can I say? I'm inquisitive. Born like that.' Even she was convinced by the words that were tumbling out of her mouth with a peculiarly unexpected brashness.

'So you're just stupid then? Is that what you're trying to say here?'

'Perhaps.' She was beginning to get a perverse enjoyment out of all of this. Yes. She was getting a kick out of it.

*

Dima motioned with his hand and turned left into Ivana Kozlovs'koho Lane. On the right, expensive cars stood outside elegant apartments. On the left, a small park. Rooms with views. Kyiv spread out before them. He jumped up onto the low wall that surrounded the park; old rough stone topped with new slabbed concrete. Sasha and Alyona followed. A piece of land, park benches, most importantly a vantage point; the barren trees not obstructing the view before them.

Dima stood for a moment, his hands on his hips, scanned the area, nodded his head. 'Okay. We're good. Come on.'

They were in Pechersk. He could see the buildings of Khreschatyk. It wasn't far. If they could make it down there, mix in with the people, get lost amongst them, they should be able to lose any tail they had. A couple of twists around corners, doubling back, not doing the obvious.

He thought momentarily about hiding, waiting, watching, but that had gone so very badly wrong the last time. No. He would keep moving. They would keep moving. They hurried past the buildings of the Ukrainian Humanitarian Lyceum, around the corner, up Kruhlouniversytetska Street – wider, more exposed – keep going. It wasn't far to Liuteranska Street. Turn left down the hill. Wider still, four lanes. Vulnerability.

Militsiya. Berkut – the special police force. A law unto themselves. Brutal – Men in uniform seemed to be everywhere. Their weapons dangling casually from their belts, draped over their shoulders like fashion accessories. Cars with flashing lights.

They had to be very careful. To run might draw attention to themselves, to walk meant Lezo could catch up, assuming it was Lezo. No. Of course it was.

269

Though, by now there must be others. Surely there were faceless others after them. Try not to look. Try to appear normal. Heads down, hurrying through the cold just like everyone else. Don't look. A cold indifference.

At last they reached the bottom of the hill, the archway, the steps, the square, and Khreschatyk. It was busy enough. Shops, people, traffic, places to disappear into.

Chapter 43

November 2001

The next morning, when Nadia opened her door, she found the most peculiar thing that had been left on her mat. A collection of leaves in deep reds and oranges. Some berries. A feather. A piece of ivy twisted intricately through them, holding them together. It was beautiful. She picked it up carefully, not wanting to spoil it. To damage it. At first she thought it had been Artem. Perhaps this was some Ukrainian autumnal offering? Some country thing? No. He would have knocked louder. Phoned. Found a way to get in. Surely? She called him.

'Hi, it's me. Nadia.'

'Morning. This is a nice surprise.' His voice was tired, sleepy.

'I didn't wake you did I?'

'My day off. I was just having a lazy, long lie. Should be up anyway. You're not calling off tonight, are you?'

'No, no. Sorry. I forgot. About your day off I mean. Listen, you didn't leave something at my door did you?'

'Other than my heart?' he replied in a silly over romantic tone.

She giggled. 'Seriously. Did you leave something?'

'Um. No. Now you're beginning to worry me. Do I have a competitor? Is there another suitor? I shall draw pistols with the man!'

She laughed. 'How can you be so jovial after just having been rudely woken up?'

'Ah. That is because I have you.' He back-peddled. She didn't appreciate the possessive thing. Strange Western ways. 'I mean, because it is you doing the waking. If it was anyone else I would be angry and short tempered!'

She sighed. 'Incorrigible! Sorry I woke you. Look, I need to run. I'll see you later. Bye.'

Her curiosity had turned to guilt. The whole thing had been soft and gentle...different. It had to have been Alyona. And she had left her standing on the doorstep. She should have at least tried to find out who was there. Damn it!

She had time to do a quick detour across Kontraktova and up Andriivs'kyi on her way to work. With a bit of luck she might bump into Alyona and be able to offer apologies and thanks.

The morning was crisp and bright. The sunlight harsh. She slipped on her sunglasses to lift the frown from her forehead. There was no sign of Alyona or Sasha. She pondered over going to the old house. The basement. What harm could it do? She walked through the alleyway, the courtyard, and onto the grounds of the house. It appeared empty. Quiet and foreboding. A shiver crept up her spine.

She hesitated at the entrance to the old house and looked around. Listened. There was something there. Something near. A peculiar noise coming from the far side of the building. She crept around.

Alyona was sitting on the ground. Birds all around her. Crows mostly. They pecked at the ground at her feet. Stood on her legs, her shoulder, her outstretched arms. Her head was tilted back and the strangest of noises was coming from her. Part bird song, part human voice. The whole thing was slightly unsettling. Unworldly. But ultimately beautiful.

Nadia stared. Transfixed. Hypnotised by this little girl and her birds. She didn't want to interrupt this, whatever it was. But she did want to record it. She crept stealthily backwards, until she was far enough away for the noise of the shutter of her camera not to disturb. Not to intrude. She stood, entranced, taking picture after picture. Memory after memory.

That evening, when she met up with Artem, she didn't mention what she had witnessed. It felt like it was something very private. A secret. She told him that she had guessed that the odd present had been from Alyona. He agreed. Nothing more was said. No questions asked.

He had advised her to wrap up well and she was glad that she had listened to him.

'It will be winter tomorrow,' he said, looking up through the straggle of golden leaves clinging on to the arches of trees. Beyond them a sky of cold, pale blue. 'I like to come up here. To say goodbye to the autumn.'

'You really are a romantic, aren't you?'

'What can I say? I love my country. I love its nature. I love this. All of this.' He squeezed her arm close into his body. Took a deep breath. 'Can you smell that? The mustiness of the fallen leaves. Old growth feeding the new. The circle of life. If loving that is being a romantic, then yes, I am.'

She was impressed. This man had a beautiful way about him. An insight. He was more than special. Exceptional. They sat on a blanket, on the hill's highest summit, enjoying beer and bread and cheese, as they watched the sun slip down below the city. On its way, surrounding hills were picked out by shadow and sunlight. Reds and greens of roofs, and pinks and blues of buildings. The dying light caught golden domes, sending flashes of brightness into the sky.

Artem reached his hand up and pretended to snatch at the gold. He mimed stretching something, twisting it and tying it around Nadia and then himself.

She laughed. 'What are you doing?'

'Now our souls are tied together.' He smiled. 'A golden thread that connects us. Unbreakable.'

'Wow, just like that!'

'Just like that.'

Any thoughts she had had of leaving him – of breaking this off – had disappeared. She had never felt so good. So free. So perfectly close to someone. It was magical. This was magical. He was magical. Yes. She was in love and for now it was all that mattered.

They waited until it was nearly dark before making their precarious way back down the hill. The dark brought with it a change of feeling. The air now somehow heavy with something different; ominous. Perhaps it was just the stories that he had told her. She shivered anyway.

He held her close. Squeezed her shoulders. 'Okay?'

'Yes. Fine.' She smiled up at him.

'Cold?'

'A Little.'

'Let's run. Come on!' He took her hand and tugged her. 'Come on!'

She laughed. Ran with him. 'You're crazy,' she whispered.

'Crazy for you!'

'Nutter!'

PART III
Stumbling

Chapter 44

December 2001

Leonid and Nadia had reached the top of the hill. He picked up his pace to almost a run, pulling her behind him. 'You need to do better than that. Move!' He knew what the children were doing. Why they were heading into the busiest street in Kyiv. Having them disappear on him again wasn't going to be an option.

'I'm doing my best, Jesus!' she complained, losing her footing, slipping, stumbling, trying to make it all look as genuine as possible. It was easy enough as she really was having difficulty keeping herself upright. She was just making a little bit more of it. Smaller steps, bigger stumbles. A few more precious seconds of escape for the children.

They had reached Liuteranska Street. Hurried down it. They stood at the top of the steps overlooking Kreshchatyk. Nadia caught the children disappearing into Tsum, the classic Soviet department store, designed in the thirties by the award winning architect Alexey Shchusev. He was more famous for Lenin's stunning mausoleum and the Kazan railway station. A ground breaking building that mixed art nouveau and Tartar design.

Tsum was a grand structure – a centre point of Kyiv. The staff as austere as the building: unwelcoming until the money was flowing. The children had barely run in through the immense, heavy, wooden doors, stepped foot onto the polished stone floors and they were out on the street again, a gun-toting security guard ushering them away like vermin.

'Fuck's sake,' Dima mumbled. He spat on the ground in protest and turned away from the shop, glancing across the road. He would have liked to remonstrate, shout, challenge, express disgust through a string of abuse, but he had to hold it in. Accept it. He couldn't afford to make a scene right now.

Alyona was staring back at the department store, confused by everything, overwhelmed by the size of the place, the people, the men with guns, the women with fur coats. Not understanding why they had been thrown out.

'The underpass. Quick,' Dima instructed.

*

Nadia had kept her gaze on the children for too long. Leonid followed it. Saw them. Ran across the road, pulling her behind him, twisting through the traffic, ignoring the protestations of angry drivers slamming on their brakes in the slushy remains of the fallen snow. Not taking his eyes off them, he watched them slip down into the underpass.

The melted snow had left dirty brown puddles on

the grey concrete floor. It was crowded. Buskers sang and played guitar, hawkers stood with bags and tables selling everything from lighters to kittens. It was its own underworld. A life different. The air was heavy with cigarette smoke mixed with the stench of stale vodka, beer, piss, and steaming bodies. Sweat fermenting under too many layers.

A *bumsh* sat at the bottom of the steps, his hands filthy, purple and grossly swollen. He was making a futile attempt at begging, his head hanging in resignation: a pile of old clothes. Subhuman. Lifeless. The stink of human piss and shit made people steer clear, create distance. The odd grunt and cough evidence that he was still here. Still breathing.

Scruffy street-kids hung around looking for *kopeks*, targets, amusement, opportunity; skipping through people, scanning coats and bags and the ground. People were careless, wasteful. The children could benefit from it. They were quick. Alert. A dropped coin, perhaps even a note, half a burger, a cigarette barely smoked, a candy, a ticket for the metro, dregs in a beer bottle – all good stuff.

'Hey Dima!' one of the children called out, whistled, raised his hand. Scampered across. A big grin on his face. 'What's up man? Haven't seen you in ages. You're in some kind of big shit, aren't you? Word's out. People asking. Serious people. The *militsiya* fucking pushed me around, man, asking questions about you. Kept my cool, didn't I!'

Dima, Sasha and Alyona ran past him. The kid joined them, running beside them. 'Who is it? Who you running from?'

'No time, man!' Dima looked uncharacteristically

scared. His eyes had that stare, that total focus on getting away. The street-kids knew it well. Running from the *militsiya,* from a mark, from someone they had just pissed off.

'Big guy with a woman?' the kid asked.

Dima stole a hurried glance behind him. Saw them maybe twenty metres away, running, catching up, staring.

'Yeah,' Dima puffed.

'Right! Owe you one. Got this. Diversion.' The kid laughed. He whistled. The whistle was replied to. More whistles. It was like they were coming from all around. You couldn't tell what was a whistle and what was an echo. It was just noise. More children came. More noise.

Dima, Sasha, and Alyona ducked behind a pillar, switched hats with three of the kids. Resumed running. There were maybe ten, twelve children, all running, all making noise. People stopped. Stared. Dima, Sasha, and Alyona kept low, beneath it all, running, across to the other side, up the steps and out.

They didn't look back. They could hear the commotion that they had left behind. Whistles. People shouting. Anger. Laughter, screeches from the other kids. Chaos.

Leonid grabbed the girl who had swapped hats with Alyona, by the collar. Turned her around. Realised he had been conned. 'You little fuck!'

'Hey! Get your hands off me! You a perv or something?' she screeched.

A couple of *babushkas* "tssk'd," stared at Leonid and pushed their way towards the girl. The interest of the ever-present *militsiya* had been piqued. They moved away from the wall they had been leaning against, ditched their cigarettes, began striding, asserting importance, presence. The buskers had stopped. The crowd that had gathered to watch them looked around. This had all gone very, very wrong. Unwanted attention was everywhere. Leonid's face was turning red. His twitch thumping angrily.

Chapter 45

December 2001

Nadia hesitated. She could break free. People were watching. There wasn't anything Leonid could do. Yes, he had the knife but he wasn't going to use it here, was he? She kneed him in the crotch. He stumbled, let go of her, bent double in pain. 'Bitch!' he hissed.

She ran, not looking back, trusting that she had enough of a head start, grateful that she was quite fit despite being a smoker. She hoofed it up the stairs avoiding the clumps of ice and snow, the frozen footprints, which she knew through experience and badly bruised knees, were treacherous. One misplaced step and she would lose her footing, fall, feel his grip. She made it up to Khreschatyk, spotted the trio, ran after them as they disappeared through the swinging doors of the metro station.

Chequered floor, marble, walls ornate with mosaics of tiles depicting sunflowers and leaves, all flew past them. Down the steps, onto the platform. The rush of air. The whirr and screech of the train. People. People piling out. Others pushing on. A chaotic rush. Push, push. Let me get there first.

Sasha had a tight hold of Alyona's hand. She was pulling back, hesitant, scared. The metro frightened her. A burly man barged in between them. Her step faltered. She slipped. Felt herself falling. A young woman reached down and righted her, smiling. 'Are you okay?' Alyona didn't seem to notice. She stared at the woman, at the people, the backs of people pushing past.

She couldn't see her brother. She couldn't see Dima. Her vision became blurred through the tears that were welling up. She hated these places. Hated the noise, the clamour. Too many people. People underground. It was wrong. They shouldn't be here. Her breath was short, hard to control. She wanted to be outside. To be high above everything. To be a bird. She closed her eyes and stretched her arms up in a "V". An arm closed around her.

*

Dima and Sasha had made it onto the train, Sasha thinking that Alyona was right behind him, suddenly realising that she wasn't. He was being forced further into the train, his eyes searching desperately for a sign of her. The hands of strangers pushing. Pushing. Bodies squeezing in. Pushing against him. Forcing him back. He tried to push back against it, towards the door. Towards where she should be.

It was too much. Too many people. Too much pushing him back. Inhaling the breath of strangers. Suffocating. He heard the doors close. A hiss and a clatter. The train began to pull away. Sasha could just make out Alyona on the platform in the arms of a man. A blur, then nothing. The blackness of a tunnel. Nothing.

'No! Alyona! No!' Sasha screeched, pushing with everything he had. Every last bit. People. Bodies. Pushing. It was futile anyway. She had gone and there was nothing he could do about it. Nothing.

Other passengers stared, muttered, tried to lean away from him, squeeze themselves into the person behind them. A street-kid high on something. Unpredictable. Dangerous.

*

Leonid had kept a tight grip on Alyona as he led her to a bench. A big brother comforting his upset sibling. The strength of the hold disguised again. 'It's alright sweetie, we'll just catch the next one. It's okay,' he said loudly enough to be overheard but comfortingly, softly. He smiled at people. Raised his eyebrows in mock exasperation. Kids!

Alyona had learned that it is usually best to be quiet, to be compliant, when you're dealing with badness. Be quiet and it goes away. It leaves a scar but it goes away. That other place. That place of safety and wildness was always there, in her head. She was there now, flying with the birds, running with the wild things. Free.

He sat her down on the bench and held her close. His arm around her shoulders. The trickle of people that had begun to drift in would soon become a river. He had to make her understand. To make her talk. There no time to take her somewhere else. Somewhere they could be alone. This had to be done now.

'Good girl,' he said as softly as he could, relaxing his hold, trying to get her attention back. She had drifted, seemingly not aware of anything any more. No anger allowed. Be nice. 'Alyona,' he whispered. 'Alyona.'

He turned her face to his, tilted her chin up, met her eyes. There was a blankness. An eerie nothingness. He stroked her face, took it in both of his hands. 'Alyona.' At last she looked back at him. Saw him. He smiled. 'You're a clever girl, aren't you. All you need to do is tell me where the bag is and you can go.' He rubbed her shoulder. 'You'd like that, wouldn't you? To go and find your brother. And Dima. Where's the bag Alyona?'

'You want to hurt me,' she replied in a whisper. Cold. Detached.

It disconcerted him momentarily. He switched back on. 'Why would I do that? No! I just want the bag. It's mine and I want it back.'

'Dima said you want to hurt us.'

'No. That's not true, Alyona. I only want the bag.'

'You're not one of them.'

'One of who?'

'One of the men in the car. One of the men in the house. I don't know you. It was their bag.'

'Ah, Gregor you mean? Gregor and his friends.'

'Yes. Mr Gregor. It is his bag. He put it on me. We had played our secret games and –' She pulled her hand over her mouth and gulped, a look of terror in her stare. 'I am not allowed to say,' she whispered.

'What games?'

'I–shh,' she put her index finger to her mouth,

smiled a resigned smile, dropped her shoulder towards him. 'Are we going to play? Is that what you want? To play with me?'

It dawned on him. He had never had any time for Gregor, but this? This was just disgusting. The vision sickened him. 'Fuck!' he mumbled, looked skyward. His twitch started thumping, his foot tapping. He bit his lip. 'No. No, I don't play those games. I only want the bag. You were telling me about the bag.'

She smiled up at him. This time with relief. 'I don't like the games.'

'No. I don't like the games either. The bag?' He was trying hard to keep his temper at bay, to be soft and friendly and trustworthy, but it was becoming more and more difficult. This was all so messed up. And this kid? This kid was something else. Something he had never encountered before. He wanted it done with. Finished. 'What about the bag?'

'He put it on me. He said it was funny. Him and the men, they laughed. And then there was a lot of noise and blood, and it was on me.' She swiped and swiped at an imaginary stain on her legs. 'And I ran.'

She looked up at him, her face innocent but haunted. Looking for something from him. He had no idea what. This girl was making him feel very uncomfortable.

'Did you see anything? Do you know what happened?'

'I was very scared.'

'Of course you were. Anyone would be.'

'I didn't look. I just ran.'

'You didn't see anything at all? Think carefully. Anything.' He was hoping for some sort of answer, clarification. A clue as to what exactly went down.

'I–I just ran.' her voice was rising again. Fear crawling back in.

He read it; knew he had to be careful. 'Okay,' he whispered reassuringly. 'It was okay to run. Anyone would. I would.' He smiled. 'But the bag, Alyona. Where is the bag now? Do you know?' Soothingly, softly, gently.

'Dima has it.' She giggled, swung her legs back and forth, put her finger to her lips again. 'Shh, it is a very big secret.'

'Sometimes secrets are bad. Like the secret game you play with Gregor. This is like that. Not a good secret. A secret you should tell.'

'But Mr. Gregor says that very bad things happen if I tell secrets. Bad things will happen to me and to my brother. I don't want that to happen.'

'And do you trust him, Gregor? Do you like him? Is he a good man?'

She paused. Stopped moving. Stared at the wall opposite. Shapes and shadows in the tiles. 'No. He is not a good man.' She turned and challenged him with her eyes. 'And you. You are not a good man either. My brother and Dima are scared of you. And Dima isn't scared of anybody! We ran from you because you are a bad man.'

He forced a laugh – a soft bemused one. 'I'm not bad.' He raised his eyebrows. 'I do what I have to do, just like you do.'

'No. Your life is empty. Your soul is dark. I know. Why do you keep your soul like that? Dark? You must be very sad inside. It is not a good way to be.'

He couldn't believe what he was hearing. Being

preached at by a little street-girl who lives in a derelict basement, who gets used and abused and is, by all accounts, not all there. It dawned on him. Stung a little. She felt sorry for *him*! He blew it out with a deep exhalation, shook it off. Stay on track. Get it out of her. 'I only want what's mine, Alyona. That's not a bad thing is it?'

She shrugged and looked away again. Looked up at the lights that were stroking the ceiling, the shadows that crept along beside them. 'Do you see?'

'Do I see what?'

'The lights. How beautiful they are.' She smiled at him, her legs swinging back and forth again, under the bench.

Irritation. Bottle it. It looked like he wasn't getting through to her at all. He didn't have time to mess around looking at lights. The platform was filling up, noise, people, distractions, danger. He had to make her trust him somehow. Get through to her.

'Here's what we'll do. You take me to the bag and I'll help all of you. You, Sasha and Dima. There are many people, really bad people, they want the bag and they will kill for it. They won't be nice like me. They'll hurt you and they'll kill you. All of you. They won't stop until they get the bag and you're all dead.' As the words fell from his mouth a taste was left. He didn't like it. 'The bag, Alyona. Take me to the bag and it's all over and everything will be okay.'

'I don't have it.'

'I know, but you know where it is. You know where Dima has hidden it.'

'Yes. I know.'

Chapter 46

December 2001

Nadia was on the train. She stood on her tiptoes, trying to get a better look. There. Halfway along the carriage, she thought that she could see Sasha and Dima, but no Alyona. Their backs were to her, though. She couldn't be sure. She began trying to squeeze her way through bodies and dirty looks, knowing smiles and exasperated faces. No. There was no way she was going to get to them just now. She would wait until the next stop. People would get off.

It only took a few minutes to reach Poshtova. A trail of people alighted. Fewer got on. There was room to breathe, space. She could move now, and she made her way to the other end of the carriage where Dima and Sasha stood. No smiles. Angst written all over their faces.

'Where's Alyona?' Nadia asked. 'She was with you, wasn't she?'

'She got left on the platform,' Sasha answered forcing the words out. 'She was there. Right there. But...We got separated.' His head slumped. He lifted his shame-filled eyes to meet Nadia's. 'I dropped her hand. I saw her – I saw her with that man as the train left the station.' He was fighting back tears.

'Lezo,' Dima cut in. 'Lezo has her.'

'Lezo?'

'The man you helped Dima escape from,' Sasha explained.

'Oh, my God. I am so sorry. What do we do now?'

'She knows. She'll tell him,' Dima said. 'Why the fuck did I tell you two where the bag was? It's all finished. Everything's fucked up and finished.'

'She'll tell him, yes,' Sasha confirmed, his angst lifting. His faith in his little sister breaking through. 'Not just because of the bag, because she knows we'll go there too.' He was playing this over in his mind. Working out what she would do. Of course he couldn't be sure. She drifted, followed her imagination to far away places and if that happened? Well, there was no telling. He tried to tune in, to talk to her, to reach out to her. Sift through all of the rubbish and connect. *Come to me Alyona. Come get the bag.* 'But we get there first. We're ready for him. We do him over, get Alyona, take the bag. Leave.'

'What bag? Is that what all of this is about? Some bag?'

'You should leave lady. We're all dead. You will be too. Just go.'

'No. I've crawled through sewers and God knows what following that creep. He knows me. I'm in this with you now.'

Dima shrugged. 'Your death wish.'

'I need to make a call. When we get off I need to call someone.'

A smartly dressed man beside them was listening. He caught Dima's eye. 'Yeah!' Dima snarled, jerking his head towards him provocatively. The man returned his stare briefly, so as not to lose face, then turned away, a "pff" of derision as he did so. A look of distaste.

The train pulled out again. Next stop Kontraktova. The carriage emptied even more. It was comfortably quiet now.

When the train pulled in at Shevchenko, they checked up and down the platform, before jumping out and hurrying towards the exit. Huge clumps of odd shaped bulbs hung from the ceiling – almost chandeliers but not quite – and lit the way past immense, square marble pillars, a myriad shades of grey. The walls red marble, highly polished. The white bust of the writer and artist, Taras Shevchenko, watched them from the end of the station. But his weren't the only eyes following them.

Dima led, Sasha and Nadia followed, hurrying along side streets again, twisting again, checking for anything that might be a threat, a warning, a danger. A few people hurrying through the snow from A to B, here to there, heads down. Nothing going on.

But there was. Just out of sight, two men. 'Can see them clear as day,' the taller of the two said into his mobile. 'They're not going anywhere, Boss.'

'And Lezo?'

'No sign, Boss.'

'Stay on them, but don't do a thing until I say so.

You got that?'

'Yep.'

*

'Your phone call, lady,' Dima said casually, a
cheeky grin on his face, holding up a Nokia 3310.
'Who you calling?'

'Who did you nick that off?' Sasha asked,
managing a smile. Dima was something else!

'The man on the metro. Gave me a dirty look so I
took his phone.' He shrugged, pulled a face that said
"so what?" 'Good to share, isn't it! Bit of give and
take.' He grinned.

Despite the gravity of their situation they all
laughed. Perhaps because of it. It felt good. Broke the
tension. A momentary slip out of the madness.

He pulled the phone back close, held it tight. 'First,
who you calling?' Serious now.

'My friend. I need to let her know I'm okay. She'll
be worried.'

'You got one minute,' he replied firmly, holding
the phone out for her. 'No saying nothing about us.
No saying nothing about where you are. Right?'

'Okay.' She took the phone, closed her eyes as she
tried to visualise Maggie's number. It came.

'Maggie. Hi! It's me.'

'Nadia! Where are you? I got a call from school
asking if I knew where you were. You didn't show
and they're worried. Me? Not a problem apparently.
Holed up here in pain and no-one gives a shit. But
you? You not showing up is a biggie and they're all
concerned. What are you up to? I hope it's good!'

'I can't explain now. We're going to –'

'We?'

294

Dima snatched the phone off her and hung up. 'No!' he insisted, pointing his finger at her reproachfully. 'You don't tell no-one nothing! And you're going home. Enough all right! This isn't your deal. You need to leave.'

'Just go,' Sasha added. 'It's best.'

'But–'

'Go!'

Chapter 47

December 2001

Leonid and Alyona stood at one of the kiosks near the bus station. He was holding her hand.

'You are absolutely sure it's near here?' he asked.

'Yes. In an old building.' She stood on her tiptoes, pointed to a piece of waste ground, some trees, and the small remains of a building in the distance. 'Just up there.'

Leonid scanned up and down the dual carriageway behind them, busy with cars and trolleys and trams. Nothing of any note. The bus station – a couple of out of town buses idling, a scattering of people. The place was almost empty. But there. On Zhytnorzka Street. Hurrying towards the bus station, Dima, Sasha and Nadia.

Alyona saw them too. Her face broke into the biggest of smiles. She lifted her hand to wave.

He pulled it sharply back down to her side. 'Not

yet!' he snapped, regretting it, *keep your cool.* He turned them away. Away in the wrong direction. Away from the people she wanted to be with.

'Why? Where are you taking me? I want to go to Sasha!' she squealed.

'Shh. You need to trust me, Alyona,' he said firmly, tightening his grip around her fingers. It was too tight again. Not friendly any more.

'But you promised!' she spat, pulling back from him, stamping her feet. 'You promised me!'

He tugged her on. 'And I'll keep that promise.'

He had to make sure she kept quiet. She couldn't make a scene. Make people notice. Draw attention. Stay calm. Stay friendly. Christ! How had this come about? He knew nothing about kids. Nothing other than they were a pain. Noisy and a pain. And this one? She was something else, and it took a huge amount of effort not to lose it with her. It didn't do to lose it with her. He had learned that today. Be soft. Be gentle. Keep her calm.

This was all so new to him. So alien. His forte was to frighten people. To slice people. Shit! Carry on. Mister nice guy. 'There are people following them. The bad people I told you about. We need to get them away from here.'

'They will hurt Sasha?'

'No. Not until they have that bag, and if we get there first we can stop it. But they mustn't see us. We have to keep hidden. Do you understand how important that is?'

She shrugged. 'I am always hiding.'

Crows flew up from behind the wall that separated the station from the hill beyond. They circled in the air, cawed, swooped, falling and rising again in a constant wave. A small, black ocean. Alyona cocked her head, stared, listened, swayed. The motion, the story.

'This way.' She tugged at Leonid's sleeve. 'Come. The birds are dancing. See?'

He stared down at her, looking quizzically. Dancing birds? This was ridiculous. But something had changed in her. He could feel a strength that hadn't been there before. She knew something. And that was where he would have headed to anyway.

'Come!' she insisted.

They hurried along the side walk behind kiosks, parked buses, billboards advertising meat and beer from a supermarket, cigarettes, sultry women. Past the last bus stop, people standing, shuffling, kicking the snow off their boots, looking up the road, straining to see the number on the approaching bus through the swirling snowflakes, clutching tickets in expectant hands.

Alyona and Leonid slipped behind the fence, keeping their backs to the wall. It jumped from the cold concrete of an apartment block to the ancient weathered stone of a two metre high wall – a mosaic of pinks and browns, greys and blues of all shapes and sizes. A gap in the wall just wide enough for them to squeeze through. Trees, a hill, a place to stay hidden, to observe from. Something scurried past their feet.

*

'That's them. Leonid and Alyona. Where are they going?' Sasha asked. A lump in his throat. A panic rising. They were heading away. Not coming towards them as they should have been.

Dima glanced over his shoulder. 'We've got a tail, man. No time to do anything now. They're right on our fucking tail. When we get to the corner of the bus station we run right around it. Get behind them. Find a way to get over that wall.'

They ran around the building and waited, pushing themselves against the white of the wall. The men hurried past them, past the bus station, up to the cross roads at the *rynok*. Stopped. Looked up and down. Cursed. Arms held out in exasperation. They were having a hurried, heated discussion. One of them got out his phone. Dima, Sasha and Nadia took advantage of the temporary distraction and bolted to the shadow of the old wall. Found a leverage point – larger stones sticking out, just big enough for feet – and clambered over.

A *militsiya* car pulled up. The officers jumped out and started having an animated conversation with the two men. They were pointing back towards the bus station. The group split up: the *militsiya* walking back towards the bus station, the others around the outside, in the same direction as Leonid and Alyona had gone. They were closing in.

Chapter 48

December 2001

The Nokia began vibrating in Dima's pocket. He panicked, fumbling to reach the phone before it started ringing. He didn't know how to turn the thing off. Idiot! The first four tell-tale notes had chimed out before he managed to press the right button and silence it.

Nadia tried to protest. 'That could have been–'

Dima simply stared at her as if she were stupid. 'You're going home now, lady. Get the fuck away from here and leave us alone. Not your country. Not your business.' He pushed her backwards, a look of distaste on his face. 'Fuck off!'

She stared. First at Dima then at Sasha. Sasha confirmed that she shouldn't be here. This wasn't her place.

'Go.'

She felt sick. Of course they were right. What was

she thinking? Playing some irresponsible role that wasn't hers to command. 'You know where I live. Let me know you're okay. Please?'

Sasha nodded. 'Just go.'

She took one last glance over her shoulder as she slipped along the wall, turned the corner, found her exit and walked out. There was no way she was going into work. She had missed most of her shift anyway. Right now she couldn't see past that bottle of vodka sitting in her apartment.

*

'Right,' Dima said. This is it, man. This is it. The bag is two minutes that way.' He pointed through the trees and ran off.

Sasha followed, scanning the trees, the hill. Eyes wide, heart pumping.

Alyona. You need to listen Alyona. You need to show me where you are. Show me. She was close by. He could feel that much, but he couldn't see her in his head. Couldn't work out exactly where she was. There was a confusion to it all. A distortion of the connection. An interference.

*

'My brother. I need to go to my brother,' Alyona whispered.

'Not yet. You need to wait. You have to trust me, Alyona.' Leonid squeezed her shoulder a little bit too firmly. She winced, stared up at him, her brow furrowed, her eyes asking why he had done that. He ignored her. Focussed on what was around them. He could see the outline of the derelict little house through the trees. The boys had to be here somewhere.

A crackle of twigs. Feet running. He stared through the mass of twigs and branches. There. He put his hand gently over her mouth. Pointed. 'There,' he whispered in her ear. 'Don't make a sound.'

She nodded.

'Good girl.'

About fifty metres below them Sasha and Dima were skulking through the trees. Alyona could hardly bear it, to be this close yet so far away from her brother. It was like he was in another world. A world she could see but not be in. She stared hard. *Up here Sasha.*

Chapter 49

December 2001

Nadia shuffled along the side of the dual carriageway feeling disconsolate. Not bothering to check, to look. There was no need now. She turned into Voloska, glanced up at the Juliet balcony that was hers. A sense of belonging, if only tentatively. So many memories. Good ones.

She closed the door to her apartment behind her, kicked off her boots, threw her jacket on the chair. Poured herself a large vodka. Sat down. Realised she smelled. Looked at herself with distaste. She was dirty.

'Bloody stupid woman!' she cursed at herself, feeling very alone, very foreign. Useless. She could call Maggie. Call Artem. And what? How would she explain her last few hours when she couldn't even make sense of them herself? No. She downed the drink and settled on a shower. A cleansing.

The heat. The steam. The sound of nothing but water. It was good. She stood there thinking. Trying not to. Not knowing how to feel. She scrubbed herself clean, washed her hair. Lather and flowery perfume and luxury, so the bottle said. Luxury. She smelled good but felt like shit. No luxury in that. She wrapped her dressing gown around herself, tied the belt and padded through to the sitting room leaving soft, wet footprints behind her.

Angry music. That was what she wanted. Loud thumping rebelliousness. She flicked through her CD's. System of a Down. Toxicity. Perfect! The rhythm. Gentle. Menacing. She nodded her head to it. The swell of the music. The drums. The anger. Written for her. This moment. Right now.

She sang. Loud, almost a scream.

She thought she heard something. Ignored it.

Again a sound. A banging. A banging at her door. 'Shit!' She turned the music down. 'Okay, okay.' More banging. Louder. Insistent. She tiptoed over to the front door. Slid the spyhole cover across. The tiniest of squeaks. Peered out. Nothing. Black. *Bloody stair light!*

'*Militsiya!* Open up!' A command. Not a request.

She paused. It wasn't like she could pretend she wasn't in. *Shit shit shit...*

'I'm sorry. I don't speak Russian,' she lied.

'Open!' in English.

She paused. Held her breath. Heart pounding.

Again. 'Open!' Stronger.

She slipped the safety chain across and opened the door a crack, one foot and the weight of her body behind the door, securing it. 'Yes?' Innocent.

Too strong a force to the door. The chain flew off and slid across the wooden floor. She stumbled backwards. A hand. Leather clad. Across her mouth. Her feet scrambling in a vain attempt to keep up with her body, to stay upright, as she was dragged backwards into the bedroom.

Chapter 50

December 2001

Dima had the bag slung over his shoulder again. The scene in front of him was not what he had wanted. This wasn't going to plan at all. *Fuck's sake!* Lezo had found them. He had one arm around Alyona, like they were having some weird chat. Old friends. It was meant to be the other way round. He had had it all planned in his head. He would be waiting, hiding, have a hunk of tree. A branch. He would swing it at Leonid's head. Take him out. Cold. Give him a kicking. Teach him a lesson.

Lezo was smiling at Dima and Sasha. Summoned them with a flick of his gun. *Fuck!* Pulled his finger up to his mouth, pointed to the wall. Dima cocked his head, listened. Noises from beyond the wall. The heavy stamp of confident boots. The crackle of a *militsiya* radio. Yeah, he could hear them too. Talk about a rock and a hard place! He sauntered across to

Lezo, resigned to a fate that was as shit as his life had been to date.

Leonid clicked his fingers and held his hand out for the bag.

'Hand it over,' he whispered.

'Yeah, yeah, you win.' As he gave him the bag he felt like he was handing over his life. It was done. As if there could ever have been a different ending. As if anything good ever happened to any of them. Life was shit and it had just got shittier. That was all.

'You know this place?' Leonid whispered.

'Yeah. And?'

'So get us out of here.'

'You're not with your buddies then?' Dima nodded his head towards the sound of the *militsiya* behind the wall.

'Why would I be whispering if I was. This would be over. Now get us out of here. Move it.' He prodded him in the back with his gun and pushed him in the direction away from the wall.

Dima had no clue as to what was going on. Since when had Lezo switched sides, if that was what was going on? It didn't make sense. They should be dead. Bodies mangled, throats slit. A message sent out. You fuck with the Mafia, they fuck worse with you. That was how the story should have gone. It hadn't and he had no time to think about anything other than getting them out of here. He led them along the back of the buildings of the main road, away from the wall, the *militsiya,* whoever else was out there. This would be safer, easier than running into the woods again. He had learned his lesson there.

The space behind the buildings was nothing like

their frontage. Large windowed shops and offices replaced by rubble, piles of garbage, tangles of sleeping vegetation. The covering of snow made it all the more treacherous. Difficult to walk on; to find a way through. Broken bottles, sharp-edged cans. Still they pushed on. A tall green metal fence – as high as the last building they had scrambled past – blocked their way. There was no way out down here. Dima gestured up the hill. Lezo nodded in agreement. Sasha and Alyona followed, now wrapped together, arms around each other. Gentle smiles.

They pushed on up the incline, but keeping to the fence, listening for unwelcome sounds on the other side. Their way was blocked by a rough metal gate, the hill to its side too steep to climb. This had to be the way out. There was a strange impasse as Dima and Leonid weighed up who should climb over first.

'Give me a leg up,' Dima said with a shrug.

The metal was thin and sharp, but nevertheless he balanced his waist on it, checking the street beyond. It was narrow and steep and deserted. He hoisted himself over and jumped down. 'Okay,' he called quietly.

Down the hill would be trams, buses to jump onto, but their pursuers were down there too. Dima hesitated, looked down at the main road.

'Up. We go up,' Leonid said, pointing.

As they made their way up the hill, moving as quickly as the untreated surface would allow, the city seemed to fall away behind them and they were in a place of small houses that looked as if they belonged in a country village. Wooden houses, old brick buildings, no pavements, patches of trees and barren shrubbery.

At the top of the hill stood a huge house that looked like it had been laying empty for a long time. Outside, a sign advertising that it was for rent. They stopped. Leonid looking up at it. Thinking.

'No,' Alyona said forcefully. 'I don't like this place. It is not a good place. We should leave.' She tugged back on Leonid's sleeve.

'Just to hide out in. For your friends to wait in while I shift this.' He patted the bag. 'I can't be dragging all of you around.'

'No!' she insisted.

'You should listen to her,' Dima said, not believing the words that were coming out of his mouth. 'She knows stuff.'

Chapter 51

December 2001

Nadia was thrown onto the bed. Pinned down. *Jesus. Not again. This can't happen again.* She called on everything she had. Every last piece of bravado. Of strength. 'I am a British citizen. You have no right – '

'You hear that?' He laughed. 'We have no right! What? You think this is your country? You come here and think you can do whatever you like? No! We do whatever we like. Our country!'

'I told you. I don't understand,' she managed to drag on her strength and blurt out. 'English. I speak English.'

He sighed. Put his hand around her throat. Squeezed. Smiled. 'We know, Nadia. We know who you are. We know you speak Russian. We know you make friends with children from the street.' He signalled to his colleague who strode out into the sitting room. Turned the music back up. What the hell were they going to do that needed muffling; hidden by music?

Furniture being tipped over. Ornaments crashing. Splintering. Books falling. A vase of flowers breaking, water spilling amongst the debris engulfing a fallen picture of Alyona sitting amongst the birds. The water seeped into the paper. Distorting.

The man beside her took his gun. Held it to her head. Stroked her forehead with it slowly. So slowly. Disgustingly seductively. Perverse. The metal so cold and hard against her skin, soft and flushed.

'The girl. Alyona. Where is she?'

'I don't know what you're talking about.'

The gun stopped. The man stared. Made to fire it. 'You want this? You want me to shoot you? Yes?'

The other intruder returned from the sitting room. The bottle of vodka held aloft in one hand, the picture of Alyona in the other. He handed the picture over.

'I will ask again,' he said, holding the picture in front of her face. 'You will answer. No more lies. Where is she?'

'I don't –'

He slapped her hard across her face. The force, the noise, making her ears hum, her cheek sting. He smiled. 'You like our vodka, yes?' He turned to his partner. 'She likes our vodka. The little English girl likes our vodka.'

He clasped her jaw. Clicked his fingers, gesturing at the vodka. The man holding it grinned. Handed it over. Her mouth was forced open. Filled with vodka. She coughed and spluttered against the burning liquid. Eyes wide. Staring. Her lungs felt like they were on fire. Her head was screaming.

Leonid shook his head. 'What are you suggesting then? A nice little hotel somewhere, huh? Anyway,' he nodded towards Alyona. 'She comes with me.'

'Alyona stays with us! You can't take her away again,' Sasha replied, pulling his little sister in to him.

'Let's be smart about this, okay? If I'm seen with the girl and the bag it'll be assumed that I've been telling them the truth. I've caught her and this is over. No-one will bother us. On my own they're still looking for her–and you.'

'How do we know you'll even come back?' Dima retorted.

'You don't. But seems to me you don't have a choice in this. Just do as you're told for once.'

'It's okay. I will go,' Alyona piped up.

'Right. Smart girl.' He held his hand out and she slipped hers into his. A peculiar gentle squeeze, as if she was reassuring him. The trust. The squeeze made him pause. Momentarily taken aback. 'Now you two need to hide out somewhere.'

'Over there. The house over there is better.' Alyona suggested, pointing further along the road where a little track cut off into the trees. Birds flew.

Nestled, almost out of sight, was a small wooden cottage. It looked like it was about to collapse in on itself. The roof was sagging, the timber splintered, untreated, uncared for. The garden nothing but a tangle of overgrown plants. Even the pathway to the door was concealed. That was good. Less chance of footprints being spotted. They forced a way through, roughing up the snow behind them with a handful of twigs.

Avoiding the front door, they made their way around to the back of the building. The back door wasn't locked. Inside there was still furniture. Ancient, smelling of damp and neglect. A range with a blackened kettle atop, some pots and pans. An oil lamp.

Leonid looked around, his expression one of distaste.

'Okay. You tuck yourselves in here for a few hours. We come back and we all get the hell away from here. Sound good?'

'Sounds too bloody good. Why would you come back for us, eh? You'll sell us to your cronies or just kill us. That was what was meant to happen, wasn't it? You kill us.'

'Well, the thing is Dima, I could just as easily have taken away your scrawny little lives down where I found you. I didn't. You know why I didn't? I haven't got any cronies. It's just me now. And let's be honest here, I'm way closer to you than I am to any of them.'

'Sure,' Dima retorted scornfully.

'And you? You are so like the kid I used to be. Same cheeky little fucker. Same shitty place to live in. Same worthless life. Thing is, I could help you. Help all of you. You're going nowhere without me. Just use that brain of yours, Dima.' He tapped on the side of his head.

'Fuck off!' Dima spat, pushing the humiliating finger away.

Leonid laughed at him. He took pictures of them all. Head and shoulder shots, added the Nokia's number to his phone, took the bag and left saying, 'If we're not back by tomorrow night you're on your own. Leave Kyiv.'

*

Dima and Sasha explored cautiously, taking tentative steps into the rest of the house. Everything creaked and groaned. The dust was almost as thick as the snow outside.

'You know, she'll be all right, man,' Dima said, punching Sasha's arm. 'She'll be fine.'

Sasha didn't feel it. None of this felt fine. But he nodded. Forced out his worry, his fear. He had to keep positive for her. What was the point in being negative anyway? It didn't serve anyone. Especially not Alyona. She would pick up on his feelings.

*

Leonid took the first turning left and hurried down to Nyzhnii Val Street where he jumped on a tram heading away from Podil, Alyona and he hand in hand again. Everything was flying through her head. All strangeness. Too much. Too fast.

They got off at Peremohy Avenue. Alyona stood and stared. Her head struggling to process this place. Row upon row, block upon block of faceless buildings. Thousands of houses, people, lives. She didn't like this. It was cold and ugly. Concrete stretched so high that there was nothing else to see. Nothing else to feel. No birds. What could she do when there were no birds? Where could she go?

Leonid tugged at her. 'Come on. It's okay. I know this place.'

She looked blankly past him, as if she hadn't heard him, as if he wasn't there. 'How can you? How can you know? All of the buildings are the same. Everything is the same.'

Yeah, she had a point. They walked past a long stretch of grey buildings and went into the tower block where his contacts lived. These guys were from Belarus. Not friends of Igor's. The opposite. Leonid had had his eye on them. Dodgy guys with ambition who dealt in drugs and counterfeit anything. You wanted it. They could get it. Most importantly, they had access to shit loads of cash.

He reckoned that this was his best bet, doubting questions would be asked. Cheap drugs were cheap drugs and money was money. They dealt in forged papers as well. That was a risk, but one he was prepared to take. The people he knew who made top quality documents were part of Igor's network. He couldn't use them. These guys? He didn't know about the quality they could get hold of and time was of the essence. He had to hope. To trust. Not good, but necessary right now. The only other problem he could foresee was the haggle. He was in a hurry. He was asking for a lot to be done. They would take advantage. He had to get the best deal he could. He had to be smart.

'When we go in here you have to be silent, okay? Not a word. No matter what you hear or see, you be quiet.'

'It is always that way. I know what to do, Leo.'

There it was again. Leo. Someone young and vulnerable. Someone else. He wrestled with it. That other person. No. Not him. Not now.

Chapter 52

December 2001

Nadia's drawers were being emptied. Clothes tossed to the floor. Underwear picked up, deliberately, slowly. Sniffed at. A lascivious grin. Her dressing table cleared with one swipe of an arm. Perfume, make up, swept to the floor. The framed photo of her and her dad at her graduation thrown against the wall. Glass exploding.

She couldn't think. A blackness. A terrible fear. More vodka poured down her throat. She felt like she was drowning. Pinned down. Couldn't move. Couldn't breath. Spluttering. Wheezing.

Derision. From them only derision.

'Where does she live?' The gun stroked its way down her neck now, her chest, slipped her belt undone, opened her dressing gown. A pause. A sigh.

Grab something Nadia. Anything. Stop this. 'Up near Poshtova. A basement behind Poshtova. That's all I know. I swear.'

'Where exactly?'

'Pink building. Borychiv Descent. In the woods.'

'By the steps?'

'Yes. Yes. By the steps.'

'Good girl. That wasn't so difficult now, was it?'

He poured the rest of the vodka over her body, over her bed. Stood up. Lit a match. Made to flick it at her.

She squealed. Rolled onto the floor. Winced as splinters of glass pierced her skin.

The music.

I don't think you trust
In my
Self-righteous suicide
I cry
When angels deserve to
Die

He laughed. Blew the match out. 'Next time. Next time we do all of this.'

A buzz of noise, of confusion as they left. Amongst it she thought she heard, 'Call Lezo,' as the door closed behind them. Footsteps on the stone stairs. Becoming muffled. Disappearing.

She curled into a foetal ball and cried. Screaming and crying. Screaming and crying.

Her head was pounding. Heart thumping. 'The door. Lock the door.' She crawled her way to the front door like a wounded animal. Stretched for her keys. Turned all of the locks. Slid the bolts.

*

'Shit, it's fucking freezing,' Dima grumbled. No centralised heating system here. 'And we can't even light a fire now. Fuck's sake.' He rubbed at his arms, then slapped his body to emphasize the point.

Sasha had taken first watch from the small attic window. Peering through the trees. Searching for anything. Hopefully nothing. Below he could hear Dima checking through the little house. Doors opening. Squeaks and clicks. Quiet curses. Exclamations.

He froze. Stared. A man was walking along Olehivska Street, another man behind him looking around, searching, two *militsiya* taking up the rear. They went into the grounds of the empty house Lezo had first suggested that they hide in. The door was opened, the house searched, loudly, no fear, no attempt at keeping hidden.

'We need to move. Now!' Sasha said, rushing back down to the ground floor, a trail of dust in his wake. He didn't need to stress the urgency. They both felt it. They both knew. Their saving grace was that the house across the street was big. It would take time to search through it all. They hurried to the back door.

'The snow. Tracks. We can't leave any,' Sasha whispered.

'Uh-huh.'

The back of the house wasn't as overgrown as the front. The shells of discarded cars, left to rust and decay, were scattered around, tangled up in weeds and shrubs. Rubble, old metal pails, a dog kennel, enough detritus to allow them the chance to obscure their path, disguise their tracks. They used pieces of a large cardboard box to place on the snow and stand on, lifting it after them, laying it before them. It was slow, cumbersome, but effective enough. There were marks, indentations in the snow, but nothing you could call a track. Nothing you would identify as having been made by people. Not really. And it was still snowing. A few minutes and there would be nothing.

At the bottom of the garden a low wall separated the property from the woods. They scampered over, crouched down, pulled the cardboard over themselves and leant it against the wall to make an impromptu lean-to. They were covered. Just. It would have to do. They listened. Angry voices. The sound of the cottage door splintering. Footsteps. The back door.

'Nothing here.'

'They could be hiding in any number of places. There are plenty of empty buildings on this street. We keep going.'

'Have they got a track on the mobile?'

The voices trailed off as the men left.

Dima slipped the phone out of his pocket. Were they talking about this? Surely not. He hadn't let that woman use it for even a minute. He didn't know anything about mobile phones and this even belonged to a stranger. Someone with no connection to them at all. No. It couldn't be this phone they were talking about. He shook his head; stuffed the phone back in his pocket. This was the only time he had ever had a phone. No-one he knew had one. It was cool. He was keeping it.

They waited in silence, neither of them daring to speak, barely daring to breathe.

Sasha's thoughts were with Alyona. How he'd so easily allowed her to go off with that man. Leonid. Leonid Lezo. Leonid the blade, for Christ's sake. A killer. A Mafia hitman. His little sister whom he had sworn to protect – always – was with him. Lezo had the bag, he had Alyona. Why the hell would he come back? He didn't feel anything bad from her, though. He would feel it, wouldn't he? He always knew. Sometimes that made it so hard. That he knew. Right now he only felt normal from her. Normal scared, normal confused. Alive. He had to send good feelings back to her. Positive, safe feelings. He did his best.

Dima was going over what Leonid had said about them being alike. About him being closer to them than to the Mafia. Was it true or just some clever line to trick a stupid street-kid? That's what he was, wasn't it? Just some stupid street-kid. Why did he ever think anything different? Stupid! He had really proven it over the past day. Stupid mistake after stupid mistake. He bit his lip, chewed on it. Stupid.

Minutes passed, noises slipped into the distance carrying with them the weight of fear that had been sitting on Dima's and Sasha's shoulders.

'Shall we go back inside?' Sasha asked. 'I mean, they've searched the place. They won't be back, will they? And we can't see anything from here.'

Dima liked the fact that Sasha still looked to him as the one to make decisions. At least Sasha still thought he knew stuff. He was smart. Worthwhile.

'Yeah. Yeah, I was just thinking that. Let's go.'

*

Alyona clung on to Leonid's arm with both hands. He felt safe. This place didn't feel safe, but he did. The building was tall and they were taking the stairs. She didn't mind that. Lifts were scary things. They locked you in. She didn't like that. Locks and keys and no way out places were bad.

When they reached the top floor Leonid

320

straightened himself, took his hat off, ran his fingers through his hair. He smiled at Alyona and did his best to smarten her appearance up. There wasn't much he could do. The kid was dirty.

She smiled. Copied him. Swiped at his coat. The dust. The dirt.

Shit! He was dirty too. That wouldn't do. That wouldn't do at all. He did his best to get himself closer to the man he should be. She helped. Checked.

'There! You look better now,' she said to him. Her hands on her hips. A satisfied look on her face.

This was it.

'Okay,' he said. 'Remember, stay quiet. Right? You can't speak or hear. That's what we're going to say.'

'Okay Leo,' she whispered back with a smile.

He felt it. The smile. It warmed him. Made him feel. Something he didn't know. A strange warm pull. A tug at something buried deep inside him. He looked away, called a number from his mobile and let it ring three times before hanging up. He called again. Repeated the code. The door clicked open and they were hurried in by a man in a tracksuit, sporting an empty holster. The gun drawn, ready in his hand. No words were said until they were inside and the door had been locked behind them. Four mortice locks, two heavy bolts, one at the top and the bottom of the door, two security chains.

Alyona stared. Eyes wide. Danger. She tried to be brave. Pretend. It was as if Leonid knew. He squeezed her shoulder, softly, reassuringly, not looking at her.

'Lezo! Welcome, welcome.' Another armed man led the way along the hall and into a sitting room. Two more armed men stood at the door.

Sitting on a leather armchair, hand slapping his leg to Johnny Cash, a moustachioed man with his greased back hair in a straggly ponytail. Leather waistcoat, blue denim jeans, cowboy boots. He stood up and held out his hand. Leonid took it between two of his.

'Why the fuck have you brought a girl with you?' he muttered disbelievingly into his ear.

'Little mute thing. Good to have. No-one bothers you if you've got a little mute girl with you.' Leonid laughed, pulled a face, shrugged.

'Fucking Ukrainians! Shit man. So, what you got for me?'

'The very best cocaine. Straight from South America. The real deal. You're gonna love this shit!'

They talked. It was friendly enough. A business deal with an edge. Numbers were thrown back and forth. Smiles, scowls, nods, shakes of the head. It was a game and they both knew how to play. Leonid had learned from watching a master, Igor. This was the first time that he was the one doing the deal. Not just the bodyguard. His own boss. He could get used to this. The buzz. The excitement. The scheming. One step ahead. Each word carefully chosen. A verbal game of chess.

Alyona stood, silently staring out of the windows. She had never been so high up in a building before. The height was good, exciting. It was like being up in the sky. Her eyes followed the oblong roofs of lower buildings, the grey snakes of highways twisting through the snow encrusted landscape around them. Her focus settled on a hill in the distance, coated with skeletal trees. It looked familiar.

Terms were agreed. They would have to wait. The

money, the documents, it all took time. The sun was going down. The light changing. Everything changing.

Chapter 53

December 2001

Nadia staggered back through to the bathroom. Her head spun. Her stomach lurched. She just made it to the toilet in time. She retched and retched, her body heaving, until there was nothing coming up but a nasty yellow bile. Still her body kept forcing it out, acidic, foul. It felt like she was going to die.

Finally she managed to control it. To stop the heaving. To breathe. She stretched across the bath and fumbled for the shower. Turned it on. Sat under its stream. The water doing nothing to wash away the violation that she felt.

She had no idea. No idea of what to do. Her brain was so fuddled by the alcohol. Her thinking wrecked by the fear. Everything was jumbled, spinning. Flashes of nonsensical thoughts. Images. She had to get a grip. Get a hold of herself. She scrubbed and scrubbed at herself with soap until it hurt. Her skin red, raw. She stared at herself. At what she had done. The red seemed to crawl around her, slithering like a serpent. Biting at her. Making her feel dizzy again. Swaying.

She screamed. 'Fuck you! Fuck you! Fuck you!' Her voice cracked, crying, fighting it. Her fist pounding against the tiles. 'Fuck you!' More pain, but a sobering pain that snatched her back. Stopped the spinning. She turned the shower to cold. The shock of it made her screech. Made her focus. Was she safe? Was she sure that they had gone? Was the door locked? Closed even? She didn't know, couldn't remember. Everything seemed distant. Messed up. She had no idea of what was real.

She stepped out, shivering, pale from the cold. Legs unsteady. Lurched for the towel rail. Gripped it. Snatched at the towel. Dried herself. Walked cautiously out of the bathroom, using the walls for support, checking all around. A sigh of relief. The door was shut. The bolt pulled.

Water. She needed to drink water. She took a bottle out of the fridge and gulped at it. It felt like it was going to fire straight back out. Her stomach fighting against everything. She fought back. Swallowed hard. Held it down. Her body calming. Her insides cooling.

It was creeping back in flashes. Her memory. Exactly what had happened. She had to work through it, past it, beyond it. She rummaged through her cupboard, pulling out clean clothes. Untainted.

As her thoughts cleared she suddenly remembered Bogdan's package. The wedding dress. A further panic. It had to be all right. It had to be!

She had left the package in one of the big wall

units that had been ransacked. Contents strewn across the floor. She couldn't see it. A desperation now. Searching through the mess. Eyes misted. It couldn't be gone. After so much. It had survived through so much. It had to be okay!

There. Under the curtain, she glimpsed something. The brown paper. She bent down and gingerly slid it out, her fingers trembling, praying that it would be in one piece. Undamaged. Afraid to look. Yes. It was intact. She sighed and clutched it to her chest. A tear dripped from her face onto the paper. Was absorbed. A small stain.

Everything had changed in her apartment now. The feelings, the memories, everything. It was dirty, a hideous place of fear and brutality. Everything decent gone. She had to get out of there. Anywhere else would be better than here. She felt the need to be amongst people. It didn't matter who, or where. Just not *them* and not here. She grabbed her passport. Money. Pulled the phone from its charger. Opened the Juliet balcony. Leaned out. From here she could see up and down the street for a decent distance. Daylight disappearing. Street lights taking over. No *militsiya*. She couldn't see anything untoward.

She rushed down the stairs. Dust. Age. Nasty. Opened the door. The blast of cold snatched the breath away from her. Punched her. She checked left and right across the courtyard, the car park, the gardens. No-one. Through the alleyway and out onto the street. Hood pulled up. Scarf over her face. Only her eyes showing.

She hurried along Voloska, scanning, checking everyone, everything. She had no idea of what, or who, she was supposed to be running from. Right now everything was a threat. Definitely *militsiya* but who else? Everyone. Right now it felt like everyone. The people she had needed to be amongst were all potential enemies. Threats. They walked past. Heads down against the snow. Chatting. What were they talking about, whispering about? Were they glancing at her as she walked past? *"That's her."*

Militsiya cars. Always around. Creeping, searching. Speeding, screeching. One was coming towards her. Slowed down. Crawled past her. She looked away. A danger? Nothing? She didn't know. The junction was right there. She turned the corner. Closer to Kontraktova. More people. Trams. Noise.

Where should she go? What Maggie had said about the English speaking bar. The familiarity. That all made sense now. She should call her. Call Maggie. Not now. She didn't want to be speaking English. Be drawing attention to herself. No. But she should go somewhere where she felt safe. She thought first of the bistro, Mishka's. Not an expat place but familiar. It was right there.

She would walk in.

'Coffee?' the waitress would ask.

'Please. Yes!'

She would take her usual seat at the window. Long net curtains from ceiling to floor, the nicotine staining making them look closer to brown than white. The whirr of the heating. The clatter of the kitchen. The chatter of the women. But there would only be locals. That wasn't what she needed right now. She hurried past. Another life. Someone else.

Across Kontraktova – *summer nights, beer and*

buskers.

Up Andriivs'kyi – *gentle strolls, laughing, searching out odd little gifts, mementos. A Red Army hat for her father,*

Avoid the main streets. Cut through the park. Longer but safer – *Alyona dancing with the birds. Rustling leaves. Sunshine mottling the ground.*

Down to Maidan. Too busy. Don't look up – s*itting at the fountains. Buying dodgy cigarettes and vodka from the line of hawkers. Steaming pots of home-made pies. Street-kids and lovers. Old men and women reminiscing.*

Keep it. Keep it all. Everything.

*

At last she reached Mykhailivs'ka Street, a dash up the hill, and finally O'Brian's. A quick check for anything untoward. The overly lingering stare of a stranger. *Militsiya.* A crawling car. She couldn't see anything obvious. Clutched the handrail. Took a deep breath. Settled herself. Control. She needed to be in control. *It's okay. It's okay.* Steps down before the steps up. Irish music. English and Russian. Laughter.

She walked across the wooden floor, her footsteps sounding too loud, like they were announcing her presence. Invisibility, that was what she wanted. Needed. *Don't look. Don't look at anyone. An empty table in the corner. Focus on that. Get there.*

The bar was full of its usual clientèle. Loud Westerners flashing their cash; hookers blatantly working the punters; girls in skirts too short and heels too high looking for visas; men in suits doing dirty deals behind shot glasses.

No. Nadia didn't like it. Yes. It felt somehow

secure.

*

Alyona was sitting down now. The man in the cowboy boots had brought a wooden kitchen chair over for her.

'Funny little thing, isn't she?' he'd said, rubbing the top of her head.

It was dark. The view from the top floor now nothing but lights and darkness. It was easy to dream, to be somewhere else, something else. Alyona just flew amongst the lights, looking down on things distant.

Cowboy Boots and Leonid had downed some shots of vodka, toasting each one in turn. There was no choice in the matter. This was how business was done and a refusal would have been an insult, insinuating one didn't trust the other. In this business trust was essential. No trust, no deal. No. Leonid had to keep face.

'To business!' Leonid.

'To our mothers!' Cowboy Boots – Leonid cursed inwardly at that one. Smiled, made eye contact, clinked glasses nonetheless.

'To money!' Keep it impersonal.

'To our grandmothers!' *This is getting fucking tedious.* Still smiling and clinking. Smiling and clinking. Slamming down glasses with a burst of masculinity. Testosterone bouncing from one to the other.

They didn't have to wait as long as he had feared. His head was slightly befuddled by the drink, but kept clear enough with a decent amount of bread and fish. He still felt in control. In charge. The documents were

329

good. The money slightly light. A shrug from Cowboy Boots. What are you going to do about it? A heavy handshake and a firm hand on each of their shoulders.

'Good doing business with you.'

'And you.'

Leonid took Alyona's hand and they hurried down the stairs. He checked up and down the stairwell at each landing, his gun drawn. Of course the double cross was always possible. Only a fool would think otherwise. Alyona acted like his shadow, slipping behind him, barely visible as a separate entity, totally silent. It was as if she knew what to do, how to behave. An enigma.

They had reached the second bottom floor. He was almost relaxing, almost thinking it was okay – they had made it – when a door above them squeaked open. They pulled themselves back against the wall and listened. No voices, but no sound either. It was too quiet. Someone else was trying not to be heard. The door at the exit below them opened as well. It could be anything. Kids playing hide and seek. Lovers sneaking to secrecy. It could also be someone after them. They would have to get out of here. Now.

Leonid opened the door to the landing slowly, slowly, just wide enough for them to squeeze through. He held the door until it closed. No sound.

What to do now? There was the lift. Too dangerous. He looked up and down the landing. Strip lighting. Six doors to people's lives. Heavy pipes running along the walls. Alyona pointed to the window at the end of the landing. *Smart girl.* He nodded back at her and they dashed to the window. It was low to the floor. A simple latch, easy enough to open and clamber out of. What concerned him was what was on the outside. He knew he could jump and roll. What about the girl? There was no choice.

'You can do this. Just copy me. Jump and roll,' he whispered. As the words left his mouth he felt the strangeness of it. So concerned with the welfare of somebody else that he was putting his own life at risk. He would normally just have jumped. Run. Saved his own skin.

Out of the window all he could see was snow. Not deep enough to break their fall, but covering the ground. It could be concrete, dangerous, or, if their luck was in, the remnants of a piece of grass, mud, something that wouldn't break a leg; crack a shoulder. He jumped, rolled. Nothing too hard. It was okay. Alyona didn't need any encouragement. She stared at the ground. Breathed in. Copied. Landed safely. Reached for his hand. No-one had ever done that before. Reached for his hand.

'Well done!' he mouthed, with a smile, eyebrows raised in appreciation. Something more. Something deep.

She nodded back at him, feeling proud, pleased with her bravery. The leg she had cut yesterday nipped, but she was okay.

They hurried back towards Peremohy Avenue and jumped on the first trolley bus that came along. Where it was going was an irrelevance. The trolley bus was cold, the icy air blowing in through ill-fitting doors, whose rubber sealant had fallen off along with chunks of rusted metal. The lights were dim and flickering as if they might just give up and die at any moment. The machine screeched.

Some loud youths, smelling of alcohol, cigarettes, and stale clothing, sat at the back. Two chattering *babushkas,* tutting and shaking their heads. Old men not looking. Staring ahead at nothing through eyes that didn't want to see any more.

The seat nearest the exit, halfway up the bus, was empty. It was the coldest place on the bus, but also the quickest way out. They would take it. The windows were frosted over, leaves of ice clawing their way across the glass like a miniature forest. A place of wild things. Alyona traced the shapes with her fingers. Lights blushed outside, sneaking past them in a rhythmic blur – an out of focus movie running at the wrong speed.

'We will see Sasha soon?' Alyona asked, whispering in Leonid's ear, her hand cupped around it, her legs swinging back and forth. Gently, rhythmically.

'Yes,' he replied. 'Soon enough.' He felt this strangely unfamiliar desire to protect her. It was...good. This strange little street-girl made him feel good.

They jumped off two stops along and crossed the street through the subway. It was quiet. Empty, grey and quiet – the only sounds the hum of the traffic above and their footsteps echoing back at them as they splashed through the puddles of dirty melted snow. Leonid led them to the metro, constantly alert, scanning faces, bodies, everything. Alyona was copying him.

He wondered who or what she was looking for. If this was just a game to her, or if she was aware of the danger they were in. An overly lingering glance, a glimpse of the *militsiya,* former acquaintances, colleagues. Everything was potentially dangerous now. Who had spoken to whom, double-crossed. He didn't know. He had been giving Igor regular updates. Yes, he was on their trail. Yes, the bag was with them. Yes, all of their little bodies would be dealt with. No, he didn't need any back-up. It would be finished soon and he would return with the bag and the evidence. Job done, as always. But something was wrong. The tone of Igor's voice. Different. A distance. More than usual. He knew that something was up. Leonid was sure of that now. All ties had to be cut. Everything was a danger.

They got off at Kreshchatyk. A heavy *militsiya* presence, like normal. Heads down and inconspicuous wasn't what Leonid was comfortable with, used to, but it was what they had to do now. He loved this place. He really did. More than anywhere else in Kyiv. Others spoke of the Lavra, the churches, the hills, the river, the lilac blossoms and chestnut trees. Not him. Kreshchatyk was it. It was grand and broad and impressive. There was a strength to it. Power. It felt so wrong to be hiding from it.

Alyona could feel his apprehension. She followed his glances. Checked the faces he checked, the doorways, shadows. So many strangers that she would usually be oblivious of, oblivious to. Her eyes caught the sparkle of the Christmas tree lights. A huge pyramid of colour and brightness.

She lingered. Leonid tugged her on.

'Where are we going, Leo?' she asked, her head turned back, still watching the tree, the lights. Her breath drifting up, disappearing into the brightness.

'To get my car and then your brother, okay?' He knew the car was risky, but he had weighed it up. Five minutes in his car or forty five on foot and public transport. The car won.

'Okay.' She looked up at him, hunched her shoulders and smiled.

They turned into Kostolna. Leonid's Mercedes was parked in its usual spot at the bottom of the street. When Alyona saw it she stopped, stared, dropped his hand, stepped back. A familiarity with the car, the number plates, the blacked out windows.

'What is it?' Leonid asked. 'Come on,' he said encouragingly. He opened the passenger door for her and gestured that she should get in.

'I don't want to.' Her voice was quiet, hurt. 'I don't–I thought. I don't want to play those games mister Leonid.'

Oh, for Christ's sake! 'It's just my car. I don't play those games. I told you. Come on. I'm taking you to Sasha, remember?' There wasn't time for this. He grabbed her wrist, pulled her to the door. 'In!'

She started to cry but climbed in, her head low, her body slumped. It felt like she had been betrayed. She had let herself like him; get close to him. And now he was just one of them.

He pulled the seat belt across and strapped her in. Hurried round to the driver's side, eyes checking all around. Nothing. He jumped in, started the engine, and pulled off.

'It's all okay, Alyona. You don't need to be scared.'

'They always say that. Everyone says that, but they don't mean it. I know.' She was glowering.

He shook his head. What was he supposed to do

334

now? This was all new to him and he had no idea. Her being upset, scared, it bothered him, but he didn't know how to deal with it. He focused instead on driving, on what was happening outside, on getting the job done. That was what he did. Got the job done.

Chapter 54

December 2001

Nadia lit up. Took a deep draw. Felt the buzz of nicotine. She picked up her coffee. Her hand trembled. Coffee spilled. Splashed onto her jeans. She cursed inwardly. Glanced around. No-one was looking her way. She put her other hand around the cup, cradling it, supporting it. Two hands better than one. Strong coffee began to replace the foul taste that had been stuck in her mouth. She drained the cup, eyes constantly scanning. What for? That was what made it all worse. The unknown.

Focus on the English. The familiar. The Americans, effervescent, always something to shout about, enjoying life. Laughs. The music. Whiskey in the Jar. Tap her foot. Try to be normal. She finished her cigarette. Lit another from it before stubbing it out in the Guinness ashtray. *Okay.* She had pulled herself together enough. She could call now.

'Hi Maggie. It's me again. Are you okay?'

'Shit girl! Never mind me. What happened to you? Hanging up like that! Artem called, "Do you know where she is?" all worried boyfriend stuff. What's happening with you?'

'Are you at school now?'

'Yeah. Mid lesson. Getting dirty looks from the students. Ha! So?'

'I can't really speak now. I'm okay. Just be careful. I don't know what's going on, but the *militsiya* turned my place over. Threatened me –'

'Jesus! What? Why? But you're okay?'

'Yes. I'm in O'Brian's. I've got to go. Just be careful. Be very careful.'

Nadia called Artem. She kept it brief. Just enough to make sure he would hurry; he would understand her urgency. He told her that he'd be there in five. She wasn't to go anywhere. Right now she didn't think she could move anyway.

After what seemed like ages she finally spotted him. The dancer's gait. The gentle strength. He stopped at a table of men. A hand on a shoulder. Strong handshakes. Smiles. A shared shot. Finally he was there. She jumped up and threw her arms around him.

'Oh, thank Christ. Thank Christ!' She tried so hard to swallow her tears but they came. His neck wet with them.

'Nadia. It's okay. It's okay. What has happened to you?' He held her tight. Stroked her hair. Whispered. 'Shh. Shh. Come. Sit down.'

He pulled her seat out for her. Sat her down. Pulled his chair close to hers. Took her hand.

She inhaled a deep breath. Composed herself.

He lit them both a cigarette. Handed one to her. Listened as she told him everything in a conspiratorial whisper. It was as if she were a reporter, a story-teller. As if it hadn't happened to her.

'You have to leave. You have to leave Ukraine.' His voice was strange. Detached.

'No! I can't. Why should I? I won't be bullied like that. Not any more I won't!'

He sighed. 'You don't understand, Nadia. They will kill you. If you stay, they will kill you.'

'Screw them! I won't let them. I'm not going anywhere!'

'Nadia.' He took her face in his hands. Held her stare. 'You need to listen to me. You don't know. You don't understand the way of things here.'

'So I've been told!'

'It is true. You cross people like that and they will kill you.'

'But –'

'The match. The threat of fire. It is a message and you have to follow it.'

'Screw them!'

'You need to call your Embassy.'

'I –'

He picked up her mobile. Handed it to her. 'You need to call your Embassy now.'

Chapter 55

December 2001

Leonid pulled up in the car park of a small shop. It was at the back of the building and secluded. A good place to be unnoticed; better than sitting on the road. They were about a hundred metres away from the lane and the cottage where the boys were waiting.

'Why are we staying here? I want to see Sasha.' Alyona's voice was still upset, distrustful.

'We just need to make sure that no-one else is here. Look around for a minute or two. Okay?'

She didn't reply, just sat staring out of the side window. There was nothing to see but darkness.

'When we go outside I need you to be very clever, to listen and look, but pretend that you're not. Do you understand?'

She nodded. Climbed out. The hoot of an owl. The velvet swish of its wings. She smiled.

They walked back towards the lane, hand in hand.

Leonid checking, listening. Alyona looking up at the trees, the sky, her own checking and listening.

A shadow bled out of the bushes.

Leonid stared through the darkness trying to make out what, or who, the shadow was. He held her hand more tightly. Tugged at her, closing the distance between them. As they drew closer, the shadow took form.

Alyona sucked in a deep breath. 'It is okay. It is Sasha!' Alyona called, in an excited whisper, pulling on Leonid's hand. 'It is Sasha, Leo. Look!'

He smiled. He was Leo again. 'Shh. I see him. Go.'

They hurried along the road to where he stood, Alyona running ahead, only with eyes for her brother, Leonid checking up and down, up and down. Sasha and Alyona wrapped their arms around each other. Became one.

'Come on,' Leonid instructed, looking over his shoulder. 'In.'

Dima was waiting inside, surprised at Leonid's return. Sceptical, doubting. He hadn't dismissed the thought of them ending up as fish food. Not yet. He grunted an excuse for a greeting at Leonid. Rubbed Alyona's head.

Leonid chuckled. He could read what was going on in Dima's mind. He would be dubious too. No time for messing up now. The kid had to know who was boss. He pulled his gun. Pointed it at Dima. 'Sit.'

Sasha and Alyona stood back. Watching. What was going on?

Dima stood his ground. 'Give us our papers,' he demanded, holding out his hand.

Leonid smirked. Shook his head. 'They stay with me for now. And you sit down. I won't ask again.'

'Aww, come on man!'

'You get what's coming to you when it's coming to you.'

'What the fuck does that mean?'

'It means shut up, Dima. Sit down right where you are and shut up. You listen. Do as you're told and you might just get out of this alive. Got that? You're helping no-one right now.' He crooked a finger at Sasha and Alyona. 'You two. Come here. Sit.'

They didn't hesitate. Sat down beside Dima, as one.

'Fuck's sake,' Dima mumbled from his place on the floor. 'At least let us see. The money. The papers. Let us see.'

'Fair enough.'

He took a wad of dollar bills from his bag. The papers from his inside pocket. Wafted them in front of Dima. 'There. Happy now?'

'Yeah, right. Sitting like a fucking dog on the fucking floor. Happy as shit!'

Sasha nudged him.

'What?' Dima complained.

Leonid checked his watch. They had time. Just. 'We need to hurry. No funny stuff. No messing around. Just do as you're told. You can manage that, right?'

'Hurry where?'

Leonid sighed. 'Can't you just be like your two friends here? Just nice and quiet. Can't you?'

'No! No man, I can't. I want to know.'

'Zip it!'

PART IV
Falling

Chapter 56

December 2001

The British Embassy was a ten minute walk away. Nadia and Artem hurried down O'Brian's stairs and out of the entrance, entwined like two lovers with an innocently ulterior motive. Snow was blizzarding down, bringing an urgent hush with it. They didn't speak, as if that would somehow hasten their progress, make their passing less conspicuous. Buildings were blurred, bodies indistinguishable shadows. A drunk stumbled out of an alleyway, stinking of piss. Nadia's heart jumped.

They reached the top of Mykhailivs'ka Street and headed across the square. The gold domes of St Michael's stared down at them with their nefarious opulence. What appeared to be a pile of discarded clothes became a *babushka* lying crumpled at the foot of the statue of Princess Olga. Nadia heard her crying. Strings of tiny, almost silent, pleadings. She hesitated, wanting to stop, but Artem pulled her on.

The Ministry of Foreign Affairs loomed in front of them. Its immense pillars and formidable structure serving to intimidate. Bright lights. *Militsiya*. Hurry past. Two minutes now. So many memories snatched at her. She wanted to catch them. To hold them.

The curve of the hill. The split in the road. Finally the Embassy. The Union Jack had never been such a welcome sight. Such a relief. Safety. She could see the security guard's shelter of metal and reinforced glass; the pale green façade of the main building illuminated by a single spotlight.

They asked for her business. For her ID. She handed her passport over. Explained that she had spoken to the vice consul. She was expected.

'Okay. Okay. You come in.' The guard pointed at Artem. 'He stays outside.'

'But he's –'

'He doesn't come in.' The guard gestured towards his colleague.

'No,' she whispered.

Artem. His arm around her. The feel of him. The smell of him. His breath. The softness of his smile.

The guard took Artem by the arm and pulled him away. His arm left her. His hand ran down her arm.

'The thread. It doesn't break. We will be together,' he said softly, confidently. Their fingers touched and parted.

As he was led away, she was ushered through the door.

This was all happening too fast. Everything changing. She was caught between safety and loss.

'Artem!' she called.

He turned back to face her. 'It will be okay.' He smiled.

The door closed and he was gone.

She was crying now.

Chapter 57

December 2001

Leonid had risked the car again. Dima sat beside him in the front, Alyona and Sasha cuddled together in the back, whispering to each other in that odd way they had. Leonid kept to small side roads as much as possible. Innocuous streets of sleeping houses. Away from the routes patrolled by the *militsiya*. Leonid knew the place so intimately. Where to go. What to avoid.

He pulled into an underground car park near the circus.

'Why are we stopping here? What are you doing?' Dima asked. Suspicion snipping at him, as always.

'We get out here and we walk just across there,' Leonid answered, pointing up the broad street, its confusion of lanes and junctions now almost devoid of traffic. 'And we get on the bus to Minsk.'

'A bus?' Dima complained, failing to mask his

disappointment. 'Why are we going on a fucking bus?'

'Because, no-one in their right mind tries to do a runner on a bus, now do they?' Leonid replied. 'They'll be checking the airport, train stations; the *militsiya* will be pulling cars leaving the city, but buses? Nah. Safest way to go for sure.' He handed them their fake passports, complete with visas, and their tickets.

'Right, yeah, course. But why Minsk? Why not somewhere cool? Belarus is shit!'

'Christ!' Leonid laughed. 'What is it with you? Because we need to hide, to disappear, right? We can do that there, then we move on. To somewhere' – he sighed patronisingly – 'cool.'

Dima smirked in reply.

Igor's influence was to the west and south, not north and east. Where they were going was dodgy, even more closed than Ukraine but, again, unexpected. They wouldn't be there for long. A quick switch of transport and by this time tomorrow they should be safe enough. The Baltic States, mainland Europe. It could be done.

'On to where?'

'Right now, the less you know the better, so just shut it, will you?' He slapped Dima's head.

Dima refused to flinch.

'Too many questions,' Leonid added. 'And when we get to the bus stop we don't talk. We don't know each other. Any of us. Right? You need to listen to me on this. Do as you're told. Have we all got that?'

Sasha and Alyona nodded. Dima shrugged.

They stood at the bus stop, watching the queue fill

up with a straggle of misfits; poor people who'd spent their last *Hryvnia* on their tickets, backpackers looking for cheap thrills and stories, escapees. *Babushkas* stood huddled around their tartan plastic bags, which were full to bursting with God knows what, chattering excitedly. Smokers exhaled, watching the fumes drift up into the cold night air, dissolving, disappearing. The bus pulled in, the doors hissed open and bags were loaded amidst much huffing and puffing, arguing and gesticulation.

Dima got on first, followed by Alyona and Sasha. Leonid waited until all of the other passengers were on board, checked up and down the street, before climbing on himself. A last casual glance from the door. Nothing. A smile and a nod at the driver. They made their way to their seats, doing their best to pretend that they were unknown to each other.

Alyona looked around anxiously. She didn't like sitting beside a stranger, but they were lucky to get any seats at all. Straining her neck, she saw Sasha four rows behind her. She smiled and waved as a child might wave to its mother. He put his finger to his mouth *shh...* and gestured for her to sit back down, as the bus pulled off.

Kyiv trickled away into the distance on its black river, glistening like oil. Shadows danced on its surface, twisting and turning, contorting themselves into monstrosities. A dissolving haze of dirty orange light. Blackness. It was gone. Behind them.

The woman next to Alyona was peeling a boiled egg. 'Here,' she said. 'Look at you. All skin and bones like a little bird.' She poked at Alyona's legs. 'You should eat. Please? I have plenty, and look at me!' She laughed and patted her expansive belly. 'I don't need them.'

Her smile was warm and genuine but Alyona, hesitated. Yes, she was hungry, but she didn't know what she should do. Everything had changed. Her parameters, the framework to what had been her life had slipped away. Left back there. Was this okay?

'Please?' the woman said again, holding the egg out.

'Thank you,' Alyona eventually replied, accepting the food with a soft smile. 'You are very kind.'

'Pff. It's an egg. Nothing!'

Sasha gnawed at his fingers as he watched his sister in conversation. *Be careful Alyona. Please.*

The woman stretched around and peered above the headrest. She gestured to Sasha to come forward and offered to change places so that Alyona and he could be together.

'Thank you so much,' Sasha said, accepting her offer and sitting down beside his little sister, feeling Leonid's disapproving stare behind him. But what else could he do? This was safer, surely.

'She is a very nice lady!' Alyona sighed. 'Very nice.'

Internal lights were switched off. People began to fall asleep, heads flopping, mouths drooling, whispers, uncomfortable twists, the odd snore, a cough.

None of them slept. Too much going on. All alert. Watching. Wondering. To the children it was all so new. Something other than Podil, than Kyiv. They stared out of the windows but could see little other than blackness, shadows, the odd streak of light from passing traffic. A hamlet, a village, a small town. Everything quiet and dark. Most places without street-lights.

Several hours later the bus came to a halt at the border with Belarus. Getting out of Ukraine and again out of Belarus were the danger points. Brothers in corruption. Border guards in people's pockets. Favours owed. Leonid just hoped that word hadn't reached here yet. That no-one out of Kyiv was looking for them – yet.

Passports were collected by the driver and taken into the border control office. The luggage was all offloaded and checked. Guards strutted, poked and shook. German Shepherds sniffed hungrily. Most of the passengers stared out of the windows. Some ignored it all, others purposefully looked away. The children stared. They had no bags in there, but the searching, the feeling from the guards, set them on edge. They knew that people in uniform were dangerous. This was dangerous. It was quiet in the bus. Very quiet. Like more than just them were holding their breaths.

A guard boarded the bus. 'Alyona Gorkova,' he called. There was an audible intake of breath but no reply. 'Gorkova! Alyona Gorkova!' he demanded.

Chapter 58

December 2001

'That's you, Alyona. You're Gorkova now. He wants you to go,' Sasha whispered in a panic. He didn't know what to do. Should he look back at Leonid for some clue, or do as he had been told and ignore him? Pretend that they were strangers. He swallowed hard, watching the progress of the guard, but not wanting to. Not wanting to look. Not wanting any of this. His heart thumped so hard that he could hear it. Feel it pounding against his chest.

'Go where?' Alyona asked, confused.

He couldn't answer. Not just because he didn't know. His mouth was too dry to form words.

The guard strode up the aisle, checking the passengers against the photo in the passport. He paused as he caught Leonid's eye. Frowned. Leonid held his stare. The guard looked away. Carried on checking faces. He reached Alyona. Stopped. Looked again from passport to person. Nodded.

'You. Come with me. Now.' Slow, deep, menacing. A threat lingering with each word. He grabbed her arm tightly, pulling her to her feet.

She squealed. Pulled against him. Away from him. Her head twisted; terrified eyes staring back at Sasha. Beyond, to Leo. To Dima. To the lady with the eggs. *Help,* her stare said. *Help me!*

Sasha stood; his legs trembling. He gripped the headrest for support. Took a deep inhalation, trying to summon strength for his sister. 'I am her brother,' he managed to force out.

The guard smiled with cold satisfaction. 'Then you come too. Your baggage. Where is it?'

'We don't have any.'

'Really.' Sarcastic. Not a question.

They stopped when they came to the driver.

'Their bags? Get them for me,' the guard instructed.

'They didn't have any.'

'You're sure about that?'

'Yeah! The kids caught my eye. No bags.'

The guard nodded.

PART V
Flying

Chapter 59

Now

Nadia sits in the window-seat clutching tightly onto her brown package. The sickening knot in her stomach as the plane takes off. She stares out of the window as Kyiv becomes smaller and smaller. Lights. A golden thread. Stretching. Disappearing. Nothing. She stares at the blackness. Her heart sinks. Left down there. A horrible emptiness. She puts her hand to the window, fingers spread. 'Goodbye,' she whispers. A crack of light breaks through the sky. She plugs her earphones in; turns the music on; The Smashing Pumpkins – Aeroplane Flies High.

She lets her fingers slip inside the package. The feel of the dress. All that it has survived through. Something so special. The power of the story. The love it held. The connection that she now has with it.

The memories of that first day in the field of sunflowers.

Her fingers reach something else.

The leather of Bogdan's notebook. She bites her lip. Closes her eyes. Puts her hand on her belly. She is crying. She carries more than just Bogdan's story. This child. This child will stay with her. They will return to the fields of sunflowers.

*

Alyona blinks away tears. The woman who had exchanged seats with Sasha calls after them. 'They are just children. Leave them be.' Some stare, tut, others look away – some things are best ignored – some shake their heads offering a camaraderie in their silent protest.

The children descend the steps of the bus. Another guard is waiting at the foot of them. They head towards the hut that serves as the office for the border guards. Alyona's wrist is in the unrelenting grip of a guard. Her other hand is being held gently by her brother. She is whispering something to no-one. Head skywards. Stars in blackness.

Dima twists around to Leonid in the seat behind him, his leg thumping up and down nervously. 'Can't you do something?' he whispers desperately. Eyes demanding.

'Wait. Wait and see what happens. It may be nothing. A question about her documents. A show of strength. You know what they're like.' But he doubts it. This all has the feel of something much worse than that. The chat with the driver. The smile at Sasha being there too.

Could he offer a counter bribe? Would there be any point in it? He has a bunch of cash. He could offer so much more than the guard, or guards, will get as payment for this. For Sasha and Alyona. That feeling. *Christ*! He hates the fact that he cares. It messes everything up. And that little girl...

The driver gets out and stands next to the bus, having a smoke. Other passengers follow. Do likewise. Stretch their legs. Smell the clean air. Forest all around. Pine trees, tall and majestic. Dawn is breaking. A crack in the sky. So different from the city. Lighting up.

Dima and Leonid step off as well, their eyes following Sasha and Alyona.

'Wait here,' Leonid stresses to Dima, slipping a wad of notes into his jacket. 'If this goes to shit, keep quiet. And be smart.' He strides forward – w*hat the hell am I doing?* As he gains on Sasha and Alyona, they are dragging their heels, clinging on to the hope that something might happen.

The guards and the children are getting closer to the border control office. Fifty metres now. The sound of their feet crunching on the gravel beneath is agonising, painful, as it beats away their freedom, their lives. Sasha glances back with a desperate stare pleading for something. For anything.

Leonid swallows hard, attempts a smile in return, trying to offer reassurance. Hope. Although he doubts that there is any chance of getting out of this one. He wonders about whether to approach the guard outside. Fewer officials to deal with but more possible witnesses. He has no idea of what, or whom, awaits inside. More officers certainly, but how many and more importantly on whose side?

He knows how this plays out. This is Igor. This is the law. This is the State. Bribes only work if there isn't a fear of death alongside them. Who's he trying to kid? The more he thinks about it the clearer it becomes that he is walking towards his end if he carries on. No doubt. No doubt at all. There is no point in this.

One of the guard turns around, as if he knows, as if he is challenging Leonid to step forward. Daring him. Twenty metres now, maybe thirty at most.

'Toilets?' Leonid asks.

The guard stares, questioning, then nods towards the hut that houses the toilets.

Sasha visibly winces, biting back tears as Leonid nods in acknowledgement and veers away. Alyona still stares skywards.

The strangest of feelings descends. An intensity envelopes everything. The sound of birds. First one or two. More. It swells. Comes from all around. This is no dawn chorus. It is too loud. Too overwhelming. So many of them, birds, cawing and screeching. Not singing a greeting to the day. Something else. Deafening. Painful. The unearthly sound all around. Swirling. Sweeping. Taking over.

The trees tremble with the weight of them. The tops sway, becoming fluid. The sky suddenly fills with them. A huge swarm of birds – not just crows but corvids of all kinds – as they take off as one. They swoop and dive, a great black mass, towards the hut, the guards, the children.

Leonid stands still. Stares. Not believing the scene unfolding in front of him.

The guards raise their arms to protect their heads from the swarm of diving birds.

'What the hell?' Ducking, swiping, running for cover.

Beaks pecking, stabbing. Wings beating. Claws snatching. Tears in flesh.

Leonid crouches down and retreats. Everyone else stares. Mouths open. Eyes wide. Nothing said.

Alyona takes both of Sasha's hands. Looks into his eyes. 'Come!' she calls through the cacophony. Birds swirling around them both. 'Come with me.'

They run. The mass of birds seems to clear a path for them, swarming above them around them, swirling, screeching. Black all around. On they run, Alyona leading now, Sasha blindly following. Trusting her. Trusting this.

'What the hell did I just witness?' Leonid mutters.

Dima laughs. Jumps. Pumps the air with his fist 'Fucking ace! You go bro!' His words fly out in an ecstatic senseless stream. He pumps the air with his fist again and again, turns to Leonid, the biggest grin on his face. 'Shit man! Did you see that? Shit man!' He looks up at the sky. Dawn is seeping through in the palest of hues. The brightest of stars still shine.

They stare, as slowly the birds begin to clear, as dawn begins to break. But there is no sign of Sasha and Alyona. The shadow of deep, dark forest. Dima's elation begins to slip. He turns to Leonid.

'What?' He shakes his head. 'What do we do now?'

As soon as the birds have gone a young guard runs out, pale and shaken, looking from the sky to the ground and back again. He hands the passports to the driver and hurries away. People take their seats amidst mumbles and quiet exclamations.

'We have to keep going, Dima.' Leonid gestures to the open door. 'On the bus.'

'But–'

'On the bus!' He insists, nudging Dima in the back.

Dima feels sick. Feels dirty. Feels like a traitor. Reluctantly he climbs up the steps, bends down as he walks along the aisle, staring through the windows as he does so, struggling with the thought of losing his friends, the closest thing he has to family. Hell, they are his family.

The lady with the eggs smiles, clasps Dima's hand tightly as he passes her seat. 'This earth is magic,' she whispers, her blue eyes hold the brightest sparkle. 'Look.'

He flinches at her touch, but follows to where her fingers are pointing. The flash of something bright in the distance, running from the woods. 'Is that?' He focusses. 'Leonid! Look, man! Look!'

'Well, I'll be damned!'

Leonid makes his way back towards the driver. A brief conversation. A nod of heads.

Once in Belarus the bus pulls up and waits for the breathless Sasha and Alyona.

'On you come,' the driver calls. 'Hurry now.'

They clamber up, grubby smiles on their faces. The bus erupts in cheers and clapping as they make their way back towards Dima and Leonid.

The doors hiss closed and the bus drives off.

'The States, man!' Dima whispers across the aisle to Sasha. 'The fucking States!'

They grin at each other.

'Minsk, Dima,' Leonid chastises and lightly slaps his head. 'Minsk!'

They feel safe now. Everything has changed.

The End

If you enjoyed this story you can help other people find it by writing a review on the site where you bought it from. It doesn't have to be much. Just a few words can really help spread the word and make a big difference to its visibility. Thank you!

Acknowledgements

With extra special thanks to Joy Velykorodnyy, Hannah Shipman, and Jude Mondragon for their invaluable help. To Morag Brownlie for being my ear and constant support. Most of all to the street-kids of Kyiv who may never know that they stole my heart and inspired a novel.

About the Author

Fiona worked as an international school teacher for fifteen years, predominantly in Eastern Europe. Four of those years were spent in Ukraine – a country which left a strong impression on her. She now lives in East Lothian, Scotland, where her days are spent walking her dog in beautiful places, and writing.

Contact with the author

Twitter http://twitter.com/@FJCurlew
Facebook http://facebook.com/FJCurlew
Website https://fjcurlew.wixsite.com/author/bio

Also By This Author

DAN KNEW

A puppy born to the dangers of street life
A woman in trouble
An unbreakable bond

A Ukrainian street dog is rescued from certain death by an expat family. As he travels with them through Lithuania, Estonia, Portugal and the UK he learns how to be a people dog, but a darkness grows and he finds himself narrating more than just his story. More than a dog story. Ultimately it's a story of escape and survival but maybe not his.

The world through Wee Dan's eyes in a voice that will stay with you long after you turn that last page.

The Unravelling Of Maria

Lovers separated by the Iron Curtain.
Two women whose paths should never have crossed.
A remarkable journey that changes all of their
lives.

Maria's history is a lie. Washed up on the shores of
Sweden in 1944, with no memory, she was forced to
create her own. Nearly half a century later she still has
no idea of her true identity.
Jaak fights for Estonia's independence, refusing to
accept the death of his fiancée Maarja, whose ship
was sunk as she fled across the Baltic Sea to escape
the
Soviet invasion.
Angie knows exactly who she is. A drug addict. A
waste of space. Life is just about getting by.
A chance meeting in Edinburgh's Cancer Centre is the
catalyst for something very different.

Sometimes all you need is someone who listens.

To Retribution

He thought she was dead
She wasn't

Suze, an idealistic young journalist, is used to hiding as her cell tries to keep their online news channel open. They publish the truth about the repatriations, the re-education camps, the corruption, the deceit. New Dawn, the feared security force, is closing in, yet again.
Suze runs, yet again.
This time, however, she is pursued with a relentlessness; a brutality which seems far too extreme for her "crimes". This is more. This is personal.

When her death is finally confirmed, he is celebrating it.

Big mistake.

Retribution will be hers!

Writing as Fiona Curnow

Before the Swallows Come Back

Perfect for fans of *Where the Crawdads Sing* by Delia Owens, *The Great Alone* by Kristin Hannah, and *Sal* by Mik Kitson, with its celebration of the natural world, its misunderstood central characters living on the outside of society's norms, their survival in the wilderness, and the ultimate fight for justice.

Before the Swallows Come Back is a story of love, found family, and redemption that will break your heart and have it soaring time and time again as you sit on the edge of your seat desperately hoping.

Tommy struggles with people, with communicating, preferring solitude, drifting off with nature. He is protected by his Tinker family who keep to the old ways. A life of quiet seclusion under canvas is all he knows.

Charlotte cares for her sickly father. She meets Tommy by the riverside and an unexpected friendship develops. Over the years it becomes something more, something crucial to both of them. But when tragedy strikes each family they are torn apart.

Charlotte is sent far away.

Tommy might have done something very bad.

Printed in Great Britain
by Amazon

58583344R00219